EVERYTHING
In Its Place

Peter F. Williams

This is a work of fiction. Names, characters, places, and incidents are either products of the author's imagination or, if real, are used fictitiously.

Book edited by Peggy Peterson of Peak Editing.

ISBN 978-1-950647-96-5

Publisher's Cataloging-in-Publication Data

Names: Williams, Peter F., 1957-, author.
Title: Everything in its place / Peter F. Williams.
Description: Fort Collins, CO: Peter F. Williams, 2025.
Identifiers: ISBN: 978-1-950647-96-5
Subjects: LCSH Brothers--Fiction. | Family--Fiction. | Autism--Fiction. | Developmentally disabled--Family relationships--Fiction. | Caregivers--Fiction.| BISAC FICTION / Family Life / Siblings | FICTION / Disability
Classification: LCC PS3623 .I55 E84 2025 | DDC 813.6--dc23

Publishing Assistance by BookCrafters, Parker CO.
bookcrafters.net

Part I

Denver, Colorado – 1996

Part I

Denver, Colorado – 1996

DAMMIT! GOD! DAMMIT! The sweat was now running down my wrist and onto my fingers. The brand new starched, buttoned-down shirt I had just put on was soaked with my perspiration. I walked over to the bedroom mirror to inspect the damage. Just as I suspected, my shirt was already pitted out. The collar looked like I had just gotten out of the pool. My upper lip was not only quivering, but was a reservoir for my massive beads of sweat. This was not the way I wanted to present myself, nor the first impression I wanted to make today. I never wear an undershirt but today I was going to have to make an exception. I quickly unbuttoned my drenched shirt and threw it in the clothes hamper. I found an old, wrinkled white tee shirt at the bottom of my drawer. God only knows how long it had been in there—had to be at least twenty years. I pulled it over my head and stood in front of the mirror in amazement. It was a little tight but it still fit, barely.

I grabbed another starched button down from the closet and slipped it over my undershirt. Now it was time to move onto the next major task, trying to tie my tie. I soon realized that my nerves and perspiration were going to ruin my perfect record of tying that flawless Windsor knot. Every day for the last fifteen years I had worn a tie to work and never once had an issue getting that knot tied. Today my fingers were so damp and dripping with perspiration I knew it was just not going to happen. I guess every record must fall eventually. I threw the soaking wet tie onto the bed and grabbed my blue blazer. No tie today!

I knew Colleen, my wife, would already have the Jeep out of the garage and be waiting in the driveway on my sorry ass. *Late again, just like my brother Drew*, I thought. Running out the garage door, I jumped over one of the kid's mountain bikes, being careful not to tweak my ankle. That right ankle I'd broken in a high school basketball game against the mighty St. Patrick's of Elizabeth, New Jersey twenty-one years ago has always given me problems. I really didn't want to show up for my first appointment on crutches with a major limp. As predicted, Colleen was waiting for me in our driveway. The sun's glare on the windshield hid her face and I couldn't tell if I was already in the doghouse. I opened the front passenger side door and sat my butt down as fast as I could. Colleen glanced over at me, shook her head in disgust, and told me I might want to wipe the sweat off my face. *Great*, I thought. The doghouse was avoided for now. Colleen had more important things on her mind.

The car's A/C was just not cooling me off fast enough so I opened the window to try and slow down my perspiration issue. My deodorant would need to work overtime today. I fumbled with the radio dial to find a song or two that would take our minds off of our impending appointment. My thoughts wandered as I continued to search for that perfect song. I couldn't recall anyone in my family ever going to a shrink, I mean psychologist, before. Neither my dad nor my mom. Not my older sister, my younger brother, nor even my older brother Drew. Oh wait. I did recall a time when I was six or seven. For about a year, each Saturday my mom drove us about ten miles into Morristown. Like ducklings following their mother, we climbed up a long flight of stairs in an old stale-smelling office building and left my brother Drew for an hour as Mom and the rest of us went grocery shopping at the Grand Union. We never discussed who Drew was spending time with. That subject was always off limits. Years later, I figured out he was spending that hour with a psychologist.

I was still determined to find that perfect "take your mind off reality" song. I glanced over at Colleen, who was solely focused on getting us to Dr. Brooks' office safely. Obviously, Colleen was handling the situation much better than I was. "Baby I'm-a Want You" by Bread was not the answer to distract us today. I turned the dial to the next station. Abba? Oh, come on! Next station, Nickleback? My goodness, talk about hitting the worst trifecta ever. Next station, classic rock— yes. "Crazy Train" by Ozzy. All aboard...perfect! Colleen looked over and saw my huge grin. She just smiled and shook her head.

With only a few more minutes left in our drive across town, it was now time for me to get serious and start acting like a thirty-nine-year-old mature adult. I needed to reflect on the reason for our appointment...and the root cause of all my anxiety today. Our visit to Dr. Brooks was not about me. It was not even about Colleen and me. Our appointment today was about Mark, our third child, who was now a second grader. I always knew Mark was special, from the moment he was born by C-section in that Garland, Texas delivery room. Mark peed all over the first human he came in contact with—our delivery nurse. Mark needed to let everyone know who was in charge.

Raising our first two children prior to Mark's arrival had all seemed pretty routine. Mark brought us a new set of challenges. He gave us a new perspective on parenthood Colleen and I were not prepared for. Mark generated a whole new list of "firsts" for us as parents. For example, two weeks ago, Colleen and I were summoned to appear before Mark's grade school principal. Okay, summoned might be a little strong. We were asked to attend a meeting with Sister Agnes. Pardon me, I just now had a flashback to my sixteen years of Catholic education. Sister Agnes informed us that Mark was also creating a "first" for her. I was glad to hear we were in such good company. Sister Agnes told us that she had made a decision to move Mark from his current teacher in the second grade into the other second grade class. Sister Agnes said that in her thirty-five years as a grade school principal, she had never moved a student from one class to another during a current school year. She had never wanted to set such a precedent.

Mark's current teacher had complained to Sister Agnes that she did not have the patience to work with Mark anymore. Sister Agnes explained that Mark periodically made derogatory comments in front of the entire class about his teacher's lack of teaching experience. One specific comment Mark had recently made to his teacher was, "You don't know what you're doing. You've only been teaching for a month." You see, this was Mrs. Howell's first teaching assignment. She had just graduated from college. I knew my eight-year-old son was quite opinionated, but was surprised he was wreaking so much havoc in his class.

My first reply to Sister Agnes was, "Well, at least he's being honest." Colleen kicked me under the table. Sister Agnes recommended that we take Mark to an adolescent psychologist and have him tested. She felt that Mark might not be developmentally ready for the second grade. This is how our visit to Dr. Brooks, an educational adolescent psychologist, materialized. Colleen and I were not only devastated but also embarrassed as we left Sister Agnes's office. We were also concerned that our precious second grader might not be emotionally and academically ready for the second grade. This afternoon was our first appointment with Dr. Brooks to discuss our challenges with Mark.

Colleen brought the Jeep to a hard stop right before she hit the concrete parking block. As she turned the car off, Bruce Springsteen's "Jungleland" faded through the car speakers. Honestly, I would have preferred to stay in the Jeep and hear the rest of Clarence's amazing sax solo, but it was time to get on board and help support Colleen. For the first time in the last hour, I finally felt like I had my perspiration issue under control. I opened my door, got out and reached for Colleen's hand. There was no turning back now.

As Colleen and I entered through the front double doors of the Lakewood Professional Building, my first thought was of Mike Brady. Oh yes, Mike Brady would have been mighty proud of this seventies' architectural masterpiece. You know, Mike Brady, the world-famous architect and father of *The Brady Bunch*. This building had Mike Brady written all over it—early seventies design with burnt orange and green earth tones. I hadn't seen that much wood paneling since my New Jersey childhood family room. We checked the wall directory and hustled up one flight of stairs to Dr. Brooks' office. Usually moving that fast up a flight of stairs in the Colorado altitude would have me gasping for air, embarrassingly trying to catch my breath. Today my nerves would have nothing to do with it.

Entering the office, we were met by an extremely young and pleasant receptionist. She was not the Nurse Ratched from *One Flew Over the Cuckoo's Nest* I had been expecting. "Mr. and Mrs. Wilson?"

"Yes," I answered. "I'm Steve and this is my wife, Colleen. We're here for our one o'clock appointment with Dr. Brooks."

The receptionist asked us to take a seat, saying that Dr. Brooks would be with us shortly. The fact that the waiting room was empty didn't bother me, but the waiting room was a disaster. There were toys, games, puzzles, and educational materials strewn all over the room. It looked like a bomb had exploded. I couldn't wait to see what Dr. Brooks' office looked like. I leaned over to Colleen and whispered, "I'll bet you dinner that Dr. Brooks has a grey beard, shorter than those guys in ZZ Top, and will be wearing tan corduroy pants and old brown boat shoes. He'll kind of look like Robin Williams in *Good Will Hunting*."

Just as the word "stop" was about to come out of Colleen's mouth, the door opened and there in front of us stood Dr. Brooks. I couldn't hide the huge smile on my face as I leaned over to Colleen and murmured, "You owe me dinner."

Dr. Brooks invited us into his office and we quickly took the two seats right in front of his desk. In the uncomfortable silence that now filled his office I anxiously waited for him to speak. I was sure that at some point I was going to be subjected to a series of rapid-fire questions. As Dr. Brooks took his seat behind his cluttered and musty-smelling desk, I couldn't help but notice the number of books crammed into his office. This guy was either extremely well read or a major hoarder. I had never seen so many books with the suffix "ology" on the covers.

Dr. Brooks asked if we would like anything to drink. Colleen nervously cleared her throat before she could get out the words, "Just water, please."

I said, "I'll take a Jack and Coke." He peered over the top of his tiny Ben Franklin eyeglasses and I could tell he was not amused and did not appreciate my sense of humor. I quickly changed my order to, "Just water, please."

Dr. Brooks got up from his desk and walked to the back of his office to pour our drinks while I received a painful knuckle punch to my bicep from Colleen. All we'd done so far was place our drink order and I was already in trouble. This was going to be a long afternoon.

Dr. Brooks handed us our waters and took his seat. To be perfectly honest, he did a very nice job easing some of our tension by his initial set of questions. I'm sure the Jack and Coke I had ordered earlier would have had the same results but this was Dr. Brooks' home field and I needed to play by his set of rules. My college degree was in Psychology, so I had good intuition as to what was coming next. "I know we're here to discuss Mark, but I'd like to get some family history and background before we get into Mark's challenges at school," Dr. Brooks began. "Who'd like to go first?"

I knew Colleen with her Type A personality would jump at the chance to go first. I sat back in my chair and thought, "Time for the skeletons to now come flying out of the closet." I was impressed by Dr. Brooks' display of interest as Colleen surgically dissected her family tree. I witnessed continual head nods along with numerous utterances of "yes" while he appeared to write down every word that came out of Colleen's mouth. This guy was good! He had much better listening skills than I ever had. "You're not listening to me!" was a common complaint from Colleen almost every morning while I read the newspaper at our breakfast table.

Quite frankly, I struggled to pay close attention to Colleen's dissertation about her family because I couldn't stop thinking about what I would say about mine next. I did manage to discover a few new secrets though, that even after fourteen years of marriage I was not aware of. Colleen's dad, who died at age forty and whom I had never met, was verbally abusive to her and her siblings. The second secret I learned was that Doris, Colleen's first cousin, was gay but had yet to come out to her family. I can honestly say that both of these two confessions were not a total surprise for me, but did validate some of my prior suspicions.

After what seemed like an eternity of hearing about Colleen's mega-family—parents, grandparents, brothers, sisters, aunts, uncles, cousins, second and third cousins, and a few black sheep in her family tree—it was now my turn to talk. While Colleen's family tree is like a large mature fully-bloomed oak tree, my family tree is more like the

Christmas tree in *A Charlie Brown Christmas*—short with a few weak branches and needing support to stand up. I really struggled with where to start. Should I start with the oldest family member and go through to the youngest or should I go youngest to oldest? I could feel myself start to perspire again. Thank God I had put on that undershirt earlier. I could tell that Dr. Brooks and Colleen were growing impatient waiting for me to start. I decided there was no better place to start then at the top of my tree.

"I grew up with no grandparents. Well, I had grandparents, but they all died before I was even born. I never knew any of them."

Dr. Brooks looked up and said, "Please continue." I guess I wasn't going to get any sympathy for hereditarily, most likely doomed to expeience a short life span.

"Next, I'll talk about my parents." I wanted to be careful as I went down this road because I was sure he was going to evaluate my choice of words and read my body language as I spoke. I adjusted my chair and sat up straight. "My dad was a big guy. He was six foot three inches tall, and weighed at least two hundred eighty pounds. To be honest, I grew up in total fear of my dad. He wore a thin belt and had a mean backhand. It's sad to say, but the best times I remember were when he was out of town on business because he couldn't hassle me about my grades or the length of my hair. He hated long hair. Once he picked me up from the record store instead of Mom. As I got into the car, he ripped the new album I had just purchased from Scotti's Record Store out of my hands, studied the album cover, proceeded to call the guys with long hair on the cover faggots, and threw the album out the car window. When we got home, I got on my bike and found that Doobie Brothers album on the side of the road. I still have it today." I couldn't help but weakly laugh at this point and hoped Dr. Brooks wouldn't hold it against me.

"I remember being whipped a few times with that thin belt of his. I'm sure I deserved it. As I've gotten older, I've come to realize he just might not have liked kids very much. Growing up, it felt like we were a burden in his life. I am thankful that he provided for Mom and my brothers and sister and me, but I'm certainly taking a different approach to raising my kids. My Dad was a deeply religious man but

I struggled with some of his hypocrisy. For such a religious guy, he seemed pretty racist. He acted very different in public than he did in our house. Most of his adult life he smoked about three packs of cigarettes a day. He was diagnosed with stomach and liver cancer at age fifty-nine. He died six months after his diagnosis. That was about eleven years ago."

No other words or thoughts came to me and I stopped talking. I hadn't mean to, but I felt like I had just crapped all over my dad. I couldn't help wishing someone had slapped me across my face before I became too negative about him. I couldn't ever remember speaking so disparagingly about my father, especially to a complete stranger. As I reflected on what I had just communicated to Dr. Brooks, I started to worry that what I had just said would hurt Mark's diagnosis somehow. There were other characteristics about my dad that I could have shared to try to point a more positive image of him. I did feel like I was being honest, though. It wasn't the time to take anything back and I needed to move onto my mother.

"About my mom; you could say she is a living saint. She has always been there to support us and comfort us, in good times and bad. Growing up, I hardly ever saw my mother lose her temper. I never heard her raise her voice or swear. I don't think I've ever seen her finish an entire cocktail. Once I watched her with a whiskey sour, but I think she was just being social and only drank half of it. I never saw my parents argue. Having been married now for over fourteen years, I find that unbelievable. If they did fight it must have happened behind closed doors.

"I saw her get really get angry only twice in my life. Once because I connected two electrical wires and blew up her sewing machine. I'll never forget the smell of burning electricity. She told me to wait upstairs until Dad got home. I knew what that meant. My dad's skinny belt really put a mark on my ass that night. The second time, my sister and I broke all of Dad's cigarettes in half. We had tried to get Dad to quit smoking and we thought if we destroyed his carton of cigarettes he just might quit. At the time I couldn't tell who Mom was angrier at—us for destroying his cigarettes or Dad for going ballistic and threatening Annie and me.

"Usually on a Sunday afternoon while Dad took a nap, Mom would play catch or badminton with me. She attended most of my baseball and basketball games and was always there to cheer me up if things didn't go well. Dad never really had any interest in my sports. I always have appreciated the void that she filled in my life. Even though we now live over 1,500 miles apart, we make every effort to see her at least twice a year. I've always regretted that we don't live closer to her so she can spend more time with her grandchildren."

I could have easily gone on for another hour or two bragging about how great my mom was, but I looked at my watch and realized that I needed to speed things up. We were paying Dr. Brooks by the hour and I still had a few more people to talk about. "I want to mention one other thing before moving on, Dr. Brooks. I was raised Catholic and went to Catholic school for both grade and high school. I always thought it was cool that both Jesus' mother and my mother had the same name—Mary. I think I should stop here because I really don't want to talk about her Immaculate Conception." Again, I couldn't even get a slight grin out of Dr. Brooks.

It was now time to get into my brothers and sister. I decided to start with my oldest sibling. "John Andrew is the name of my older brother. Pretty good Catholic name, huh? He's five years older than I am." I felt stuck again and stopped dead in my tracks. I was unsure of what to say next or, more importantly, how to say it. An uncomfortable silence filled the room again as Dr. Brooks and Colleen both stared at me waiting for me to continue.

Colleen took my hand, gave it a slight squeeze, and whispered in my ear, "It's okay, honey. Take your time."

I slowly unscrewed the top of my water bottle and took a big gulp to give me a few extra seconds to gather my thoughts and develop a strategy for continuing. "My brother Drew is a little different. Today, people would say he has special needs. To be honest Dr. Brooks, I'm not exactly sure what his issues are. I only know what I saw for the seventeen years that we lived together before I went off to college. My parents never talked to me about why Drew, that's what we call him, was different from the other kids in our neighborhood. It was a subject that our family never discussed. It was completely off limits.

My dad died in 1985 without ever giving me even a clue as to what Drew's issues are. I do know that Drew and my dad didn't have a very good relationship. There was a lot of anger and frustration on both sides, not to mention some physical abuse. Drew is forty-four years old today, and I still can't get Mom to talk about his issues. I've tried, but she is a master at changing the conversation.

"When I was seventeen, I left home to go to college in Florida, over a thousand miles away. After college, I never went back home to live. All I know about Drew is what happened in our house in New Jersey before I left, and a few trips home to visit my mom with Colleen and our kids. I do know that my brother went to "special schools" growing up. My older sister, younger brother and I all went to Catholic schools. Drew attended our local public high school, but was in the "special class." I remember kids in the neighborhood continually making fun of him. They taunted him, saying he was in the retarded class while also calling him a sissy. I felt bad for him, but he seemed to deal with the comments better than I would have.

"After he graduated high school, he continued to live at home with my parents. He worked at a nearby factory so he could walk there and back. He never learned how to drive a car. In 1978, while I was still in college, my parents moved from New Jersey to South Carolina, where Drew got a job in another factory. My younger brother told me that he was fired after two months for smoking pot on his lunch break. It's been eight years and he hasn't worked a day since. I think the move to South Carolina really screwed him up.

"When we go home to visit Mom, Drew pretty much stays holed up in his bedroom. I don't get much of a chance to see him when we're there. I'll knock on his door and he'll rarely come out. He'll speak through the door, and make up some lame excuse like he's sleeping and that he'll come out later. But he never does. If we visit for a week, he might come out late at night but he'll hide in the shadows of the back of the room, facing the opposite direction so we can't see his face. On the rare occasions that he says something, he puts his hand in front of his mouth when he speaks.

"My kids find him dark and mysterious and will ask me questions about him. I don't have any answers. My kids also find it amusing that when they wake up every morning at Mom's house, all their toys and games have been meticulously organized in an orderly fashion in front of Mom's fireplace. It's like a maid came in overnight and organized all of their stuff. Crazy, right?

"Dr. Brooks, I have a very deep sense of guilt about Drew. I feel that growing up, he and I had a pretty decent relationship, though it wasn't the typical 'bro' relationship. I feel like I abandoned him when I went to college. After college, I moved on to working and living fifteen hundred miles away. I got married, had three beautiful children, and have had a pretty excellent life. Drew, on the other hand, has socially regressed, still lives with Mom, and appears to be a prisoner in his twelve-foot by twelve-foot bedroom. I feel really guilty."

I stopped to catch my breath. I had developed a terrible case of dry mouth and needed another gulp of water. My hands trembled so badly the water bottle almost missed my mouth. I was intrigued by how Dr. Brooks had been able to get me to talk so freely. I worried that maybe I had gone too deep on Drew. I still needed to get to Annie, my older sister, and Bobby, my younger brother. Dr. Brooks had been quiet and I hoped he would say something. Mercifully, he granted my wish.

Dr. Brooks cleared his throat and spoke in confident and directive voice. "I believe, based on your comments, that Drew might be clinically diagnosed with Asperger's Syndrome." I had never heard anyone ever diagnose Drew with anything before. The neighborhood kids just called him retarded.

"Dr. Brooks, with all due respect, and please don't take this the wrong way, but did you say Ass Burgers Syndrome?" I really was not trying to be a smartass or funny this time. I just needed some clarification.

Dr. Brooks slowly rose out of his chair, careful not to knock over the mountain of books on his desk, and went to the white board hanging on his wall. He grabbed a purple marker and said, "Mr. Wilson, let me spell it out for you. It's called Asperger's Syndrome." With his marker, he spelled it out in very large letters on the white board. He continued, "The syndrome was discovered by Hans Asperger, an Austrian Psychologist. It's also referred to as an Autism Spectrum Disorder or ASD for short. You've surely heard of the concept of 'being on the spectrum' Mr. Wilson." I nodded my head. I had heard of being on the spectrum before, but I hadn't understood what it meant.

As Dr. Brooks returned to his desk, I pulled out an old receipt from my wallet and wrote the words "Asperger's Syndrome" on the back of it and stuffed it back into my wallet. Dr. Brooks was not finished. He said, "I'm guessing your dad was an engineer." My jaw dropped. I feverishly went through all my comments from the last forty minutes. I hadn't once mentioned anytime during our meeting that Dad was an engineer. How did he know?

"Yes, he was an electrical engineer."

"Mr. Wilson, I'll wager your father and mother were and are both very bright individuals." Dr. Brooks was now two for two.

"Yes. My father was extremely smart. He had an engineering degree from Duke and a master's degree from MIT." That last statement conjured up a memory I had totally forgotten. I must have been about twelve years old and my father and I were arguing over a math problem I was trying to solve for my homework. Frustrated with me, he ripped my math book from my hands. He took out his own piece of paper and in about thirty seconds, solved the problem I'd been struggling with. Resembling a player who had just spiked a football after scoring the winning touchdown, he looked straight into my eyes and said, "You'll never be as smart as me." Thanks for the words of encouragement, Dad.

I went on, "I think Mom was even smarter than Dad. She never let him realize it, though. She has an honors degree in mathematics from William and Mary. In today's world that might not be such a big deal, but in 1951 she was the only female to graduate with such a degree."

What came out of Dr. Brooks' mouth next, floored me. It took the wind right out of my sails. It was a punch in the gut from Mike Tyson. Dr. Brooks said, "Your brother likes to wear the same clothes year after year, doesn't he? His clothes are all tattered, frayed, and torn aren't they, Mr. Wilson?" Dr. Brooks had hit the trifecta, but how? Was I being "punked" or something? Did Dr. Brooks have ESP? Was he a mind reader? I don't remember reading that in his Yellow Pages ad.

No one would know these facts except a family member who lived with Drew. And these realities were never discussed outside of our home. In fact, they were never even discussed in our home. Was my brother or sister going to jump out from behind Dr. Brooks' curtains and yell, "Surprise!"? I was dumbfounded.

"Yes, Dr. Brooks. You've nailed it. Everything you just said is correct. But how can you know these things when today was the first time we've met? These are all things that only my family would know." My amazement was now turning to anger. I wanted to understand what was going on here. I know we're here to discuss Mark, but after many years of confusion and twenty-plus years of guilt, I wanted to understand the mystery behind my older brother, John Andrew.

Instead of answering me, Dr. Brooks came back at me with a question. God, I hate it when I ask a question and someone responds with another question. I just wanted direct answers, not dancing around the issue with other questions. Dr. Brooks asked, "Mr. Wilson, how long has it been since you really gave a shit about your brother's wellbeing?"

For the second time in today's session, I was overcome with a tremendous sense of guilt about Drew. When I was in college, Drew had been out of sight and out of mind. In all those years that I phoned home every week he never got on the phone with me. When I came home to visit, he just stayed in his room. After I left home, he became closer to Bobby, who was eleven years younger than Drew.

During my high school junior and senior years, it was hard to be around Drew. I was playing sports and hanging out with my friends. Drew wanted to hang out with me, go into New York City, see concerts, and get high. Around that same time, I became aware of how people would stare at him and make comments about his appearance. I knew that others could see he was "different." As my embarrassment about being around him in public grew, so did my list of excuses for why we couldn't hang out. Every time I gave Drew one of my excuses for not being able to hang out together, I saw the disappointment on his face.

Honestly, I felt a sense of relief when I went to college a thousand miles away. As I climbed the corporate ladder, moved even farther away, got married and had kids, my contact with Drew became non-existent. With some quick soul searching it was obvious that I really hadn't, as Dr. Brooks said, given a shit about Drew since I left home. His question really stung.

"Dr. Brooks, you've asked the right question. I have not really thought much about my brother since I left for college over twenty-one years ago." I hung my head like a scolded fourth grader. I was almost afraid to look up and see Dr. Brooks' reaction.

To my surprise Dr. Brooks responded, "Mr. Wilson, there's no need to beat yourself up. Times are different today. The good news is that in the last twenty years there have been some major strides in the study of social interaction and patterns of behaviors with individuals diagnosed as Autistic. There also have been successful clinical studies in medicines and behavioral therapy in the treatment of individuals on the autism spectrum. I realize that all this new information might be a surprise to you, but I would recommend that you to do some additional reading on the subject. Maybe in time, you can have an informative and productive conversation with your mother on the topic. I can recommend a few books and articles on Autism that you might find interesting before you leave today."

"Now Mr. and Mrs. Wilson, let's get to the reason why we're here today. Tell me about your son Mark."

Learning the Hard Way

COLLEEN AND I BOLTED OUT of Dr. Brooks' office as fast as we could. Careful not to trip on the Mike Brady seventies shag carpet, we took two steps at a time down the stairwell. We were like two teenagers who couldn't wait to get into their car and share a secret or the gossip from our school day. I jumped into the driver's seat while Colleen rode shotgun for our drive home. Before I turned on the ignition, I locked eyes with Colleen and hugged her as tight as I could over the center console. Colleen's body started to heave and I could hear her begin to cry. I knew Colleen's tears were about happiness and not sadness. My eyes also started to well up but I fought off the tears.

Colleen didn't need to say a word. I knew she was relieved by Dr. Brooks' diagnosis and game plan moving forward for Mark at school. A good cry would relieve the stress and anxiety that had built up in her over the past several weeks. Even though Mark would need to see Dr. Brooks weekly for the next three months, the doctor reassured us that

Mark just needed some help with interpreting instructions for doing his school work. Mark responds better to visual instructions than written ones and Dr. Brooks told us he could get Mark caught back up on his homework he had fallen behind in. Still not uttering a word, I kissed Colleen on the forehead and moved back into the driver's seat, started the engine, and put the Jeep into drive.

My first priority had been to ensure that our time with Dr. Brooks would provide us with a solution for Mark to find success in the second grade. I believed that our mission had been accomplished. We now had a solid game plan for Mark and didn't have to worry about holding him back a grade in school.

My second priority was to be there for Colleen. She has always taken such ownership with our kids about their schooling. It was Colleen who was so emphatic about paying the extra money to send our kids to Catholic school. She didn't have a great experience going to public schools. I, on the other hand, having gone to Catholic schools for both grade and high school, felt public schools would have been just fine. Colleen had carried the emotional burden of Mark's issues with school and I wanted to support her in working with Dr. Brooks. I reached for her hand and gently squeezed it as we continued on our trek home.

I, too, was ecstatic about our new plan for Mark. But I also wanted to talk about the elephant in the room or in this case, the elephant in our car. At all costs, I did not want to burst Colleen's bubble. I knew she was relieved and equally, if not more, euphoric about our meeting with Dr. Brooks today. I really wanted to discuss Dr. Brooks' comments about Drew. He had opened a door that my mother and I never knew existed. Was it possible that time, technology, and advances in studying behavior and medicines changed the entire landscape around Autism? In my mind I vacillated between bringing the elephant up or waiting until later.

As usual, my impatience got the better of me and I blurted out, "So, what did you think about Dr. Brooks' comments about Drew?" I had no idea how Colleen would respond. She had never been happy with the way my mother had provided care for Drew. She couldn't understand why Mom, as Colleen would say, "Let him rot in his room." For years, it had been a source of a few major disagreements between Colleen and me. She couldn't understand why I wasn't able to "go there" with my mom and why that conversation was off limits.

We were about a mile from home and Colleen was singing along to a Madonna song on the radio. After a few minutes she responded to my question by saying, "Interesting," and continuing to sing along with Madonna. After fourteen years of marriage, I knew her answer signaled to me that she didn't want to discuss it, not now at least. I decided it was best to leave it alone and not push her. She was still riding the high about Mark and our visit with Dr. Brooks.

I focused on what was now my new order of business—getting us home followed by beginning my research. I wanted to learn everything I could about Asperger's Syndrome. I needed to get armed with information before I'd ever consider calling my mom and sharing what I had learned from Dr. Brooks today. Drew was now my first priority.

About a block away from our house I hit the remote to the garage door. We rounded the corner and drove up the driveway. I didn't want to waste my time having to move the kids' bikes so I parked in the driveway. Colleen jumped out of the car first and ran to the kids who were out back on the swing set playing with their babysitter. I ran through the garage almost tripping over our pug Murphy, who was waiting on the stairs to be let into house. We both had critical missions to accomplish. I wanted to jump on the Internet. Murphy wanted his dinner. I knew Colleen wanted to get with Mark and talk about our meeting with Dr. Brooks. Murphy would have to wait on dinner.

Much later, I awoke slumped over in my desk chair. My laptop battery was dead. I couldn't believe I'd fallen asleep. Disoriented, I wiped the drool from my chin and glanced at the clock on the wall. Christ, it was four twenty in the morning. The last time I'd checked it had been at ten thirty at night. As I gathered my thoughts it was obvious that I had missed dinner, the eleven o'clock news, and any sense of responsibility for getting my three kids their baths and to bed. I certainly was going to hear about neglecting my fatherly duties from Colleen. I plugged my laptop in and made my way to our bedroom. I walked through the kitchen passing Murphy who was lying on the floor heating vent, his usual sleeping spot at night. He opened one eye as I walked past him and glared at me as if to say, "Boy, you're in trouble."

I tiptoed up the stairs and made my way into our pitch-black bedroom. Thank God Colleen was in a deep sleep. I wasn't going to chance brushing my teeth and waking her up tonight. I tossed my clothes in the hamper and threw on my old Mott the Hoople t-shirt. I gingerly slid into our bed and adjusted my pillow with care so as not to wake her up. Six o'clock was going to come too quickly. As I lay there, my brain raced with all the information I had read about tonight. Getting to sleep was going to take some effort. It reminded me of graduating college and becoming a manager at Bennigan's restaurant where I'd frequently worked the closing shift. I'd get home at two in the morning and would spend an hour or two trying to go to sleep because I was too amped up.

Before Dr. Brooks, the world of Autism had been a foreign concept to me. I had never heard of Asperger's. Who knew that the number of children diagnosed with Autism had risen to four in a thousand in 1996? Like most people, I had heard the term "being on the spectrum," but had no idea what it meant. I learned that some people believe that Autism might be caused by the vaccinations given in a child's early years of development. Some even believe that Autism might be caused by high levels of iodine in the blood system. I had just barely scratched the surface tonight. There was so much more to learn and get my hands on.

I love the Internet. Today, I planned to take a much deeper dive while I was at work. I would have to be well-armed with information before having a conversation with Mom about Drew. Reality sunk in and I realized that I was now an hour away from that six o'clock alarm going off. I was going to need some major caffeine to get me through the day. As I finally began to drift off, I felt a deep burning passion in my heart as if I had a new purpose in life. I was now driven to figure out how to provide my older brother Drew with the quality of life he deserved. I was determined to solve this mystery. It was going to be a fantastic day.

The early morning sun was magnified through my bedroom window and hitting me directly in the face. I wiped the sleep from my eyes and rolled over to see what time it was—five fifty-five. Great, five minutes before the alarm was to go off. I turned off the alarm to avoid waking Colleen up. Most mornings I would have let the alarm go off and hit the snooze button at least three times. Today was different! If I could get to the office early enough today, I'd have a few extra hours to jump on the internet and continue my research from last night. With only a couple hours of sleep in my desk chair last night and an hour in my bed, I should have been exhausted. Instead, I felt as energized as if I had drunk a couple of Jolt sodas this morning. I was sure that I'd be comatose by the afternoon, but for now I was a man on a mission.

I quickly showered and got dressed. I let Murphy out and headed out the door careful not to wake Colleen and the kids up. I jumped into the Jeep and headed to the McDonald's Drive-Thru to grab some breakfast.

When I got into work I jumped on the internet and, with the exception of a few restroom breaks, I didn't leave my desk the entire day. The workday flew by while my work productivity hit an all-time low. Thank God our IT Department was a little behind the times and didn't really monitor our online activity. If they did, I would have been in the head of HR's office by noon having to explain my non-work-related activities. A few of the staff stuck their heads in my office and I pretty much blew them off. I used the old head buried in my computer trick and explained that I had important deadline to hit today. The eight hours I spent educating myself on Autism and Asperger's Syndrome was simply exhilarating. I read through numerous white papers, case studies, and clinical outcomes.

At the end of the day, I came to several conclusions. One, it's an absolute shame that Drew was born forty-four years ago and not twenty years ago. So much work had been done in the area of autism in the last twenty years that he might be a totally different functioning person today. He might have been a contributing member of society and not someone who was a prisoner trapped in his room. Through Applied Behavior Analysis, Relationship Development Intervention, Sensory Integration Therapy, and maybe some medication, he could have mentally developed into an adult and not the fourteen-year-old he never grew up out of.

Second, my research only deepened the amount of tremendous

guilt I was feeling. Catholic guilt is a very strong force. I had left to go to college twenty-one years ago and had done nothing to help Drew. Deep inside I felt that I had not only let him down but also myself. I had graduated college, fallen in love and married Colleen, bought a house, and been truly blessed with three healthy and incredible children. The best feelings of happiness I've had in my life, Drew has never experienced. I couldn't comprehend what it would be like to never fall in love, never know the euphoria of making love, or never know the unexplainable feeling you have when your child is born, or experience the joy on your children faces on Christmas morning. How empty his life must have been.

I remember when my father passed away, a coworker who I had only spoken to a few times came up to me and told me something I have never forgotten. He said; "There will not be a day that goes by that you do not think about your father." At the time I thought that was a strange comment, but eleven years later he was absolutely right. At some time during every day, a memory of Dad flashes before my eyes. But I hadn't had one thought about Drew for twenty-one years. What kind of brother was I?

It was now five-thirty and time to head home. I packed up and left the office. I'll be more productive tomorrow, I promised myself. Driving home, my mind was still wrapped around thoughts of Drew. I'm an optimist and have always tried to find the positive, the silver lining, the deeper meaning in everything I do. Drew was only forty-four and most likely half of his life was over. I wanted to have an impact on his second half. I couldn't change his past but I hoped I could give him an opportunity to become the person that he might be crying out inside to become. Perhaps I could open a door for him to experience a great quality of life. As I've grown older, I've come to believe in the power of happiness. I wanted so much for Drew to experience a little happiness in his life. He deserved it!

I rounded the corner and turned into my driveway. I had stopped at the liquor store and grabbed a bottle of our favorite wine. I needed to apologize to Colleen for my poor performance as her husband last night. Before the evening got away though, I had one other task to accomplish. I needed to give some serious thought to when and how

I was going to initiate a conversation about Drew with Mom. Maybe I should have bought two bottles of wine.

I Just Called to Say...

IN THE LAST CONVERSATION I had with my father before he died, he asked me to promise him that I would call my mother weekly, at a minimum. When I was in college, I called home and spoke to Mom every Sunday. Sunday worked best for me because it was the one day of the week that I didn't drink. When I was in college the drinking age was eighteen. Sunday was a day to sleep in, dry out, and try to catch up with my college courses. The majority of my call home would be spent talking to Mom. Drew never wanted to get on the phone and Dad was usually taking an afternoon nap. Dad told me how much those calls meant to Mom and he was proud that I had made it a routine.

My father was pretty old-school. He believed that children should call their parents, not the other way around. If he ever did call me, it was not going to be with good news, nor would it be a pleasant conversation. I remember once getting a call from him after he received his credit card statement. He screamed at me for the entire call because I had charged $550 to his card for a brake job on my old Mustang. At the time I was promising Dad to call Mom every week I didn't know it was going to be the last time we ever spoke. He lost his battle with cancer at the age of fifty-nine, a week later.

I kept that promise to Dad. When I started working after college, I changed my routine and called her on Monday evenings. I had switched my drinking patterns and would dry out on Monday instead of Sunday. Just kidding. To be honest, I left my drinking and partying ways back at school in Florida. Monday just worked better for me.

Through the years our weekly calls followed the same agenda. We started off the conversation discussing the weather in South Carolina and Denver. Mom loved to talk about how hot it was in Greenville and how many days it'd been since the last rain. She believed that there was snow on the ground in Denver 365 days a year. She'd say, "I was watching the Broncos game yesterday and it was snowing—in the middle of October." Little did she know that it was eighty-five degrees the next day. She was a life-long New York Giants fan while I had been a Jets fan. Growing loved she loved Fran Tarkenton, and I loved Joe Namath. On our Monday calls, we discussed how our Giants and Jets had done on Sunday. If we were lucky, one of our teams would be playing on Monday Night Football. This would result in a healthy discussion, including friendly team insults, and what we thought the outcome might be.

The conversation then moved to how the kids' school and other activities were going. Mom was always interested in how the kids did in their games over the weekend and she wanted details. How many goals did Mark score? How many hits did Steve, Jr. have in his baseball game? How had Valerie's cheerleading squad performed at their competition? Sometimes one of my kids would jump on the phone and give their grandmother the play-by-play details from their weekend games.

At least once a month Mark would get on the phone and talk with her for about an hour. Other than his soccer games, I have no idea what they talked about. Through the years they developed quite a special relationship and loved talking to each other on the phone. Mark always had a special place in Mom's heart.

There was one variation to our calls. About every six months I would throw into the mix a question about how Drew was doing. My question always generated the exact same response from her—a quick, "Fine." Nothing more, nothing less. I was then left with that uncomfortable silence signaling that Mom didn't want to discuss it and it was time to move onto the next topic.

I made a commitment to myself that I would bring up my visit with Dr. Brooks on next Monday evening call. I just couldn't wait any longer. Drew wasn't getting any younger. Even though I had only delved into the subject of Autism and Asperger's Syndrome over the last four days, I felt I had enough information to hold my ground with Mom. I spent the majority of the weekend pulling my thoughts together, jotting them down on different colored note cards. I tried to anticipate every direction my end of the conversation could go and Mom's response. I even role-played every potential scenario I anticipated with Colleen. When I was ready to turn in Sunday evening, I was prepared and as ready as I could ever be. I felt tomorrow could be the start of a new chapter in Drew's life.

Monday found me with very little appetite. I think I only ate two bites of my sandwich at lunch. My stomach was a mess all day. I was nervous about the anticipated call tonight, which was ridiculous. By the time I arrived home I was angry with myself for letting my nerves get the better part of me. I'd been calling Mom once a week for over twenty years. I kept telling myself that today was just like any another Monday, just another call with my mother. My brain and stomach appeared to know better though.

I kissed Colleen when I got home and told her not to wait on me for dinner. I made a beeline for my office and closed the door behind me. I was glad I'd put on that undershirt again this morning because I could feel the perspiration start to roll down my arms in anticipation of my call. Twice in one week I'd worn an undershirt! I took a deep breath and with sweaty fingers, hit the speed dial on my cell phone. True to form she answered on the third ring. It doesn't matter where she is in her house, she always answers on ring number three.

"Hello."

"Hi, Mom. How're you doing?"

"Oh, I'm okay. My goodness, it's been so hot here lately. It's been ninety-five or better the last three days. We haven't seen any rain for almost three months. Every day it clouds up in the afternoon and then nothing. My plants are struggling this year. My grass is starting to get brown spots. I'm really not looking forward to next month's water bill."

I was so well prepared for this call that I even checked the Weather Channel beforehand to see the current weather and forecast for Greenville. I said, "Yeah, it looks like you've been pretty hot. I did see that maybe Wednesday you might get some rain."

"I seriously doubt it. That's what the weather experts always say."

As she spoke, I decided to touch on our weather here in Denver for just a second before moving onto the main topic I wanted to get to. "Our weather here has been very nice. It's been in the seventies almost every day. For September, I'll take it."

"Any snow yet?"

"Mom, it's September. I don't think we've ever had snow here in September."

"So, how are the kids? Did they have any games this weekend?"

Traditionally, I would have started to review the kid's school activities and their statistics from their weekend games, but I couldn't hold back any longer. Enough small talk, and maybe it might be good to catch her off guard.

"How's Drew?" I blurted out.

Unfazed, she quickly responded the same way she has for the past twenty years. "Fine." And as anticipated, the uncomfortable silence began. It's not the one-word answer that bothers me as much as the tone of her voice. In that one word reply I hear, "Why are you asking about Drew? I don't want to go there. It's nothing for you to be worried about. Let's go the next topic." She was ready to move on and on every call in the past I would have obliged, but not today. She had asked how the kids were, and now I could tie things together.

"Well, Mom, remember last week I told you that Colleen and I were going to meet with an educational psychologist on Wednesday to talk about some issues Mark was having in school?" I could feel myself starting to talk faster than normal. I'm not sure whether it was nerves or that I didn't want to let her interrupt me. "Well on Wednesday, when we were meeting with the psychologist and before we got to Mark's situation, the psychologist asked us to go over our family history.

"Colleen went first as you can imagine. When it was my turn, I told him how my grandparents had all passed away before I was born. I then talked about you and Dad." There was no way I was going to share with her what I had said about Dad. "After you and Dad, I talked about Drew. Mom, I wasn't sure what to say about him. All I could share was what it was like to grow up in the same house with him for seventeen years before I went to college. What's crazy, Mom, is that the psychologist stopped me before I got to Annie and asked me a couple of questions. He asked if Dad was an engineer. He asked if you and Dad were really smart. Then he asked if Drew walked around wearing old torn and tattered clothes."

I should have waited for her to respond, but I wanted to get the rest of what I had to say out. "It was nuts, Mom. How the heck did he know this? It was like he had lived with us. He asked me if I had ever heard of Asperger's Syndrome. Have you ever heard of Asperger's Syndrome, Mom?" Now I did wait for her to respond.

In a faint voice she answered, "No."

I continued, "The doctor felt that Drew might be on the autism spectrum. After Colleen and I got home, I spent a bunch of time doing some research on autism and Asperger's Syndrome. It's amazing how much progress has been made in the last twenty years. Maybe it would make sense for him to see a psychologist. So much has changed." I stopped talking, mainly because I was out of breath.

"Oh, I don't know, Steve," Mom said. "You know doctors, they'll just tell you what you want to hear. Sometimes you should just let sleeping dogs lie." As predicted, next came her usual desire to change the subject. She was done. "So, tell me what they said about Mark."

I vividly remember the first time I got the wind knocked out of me. I was in the sixth grade and was playing peewee football. One day in practice, Larry Gebert was punting the ball. As a defender, it was my job to try and block the punt. I ran as fast as I could laying out in my best Superman pose and caught the ball right in my gut, fresh off Larry's foot. I lay on the field gasping for air like I never had before. If you'd lifted up my jersey, I'm sure the word Wilson would have been imprinted on my stomach. That's exactly how I felt, when I heard Mom change the subject. It was a gut punch! I just wanted to bury my head in my hands and cry.

I knew it was useless to go back and press her about Drew. That part of the conversation was over in her mind. I had such respect for Mom and didn't want to upset her. Growing up, my parents always kept any information about him away from us, and that didn't change even as we became adults. I answered her question about Mark and his diagnosis with Dr. Brooks. I didn't have the energy tonight to get into the Giants or the Jets, who had both lost their games on Sunday. I just wanted to get off the phone as fast as I could. I was sad and hurt and done with the conversation.

"Mom, we're getting ready to sit down for dinner. I'll call you later,"

I said. I hung up, tasting the salt from my tears as they rolled down my cheeks and onto my lips. I sat motionless in my chair feeling gutted and numb. How could she not care? How could she not want a better life for Drew?

I stared at the office wall for another thirty minutes and tried to collect myself. Feeling the need for fresh air, I headed out to the backyard, stopping in the kitchen first. I opened a cabinet and grabbed my bottle of Crown Royal and a glass. My CD player was on the kitchen counter and I grabbed that too as I headed to the backyard. On my way to the back door, I passed Colleen and the kids who were eating dinner at the kitchen table. Colleen looked up and asked: "Rough call?"

I choked up and was barely able to get out, "Same as always." Then, for some odd reason, I said, "Same as it ever was... Same as it ever was," doing my best David Byrne of the Talking Heads impression. My kids thought I was hilarious. I couldn't even crack a smile.

I opened the back door and flopped into the first available chair on our deck. The Colorado sunset was absolutely stunning, Bronco orange to be exact. I twisted off the Crown Royal cap, glanced at the beautiful view of the mountains in front of me, and took my first big gulp of Crown. No glass needed tonight. It would take too much time to pour and sip. I peeled off the plastic from the new CD I'd picked up on the way home tonight and loaded it into the CD player. That angry post punk English band Oasis was just what I needed tonight. I'd have turned the volume up to eleven if I could have.

After my second huge swig of Crown, I felt a primal scream building up inside. In my best blood curdling scream, I cried out the only words I could think of at the moment. "Goddammit! Why? Why?" It was a great question. Why did Mom always have such a negative and non-communicative attitude when it came to Drew? I'm thirty-nine years old and she still can't talk to me about him.

As I mentioned before, my mother is a living saint. I'll always give her the benefit of the doubt. I tried to understand what her motives for non-communication could be. As I continued to drink, I thought that maybe after dealing with Drew for forty-four years she was just plain tired. Tired of all the stress and work that went along with being his caregiver. Maybe the thought of making any changes in his life was too painful for her. It may have conjured up all kinds of past memories and negative feelings that she didn't want to relive. At age sixty-six it just might be that she deserves to, as she said, "Let sleeping dogs lie."

Around eleven o'clock, Colleen came out with a blanket for me and said she was going to bed. God, I love her! She also reminded me that I might not want to stay out much longer because the coyotes that roam the foothills at night probably wouldn't make good drinking buddies. I kissed her good night and told her I'd be in in five minutes. I told her that I needed to take care of one more thing before I came to bed.

As Colleen closed the door behind her, I stood up for the first time since I'd sat down and almost fell flat on my face. I stared at the empty bottle of Crown Royal on the table that was the cause of my lack of balance. Laughing at my intoxicated self, I grabbed the empty bottle of Crown and threw it as far as I could. I heard the bottle smash against the mountain rocks well beyond my fence as I walked inside, being careful not to trip on the back door step. I could feel the pain now shooting up my throwing arm as I made my way to our bedroom. The old arm just wasn't what it used to be.

Colleen had already fallen asleep so I quietly brushed my teeth and slipped on the old Mott the Hoople t-shirt. I slid into bed and curled up against Colleen's warm body. As my head hit the pillow, two questions came to me. Why did I drink so much tonight? I have to work in the morning. And, more importantly, how was I going to help Drew? I may have lost the battle over him with Mom tonight but I will never, ever give up. It's not in my DNA. I felt that for the first time in my life I could make a difference in Drew's life. I couldn't change his past, but I knew I could change his future. It wasn't right to let him rot in his room for the rest of his life. For me, it's always about doing what I believe is the right thing.

PART II

John Andrew Wilson

PART II

John Andrew Wilson

THIS TRIP TO DR. BROOKS' OFFICE today was a lot less stressful than the one last week with Colleen. I knew what a visit to a psychologist now entailed; there was no need to be nervous this time. As a matter of fact, I was excited about my appointment today. I was going to talk to Dr. Brooks about my brother Drew. Last week Dr. Brooks had blown me away when he discussed the advances in studying the treatment of people diagnosed as Autistic.

After the disastrous call with Mom, I was still not willing walk away, bury my head in the sand or look the other way when it came to Drew. I had looked the other way for the last twenty years as Dr. Brooks had so graciously pointed out during my visit a week ago. I wasn't looking for some form of closure but more for answers to a few questions I had—questions I'd never been able to ask my parents. Questions my parents would never have wanted to answer.

I was able to book Dr. Brooks for a five-hour consultation. Our plan was for me to spend the majority of our time sharing everything I could recall about Drew's past. Due to his license, Dr. Brooks said he was not going to be able to properly diagnose him or even attempt to, without spending any time with him in person. He said he'd be willing to listen to Drew's background and try to provide me with some insights into the world of Autism Spectrum Disorder.

Colleen and I agreed that this appointment should be between Dr. Brooks and me so she stayed home with the kids. She understood how important this meeting was to me and told me that she didn't want to be a distraction. I made my way past the receptionist and into Dr. Brooks' office. He looked the same as the previous week. His face was deeply buried in a medical journal and he looked up as I sat down. Staring at me from over the top of his glasses he said, "Hello Mr. Wilson. Back so soon?"

I Bless The Rains Down In Africa

DR. BROOKS SPOKE FIRST. "Steve, let's start at the beginning. Tell me about your family and how Drew came into the world."

I wasn't about to let myself be rushed today. I had five hours and I was going to take my time and make sure I left no detail out. "Sure," I said. I told Dr. Brooks what I knew of Drew's beginnings.

My maternal grandparents were born in Hungary in the late 1800s. They fled Hungary as teenagers and came by ship to Ellis Island, New York. After clearing immigration, they both settled in a Hungarian neighborhood in Cleveland, Ohio. They married in Cleveland and moved to Lima, Ohio where they raised three children. My grandfather was a custom furniture maker and my grandmother a seamstress. My grandfather died of a massive heart attack when he was just forty-five in the middle of a softball game he was playing. Mom always said that her dad left the dinner table one evening to play softball down the street with some friends and never came home. She was only eight when she lost her father. My grandmother lived into her early seventies.

My paternal grandparents were born in North Carolina, also in the latter half of the 1800s. They lived in Richmond, Virginia before settling down in Norfolk to raise their two children. They were true Southerners at heart and very proud of their numerous relatives who had fought for the Confederacy. My father told us stories about growing up with lots of money before his father lost everything in the stock market crash of 1929. His family was very poor during the Depression. He led me to believe that his father died during the Depression in the 1930s and I always suspected that it was by suicide. Dad never wanted to discuss how his father had died and, in fact, rarely spoke about his father.

A few years after my dad passed away, I found my grandfather's death certificate in Mom's basement. That death certificate documented that my grandfather died in 1951 at a Virginia state hospital in Williamsburg. I had always thought my grandfather died when my father was around five, but the death certificate revealed that my father was twenty-six when his dad died. I never was able to discuss the topic with Dad and I never brought it up with Mom. Obviously, there is more to that painful story than I'll never know. My grandmother lived to age sixty-eight. All four grandparents were deceased before my siblings and I were born.

Dad was born in 1925 in Richmond, Virginia. His family moved to Norfolk, where he finished high school and then joined the Navy. His time in the Navy helped him to develop some incredible swimming skills, but honestly, he was the most uncoordinated person I've ever met. I grew up wanting to be a professional baseball player. Mickey Mantle was my idol and the New York Yankees were my favorite team. I remember Dad trying to play catch with me once but I was so embarrassed by his lack of coordination and inability to catch and throw a ball that we never played catch again. My mother was a much better athlete so she filled that void. My father, however, could swim like a fish. Every now and then on a Sunday afternoon in the blazing heat of the New Jersey summer, he'd take us all to the community pool and we'd watch him do laps while we tried not to drown in the deep end. After his four years in the Navy, he attended Duke University and received a degree in electrical engineering. He never really talked about his college experience, but what he was most proud of was his conversion from the Southern Baptist faith to the Catholic faith while he was in college.

Mom was born on Christmas Day in 1930. She lived in Lima, Ohio until her dad passed away. Mom and her mother then moved to Norfolk, Virginia to live lived with my mom's older brother John and his wife Judy. John was a jazz musician, playing in pubs at night until he had to settle down after the birth of his son John Jr., or Johnny to his cousins. After the bar scene, Uncle John worked for the U.S. Post Office until he died in 1970. Every now and then Uncle John would send us "first day of issue stamps." I wish I had kept them. Mom graduated from Holy Trinity High School in Norfolk and then went onto William and Mary in Williamsburg. She graduated in three years with a degree in mathematics. She was proud that in the majority of her math major classes she was the only woman. She was a trailblazer for women. She met and started dating Dad when he taught history for a year at Holy Trinity High School when she was a senior. Today, he would have been fired or arrested for dating her, but it was a different time back then.

My parents were married at Holy Trinity Catholic Church on March 27, 1951. Dad was twenty-five and mom twenty. In April of 1951, Dad accepted a job with the U.S. Army Corps of Engineers. Two months after they were married, he was transferred to Casablanca in French Morocco. He and Mom lived on Nouasseur Air Base where Dad designed and built asphalt and concrete runways for B-36 and B-47 bombers. While at Nouasseur, the B-36 and B-47 bombers were constantly pointed directly at the Soviet Union, no doubt as a form of intimidation. Mom also worked for the Corps of Engineers while in Morocco as an administrator. I'm sure she ran circles around most of the generals without them ever realizing it. She became pregnant around Thanksgiving of that same year.

My older brother Drew was born on August 14,1952 at the U.S. Air Force Hospital 80th Medical Group at Nouasseur Air Base in Casablanca. His birth certificate recorded his weight at seven pounds and four ounces. There were no complications during the delivery. Because Mom's father and brother and nephew were all named John, my parents decided not to break tradition and named him John Andrew. They decided that he would be called Drew and not John. When he was ten days old, he was baptized in a Catholic Church in Casablanca.

It's hard to describe Drew in his early baby pictures. He just looks "different." It always seems to me that his eyes and face make him appear frightened. While his face was rather long, he looked chubby at the same time. As a young adult he did slim down. I always thought he looked like Ric Ocasek, the lead singer from The Cars. Later in his life, Drew would tell me he thought he looked like Adam Lanza, the Sandy Hook shooter who killed his mother, twenty first graders, and six adults in Newtown, Connecticut.

When we were growing up many of my friends made fun of Drew for looking and being different. I would sometimes say to them, "Well, he was born in Africa." I'm not sure why, but for some strange reason that would shut down any more comments made about him. Sometimes my friends would ask me to tell them stories about Africa and I would make up a story based on a Tarzan movie I had seen. It was my way of changing the uncomfortable conversation.

Africa and French Morocco seemed like a far distant planet to me. I would convince myself that being born in Africa was the reason that he was so different. Based on the stories Dad shared with me, Morocco was very unlike our world in New Jersey. It also didn't help that Dad had a Moroccan painting and map hanging on a wall in our house to prove the point. I recall that painting being of men walking in a dessert wearing turbans on their heads and colorful robes and red genie slippers that curled up at the toes. Dad always said, "Those people are absolutely crazy over there. They eat with their fingers and don't use toilet paper." That certainly was very strange and different from anything I had experienced.

After sixteen months in French Morocco, my parents' project ended and they returned to the United States. Back in the U.S., Dad took a job as an electrical engineer in Plainfield, New Jersey. My parents decided to settle down and raise their family in the sleepy suburban town of New Providence, New Jersey. New Providence was a colonial town and is about twenty-eight miles from New York City. Drew was a year old when my parents set out to start their perfect life in the Garden State.

Fiddle About – My Uncle John's House

"STEVE, YOU MENTIONED in our last meeting that you felt something may have happened to Drew at an early age, something that may have changed him. Tell me more about that," said Dr. Brooks.

When Drew was three years old, my parents took a vacation for a week in North Carolina without him. It was the first and last vacation they would ever take without Drew. They left him with my Uncle John and Aunt Judy and their only child, our cousin Johnny, in Norfolk. Johnny would have been five at the time. In a rare moment of divulging any information about Drew's past, Mom shared a suspicion that something happened to him while they were on vacation. She told me, "Drew was a perfectly normal child before that stay at Aunt Judy's house. He was never the same after."

I used to speculate about what could have happened during that week. Could Drew's separation anxiety from my parents when they left him for that week cause him not to be normal permanently? Did the change in his routine during that week in Norfolk change him so drastically, even at three years old? Did my cousin Johnny do something to Drew during that week to cause him not to be normal? Or worse, was he abused mentally, physically, or sexually by my uncle or aunt? This mystery was never solved.

Growing up, we spent little time with any of our relatives. We had a very small family and few relatives. Dad had a brother who had a couple of kids but we hardly ever saw them, even though they lived only four hours away outside of Washington, DC. Mom had a second older brother who lived in California but he did not have any children. I remember Roy, her other brother, staying at our house in New Jersey once for a day before he headed to the World's Fair in New York City. He was a cool guy who worked as an engineer for Boeing. He drove his red Corvair from California to New Jersey. I remember being fascinated that his car had no engine in the front. It was the first time I ever saw a car with the engine behind the driver's seat.

We spent the majority of our vacations in Norfolk with Uncle John, Aunt Judy and cousin Johnny. Every summer during the first two weeks of August, we loaded up our Chevy station wagon and drove the eight hours from our house in New Jersey to Norfolk. The seating arrangement was the same each year. In the front sat my dad in the driver's seat, my younger brother Bobby in the middle and my mom riding shot gun. In the back seat, Drew and Annie had the two windows and I sat between them. Windows were important in that car for two reasons. First, Dad chain-smoked the entire eight-hour trip and, second, the Chevy had no air conditioning and August was a sweltering month. Sitting in the back middle seat was brutal.

Dad, who was never fond of driving, would have us up by five in the morning so he could beat the traffic. Unfortunately, he was never able to outsmart the New Jersey Turnpike and Garden State Parkway road system and he swore at the other drivers all one hundred thirty-five miles through Jersey into Delaware. We knew the choice words we heard were never to be repeated. When Dad swore, Drew would laugh at him, making me giggle uncontrollably. This resulted in Dad flinging his right arm back at us and telling us to shut up or he was going to stop the car. And stopping the car was never in our best interest.

As soon as we hit the Chesapeake Bay Bridge, about seven hours into the trip, out of nowhere Dad's southern accent took over and remained with him for the rest of our vacation. The only time all year I ever heard that southern accent was when we were on vacation in Virginia. After eight hours in that boiling hot car, we arrived at my aunt and uncle's house. I loved the dogwood trees that lined their driveway, with their bright leaves of dazzling orange and scarlet and their bright red berries. We gathered our belongings and tried each year to figure out how nine people were going to spend two weeks in a two-bedroom, one-bathroom house.

Drew had a story about our younger brother Bobby that he brought up every chance he could. I believe that was because, for his entire life, Drew was always made fun of by other kids and the chance to make fun of someone else was a welcome event. He relentlessly reminded everyone of the time when Bobby was around age seven and pooped in his pants just before we arrived at my uncle's house. He didn't want to fess up so, to hide his embarrassment, he tried to flush his soiled underwear down the toilet when we got to Uncle John's house. Bobby's soiled underwear got stuck in the toilet leaving us with no functioning toilet for nine people. My uncle had to call a plumber. Dad was so embarrassed he made us pack up and moved us to the local Howard Johnson's for the rest of our vacation. I was overjoyed because Howard Johnson's had a large pool with a ten-foot diving board. Thank you, Bobby! When we went back over to my uncle's later that evening, Uncle John said to Bobby, "Hey, Bobby, there's a gift for you on the back porch." It was Bobby's soiled underwear in a bucket of water.

Early on, we all loved going to my aunt and uncle's for vacation. Aunt

Judy was an excellent cook and their house had air conditioning, which our house in New Jersey did not. We were allowed to get Slurpee's at the 7-11 and, best of all, one night during our summer vacation we'd get to go to Ocean View Amusement Park. Drew was always obsessed with the laughing mannequins outside the two houses of horrors. He would never go on the old rickety wooden rollercoaster ride with us because he said the motion made him sick.

For a few years, Uncle John, Aunt Judy, and cousin Johnny drove to New Jersey and spent Thanksgiving at our house. I never understood why, if my parents thought something had happened to Drew at their house in Norfolk when he was three, we still went to see them every summer and let them visit us at Thanksgiving. I have to believe that Mom and maybe even Dad, questioned my aunt and uncle after Drew's stay with them. Why, as my Mom said, was he so different after that week in Norfolk? In the end, I believe that Mom must have confronted them at some time and come to the conclusion that her brother and sister-in-law did nothing out of the ordinary during Drew's visit. I, myself, am still not so sure that something didn't happen."

Don't Stand So Close to Me

Next Dr. Brooks asked, "What was Drew's experience like going to school during those early years?"

I was starting to get the hang of how our time and the flow of our conversation would go today. Dr. Brooks was going to lead with a question and I would answer as well as possible in meticulous detail. I was comfortable with his approach and knew I could handle this for the next four hours.

Some of my first memories of Drew were of him going to grade school. He went to a lot of different schools in those years. He went to first grade at Springfield, which was five miles from our house. For second through fourth grades, he attended school in Berkley Heights in the next town over from New Providence. He went to Lincoln in New Providence for the fifth through the seventh grades. These grade schools were all different and foreign to me because my other siblings and I went to the same Catholic school for all eight years. I'm sure my parents sent him to different schools to place him in educational institutions that had the ability to deal with children with special needs, especially when they didn't have a diagnosis for why he was different. It must have been devastating for my father to send Drew to public schools over Catholic schools, even though they were better equipped to help him with life skills.

Before I was old enough to start school, I would watch Drew get ready for school and wait outside for his bus or van to pick him up and take him away. I recall wondering why he was taken away for the entire day. It all seemed very mysterious to me. Part of that mystery was solved years later when, as an adult, I found all of Drew's grade school report cards. Mom had saved all of our report cards and stored them in an old dusty box in her basement. When I discovered them, I wrote down some notes and comments I found interesting. I brought those notes with me today. I thought they might help you to put this puzzle together, Dr. Brooks.

A kindergarten report card was one of the more interesting ones because there were no A through F grades. Drew scored satisfactory in being respectful, keeping his hands to himself, in rest time, using a soft voice, good posture, keeping things out of his mouth (an interesting thing to grade), constructing things, singing, listening to music, and painting. His kindergarten teacher felt he needed to improve in the areas of sharing in group planning, listening and following directions, completing his work without wasting time, and sharing his ideas and experiences with the group.

In the first grade there was a report card where Drew's grade category is listed as Educable. It wasn't a bad report card though. He scored a C in language arts, a C in spelling, satisfactory in writing and music, a C in arithmetic, and an A in art.

In the second, third and fourth grades, his report cards consistently reported the same assessment. His reading level and spelling were a grade behind now. He did well in phonics, language, writing, math, and science. He scored from good to excellent in all fifteen categories under social adjustment but there was one area he consistently scored poor in—participation in- group activity.

In the fifth, sixth and seventh grades, Drew was satisfactory in the majority of the areas he was graded in. But he was rated consistently as needing improvement in accepting criticism, beginning work promptly, completing work without wasting time, and participating in physical activities. He scored the lowest in contributing to class activities, participating in class discussions, and works and plays well with others.

Eighth grade was an entirely new experience for Drew. For some reason, my parents sent him to a school ten miles away in Bernardsville. He was thirteen and planning to go to high school the following year. I was eight. I vividly remember that short yellow school bus driving through our neighborhood each school day. Some mornings I'd watch him waiting at the end of our driveway and getting on the bus. Sometimes I'd be playing in the yard when the bus pulled up in front of our house delivering him home in the afternoon. In both instances I would try to get a glimpse of what the other kids on the bus looked like though I was never able to.

There is a time during Drew's eighth grade year that I have never forgotten. He had a doctor appointment right after school so he couldn't take the bus home that afternoon. I was off from school that day so Mom took me along with her to pick up him in Bernardsville. In the sixties, Bernardsville was a town of rolling grassy hills and farms. To me it seemed far out in the country. To an impatient boy of eight, that ten-mile drive took forever. To get to Drew's school, we drove down a long and dusty dirt road. I was surprised by all the cows, pigs, and chickens we had to dodge in the road to get to his schoolhouse. I don't think I'd ever been on a dirt road before, let alone seen a live pig or chicken. I thought he must have been going to school on a farm. The building was an old one-room red and white schoolhouse like the ones I'd seen on the *Little Rascals/Our Gang* comedies. I believe those were filmed in the twenties and thirties and this schoolhouse looked like it could have been from that era.

When Mom and I entered Drew's classroom, I couldn't believe what I saw. Remember, I was only eight. There were about thirty children packed into this one-room schoolhouse. What startled me were the physical conditions of those kids. Some were severely mentally handicapped, most were in wheelchairs, some had their mouths wide open and were drooling on their desks, and some were even in diapers. And there was Drew, sitting in the middle of his classmates. He appeared to be truly out of place. As we drove back down the dirt road on the way to his appointment, I was very upset and felt like crying. I remember thinking that Drew was not mentally retarded. I believe the proper words today are intellectually disabled. He was nothing like those other kids. Why was he in that classroom?

When I think of that strange day in Bernardsville, I still get angry. Why would my parents take Drew, who obviously had an issue with low self-esteem and social anxiety, and surround him with children who could not communicate and who were nowhere near as mentally developed and advanced as he was? What did this do to his self-esteem? Eighth grade had to be a major step back for him developmentally.

After discovering the box with his old report cards and reading through all of them, it didn't take a rocket scientist or Sigmund Freud to come to the conclusion that Drew had major social anxiety and did not function well in a classroom setting. Going to school every day for him must have been a painful and anxiety-filled experience. He couldn't handle being around his classmates and having to interact and share any ideas or thoughts with them. I'm sure that his anxiety affected his performance in school, which resulted in his poor grades. This might also explain the other consistent thing I noticed when I read through all of his report cards. He was consistently absent over thirty days every school year.

Saturday In The Park

"STEVE, THANKS FOR ALL the detail you're providing. I'm glad we're digging deep here. Do you know if your parents ever got Drew some outside help?"

When I tell people I'm from New Providence, most have no idea where it is. When I say it's near Morristown, they nod their heads as if to say they know where that it is. It might be because George Washington made Morristown his headquarters during the Revolutionary War. It could also be that in the days when *The Wonderful World of Disney* was on TV on Sunday evenings, they dedicated an entire show to seeing eye dogs that helped the visually impaired. That Disney episode featured seeing eye dogs being trained in Morristown.

When Drew was twelve, he saw an adolescent psychologist every Saturday for about a year in Morristown. Early on Saturday mornings Mom loaded up Drew, Annie, Bobby, and me in our Chevy wagon and made the nine-mile trip from New Providence to Morristown. We arrived in downtown Morristown for Drew's weekly appointment and followed Mom into an old office building, up a massive flight of stairs, and down a long dark hallway to an office. We waited outside the office door while Mom took Drew inside and dropped him off for his appointment. I still remember how that office building smelled of old wood and stale books, like an old library. The glass window door looked like something out of a Three Stooges sketch where the lawyer's glass office door had the names Dewey, Cheatem & Howe painted on it. You know, the window with gold lettering that always breaks into pieces when the door is slammed.

The entire "drop off" process every week was strange to me. Drew was left at an office for a reason that we never discussed and for the next hour, Mom took us to the Grand Union grocery store next door to do the weekly grocery shopping. Nothing against Grand Union, but I hated going there. As a kid of seven, I preferred our A&P grocery store back in New Providence. I always enjoyed the coffee grinders at the checkout counters where they bagged our groceries. I was too young to drink coffee, but I loved the smell of those ground coffee beans. More importantly to a seven-year-old, our A&P sold baseball cards while the Grand Union did not.

After the shopping was finished, we trekked back up that long flight of stairs and collected him. Nothing about this hour was ever discussed. We didn't ask him how his appointment went and he never shared any information with us. We climbed back into the Chevy and headed back to New Providence talking about anything other than what happened in that office. I sat in the backseat of the car staring at the back of Drew's head as he sat in the front seat and I wondered what was going on inside of it. We followed that same routine every Saturday for that entire year.

Take Me To Church

"STEVE, YOU MENTIONED at the last visit that your father was very religious. Catholic, I believe. That must have been a big part of your and Drew's lives. Tell me about that experience."

In his early twenties my dad converted from being a Southern Baptist to a Catholic. He used to say, "Converts are the worst." I'm not sure what he meant but I will tell you he was the most devout Catholic I have ever known. This includes most of the priests I served as an altar boy and teachers in high school. Dad made us pray in the car on our way to Mass and on the way home from Mass. When I say pray, I don't mean silently to ourselves. I mean out loud. He had a set of prayers for all occasions and he had a specific set of prayers for getting to and from church every day.

At the age of five, we were expected to memorize and say those prayers out loud. If we forgot a prayer or a specific line in a prayer, Dad scolded us in front of the entire family. God help you if you forgot that prayer again the next time it was your turn to say the prayer out loud. It was one thing to recite prayers in front of my siblings, but the worst was when I had a friend spend the night. The next morning Dad would make my friend go to church with us. I was so embarrassed to say my prayers in front of my friends on the way to and from church. I could only imagine what my friends told my other classmates at school on Monday. I'm sure they made fun of my family. No wonder I had a hard time getting my friends to sleep over.

We went to Mass every day. Yes, I said every day, Monday through Sunday. When I tell people this, they always give the same reply, "There's no way." Yes, it's true, each and every day. Let me clarify something, though. Mom didn't go Monday through Friday because Dad believed it was her job to have his breakfast on the table when he returned from church. He'd eat his breakfast in five minutes and leave for his twenty-minute drive to work. All of us children were expected to attend Mass every day from the age of five until we either left for college or moved out of the house at eighteen.

Our weekday routine for church was always the same. Dad woke us at six o'clock by whistling "Reveille" as loud as he could. He thought he was being funny, but to this day I hate that song every time I hear it. We had to be in the car by six fifteen sharp for the ten-minute ride and prayers to church. Mass started at six thirty. Thankfully, weekday Mass lasted only twenty minutes since there was no second reading or homily. We were usually home by seven. We'd make our own breakfast and sit down in front of the TV to watch The Little Rascals from seven thirty to eight. I watched that show every day before school for so many years that I could repeat any line from any episode. When I was a senior in high school, I actually attended a Little Rascal's Reunion at the Passaic Theater with four thousand crazy Little Rascal fans. Even though I drank a little too much before the show, I won a trivia contest at the event. I have to give credit to all those early mornings going to church every day for that win.

The crowd at that early morning daily Mass was dismal. In the thirteen years I went to that Mass, the only time the attendance changed was when someone died. The same twelve parishioners were there every morning. Other than the four of us, the majority of attendees were at least seventy years old. Dad always made us sit in the first pew, front and center. During different parts of the service, he would bow his head and most of his entire body in reverence. Personally, this was the most embarrassing moment for me. No one else did this and I always wondered if the other eight people who attended Mass with us were thinking, "That Wilson family is so religious."

Drew never went with us to the early morning Monday through Friday Mass. I can only assume that since Mom wasn't there to help, Dad didn't want to deal with him at church. Deep down, I also believed that he was embarrassed by his first-born son being different. And then there was the fact that Drew had an annoying habit of taking an inordinate amount of time getting ready in the bathroom before he would leave our house. Anytime we went anywhere, he would be in the bathroom for such a long time that we'd all be waiting in the car for him. There was no way Dad would ever be late for church. It pissed me and my siblings off that Drew was excused from daily Mass, but none of us ever had the courage to say anything about it. Our only recourse from this daily event was the rare time when Dad overslept or when he was out of town on a business trip. I loved those mornings when we could sleep in an extra hour.

On weekends things were a little more laid back. Our entire family went to morning Mass on Saturday at eight and Sunday at nine. We never seemed rushed and I actually enjoyed the quiet time in church on those days. Drew's behavior at Mass on those days seemed fine, which made his being excused from daily Mass hard to understand. After church on Sunday, we drove over to Wayne's Bakery for a dozen chocolate donuts and a few crumb cakes. Drew loved chocolate donuts and probably would have eaten all twelve if permitted. Bobby and I knew that he was capable of eating all our doughnuts and sometimes on the way home, he would make us cry by taunting us and saying over and over, "All the chocolate donuts are for me."

Every other Saturday afternoon, Dad made us go back to church for confession. A few times a year he would invite the local priest over to our house for dinner. I was convinced that when I entered the confessional and began to speak that the priest knew exactly who I was. "Oh, it's that Wilson kid." I was extra careful about the sins I confessed, worried that my sins would be communicated from the priest to my father at some later time.

Sunday held another Catholic ritual for the Wilson family. As if it wasn't enough that we went to Mass at nine every Sunday morning, we gathered at seven every Sunday evening in my parents' bedroom to pray the Rosary. Many times, especially in the summer months, I'd be outside playing with my friends. When I heard Dad hollering, "Stephen!" I knew to get home pronto. We prayed the Rosary as a family, all kneeling on the hardwood floor of the bedroom. After thirty minutes, my knees were nothing but prickles of pain. I never understood why we couldn't pray the Rosary in another room, like, oh, I don't know...the carpeted family room. We actually had a formation for this ritual. Dad and Mom knelt in the front with Drew and Annie directly behind them and Bobby and me bringing up the rear. Drew would regularly get me in trouble during the Rosary. He'd remove one of his slippers and act like he was slapping Dad in the back of the head with it. This would crack me up every time.

My unstoppable giggling always resulted in Dad stopping the Rosary and warning me that if I didn't stop laughing, he'd give me a bruising with his belt. He never caught on that Drew was making fun of him behind his back.

One of the reasons I chose a college a thousand miles away was to free myself from my dad and his religious expectations. His greatest concern about me going to go college in Florida was that the Southern Baptists would try to convert me. I needed a break from him and didn't set foot in a church for at least three years after I left home. But his morning regimen of whistling "Reveille" did train my body to get up every morning by six. This enabled me to take eight o'clock classes. My dormmates thought I was crazy while I thought it was amazing to sleep in until seven-thirty every morning, just like Drew had.

Train In Vain

"Wow. Going to church every day. That was quite a commitment for all of you," Dr. Brooks commented. "Tell me about some of your early memories growing up with Drew."

Our neighbors across the street from our house had backyards that connected to the woods and railroad tracks. Drew and I spent a lot of time on those tracks when we were growing up. We walked along a path through the woods and climbed up a pile of rocks and onto the tracks where a whole new world awaited us. The tracks were mainly used for a passenger train called the Erie Lackawanna, which transported passengers from the western New Jersey suburbs past our closest station called Murray Hill and then into Hoboken. In the sixties and seventies, most of the passengers were men who commuted from New Jersey into New York City for work.

The passenger cars looked like they were from the twenties, with ugly army green paint on the outside and hard wicker seats on the inside. When a passenger train approached, we moved about twenty feet away from the tracks. Drew liked to grab rocks from the side of the tracks and hurl them at the passenger cars as they sped past us. I was always paranoid because every now and then he would hit a glass window. Sometimes the engineer or one of the conductors would yell at us as they passed by. When we got older, we flipped them the bird just to piss them off.

One day when he and I were hanging out on the tracks, we saw some sort of vehicle approaching us on the rail line. At first, we couldn't make out what it was, but as the open-air single repair rail car got closer, we knew we had to get off of the tracks. The repair car spotted us and came faster. We could now see four very burley men in the car pointing at us. They yelled at us as we ran away. They stopped right where we had previously been standing and jumped off and chased after us. We ran as fast as we could through the woods. Drew, who was five years older than I, could run like Carl Lewis. He was fast; so fast I often wondered why he wasn't running track at school. He put it in high gear and left me in the dust. When we were deep in the woods and couldn't be seen, the men gave up chasing us and returned to their repair car on the tracks. Another catastrophe avoided.

Drew knew the tracks extremely well. He knew where all the signals and track switches were. He loved flattening pennies by setting them on the tracks to be flattened by the weight and momentum of the trains speeding by. He kept a collection in his bedroom.

As we grew older, we would walk east along the tracks until we reached the Murray Hill train station. It was the quickest way to get to the station from our house. We bought tickets to take the train into Summit and later, as we became teenagers, into Hoboken. Drew knew every inch of those tracks much better than I ever did.

Once, after our sister's cat, Ralph, had been missing for a few days, Mom asked Drew and me to go look for him. After about ten minutes scouring the neighborhood, Drew suggested that we go check the tracks. I would never have thought to look there. After walking on the tracks for about five minutes we found Ralph who had just ended his ninth life and was now lying on the tracks in two equal parts. We reported our findings to Mom who asked us to go back and put Ralph in a paper bag so we could have a proper burial for him in our backyard. I did not want any part of this but Drew grabbed a shovel and a paper grocery bag and convinced me to go with him. I reluctantly went and watched Drew shovel Ralph nonchalantly and without emotion into the paper bag. I'd never seen the insides of anything that large before. I almost threw up watching him shovel both halves of Ralph into that bag. I've always wondered how he knew where exactly to look for Ralph.

The woods along the tracks also offered another great escape for us. We spent a lot of time in the woods playing, climbing trees, and building forts. My friends and I scoured the neighborhood for any wood we could find or steal to build our tree fort. Armed with saws, nails and hammers that we brought from home we went to work. Drew never wanted to help build any of our forts. In fact, I never saw him use a hammer. He did enjoy climbing trees and would eventually make his way into our tree forts when he felt it was safe to do so. Safe for him meant that he felt he was somewhat accepted and that my friends would not make fun of him.

In our pre-teen years the city carved up an acre or two and built an outdoor skating rink in the center of our woods. I tried many times to get Drew to come skating with us, but to no avail. I think there were too many people there for his liking and he wasn't going to embarrass himself on skates and have everyone make fun of him.

As he got older, the woods served another important function for Drew. In a hole he'd dug deep in the woods, a metal box where he kept his collection of "nudie" magazines lay buried in that New Jersey soil.

Friends

"DID DREW HAVE any friends growing up?"

This question made me think of a story I'd read a few days earlier about a girl of seventeen in Chicago who committed suicide. What was so tragic and gut wrenching for me was what her distraught mother said when she was interviewed. She said, "Tiara had no friends, really, not one friend. Can you imagine being a teenager who is bullied most of her life and has zero communication with any friends? We looked at her cell phone yesterday and discovered not one text, not one call, and not one friend in her contacts."

I can honestly say that Drew had no friends growing up. I get emotional every time I think about it. It's heart-breaking that he never experienced the concept of friendship and all the highs and lows that go along with it. I can't remember him ever having a friend or schoolmate at our house growing up. I didn't see him going over to someone's house to play or inviting anyone to sleep over at our house. Periodically, I had friends hang out at our house and sometimes I had sleepovers, but not Drew.

Our house was on a street named Crane Circle—literally a circle of houses. Our house was on the inner loop so all of our backyards faced each other. My friends and I built a wiffle ball field in the backyard of a neighbor directly behind our house. We made base paths with actual bases, a homerun fence in center and right field, and used the roof of the house for a homerun to left field. If we had four players, we could play an official game. For at least three summers, we played wiffle ball every day that we could. We kept stats of our homeruns and batting averages. Drew never played one game with us; not one at bat. When I stood on second base, I could see his bedroom window through the trees. Quite often I glanced up to see him in his bedroom window watching us play. He would never admit that he was watching us if I asked him about it. He just never wanted to be around people he didn't know.

My parents rarely asked me to take him along with me when I was with my friends, but there was one time that they did. I and a few of my friends from the neighborhood were invited to a sleep over in the backyard of one of my friends. They had a popup camper and our plan was to cause havoc in neighborhood after dark and then sleep in the camper until the morning. My parents said I could sleepover only if Drew went too. My friends didn't care. Drew had a pretty good time for two reasons that I remember. The first was that my friend's dad had a stash of *Playboy* magazines in their basement and my friend borrowed a few of them for the evening. Drew was in heaven and stayed in the camper looking at them most of the night while the rest of us went out and soaped our neighbors' windows.

The second was absolutely disturbing and something I'm not proud to have witnessed. Late in the evening as we were hanging out in the camper, Geno, who was sixteen and the oldest of us asked Mark, who was the youngest at nine, to close his eyes and open up his mouth. Geno said, "Keep your eyes closed. I have a big surprise for you." As Mark closed his eyes tight and opened his mouth wide, Geno took his penis out and peed in Marks mouth. As soon as Mark realized what was happening, he spat out what was in his mouth and started crying hard. We tried to shut Mark up or our sleepover was sure to be over. We were stunned by what we had just seen, but Drew couldn't stop laughing. He thought it was the funniest thing he'd ever seen.

The other time of the year that I was asked to let Drew hang out with me and my friends was Halloween. Being in full costume made it easy for him; he could be any other kid from the neighborhood. He was always more comfortable wearing a mask so people couldn't stare at the way he looked. I only remember him coming out with us for one or two years. His trick-or-treating days didn't last very long.

Going back to Tiara from Chicago, I'm still emotionally haunted by the fact that her story could have easily been Drew's.

Barbie Girl

"STEVE, WHAT ABOUT the kids in the neighborhood. Didn't Drew ever play with any of them?"

Our neighborhood was full of kids our ages when we were growing up. Most of the young families that moved into our new housing development in the sixties had at least two kids, if not three or four. There were a couple of older high school kids but the majority were between five and fourteen years old. Annie, Bobby and I always had a few of friends from the neighborhood running around with us. We spent a lot of time riding our bikes in packs around the neighborhood. There were at least ten kids the same age as Drew that also lived in our neighborhood but he never developed any connection or friendships with any of them. He didn't go to the same school and he wasn't going to develop relationships with people he didn't know.

Annie developed a close friendship with two girls who lived across the street from us. Karen and Diane played at our house on a regular basis. They listened to Beatle's records in Annie's room and talked about their crushes on David Cassidy, Bobby Sherman or Jack Wild. In the afternoons they watched *Star Trek* or their favorite cartoon, *Top Cat*. For a few years they played in a giant sandbox in our backyard where they built a large city in the sand with an intricate road system and houses that their Trolls could live in. Trolls had just entered the market and it seemed like every kid in the neighborhood had a half dozen of them. Later they would introduce their Barbies into Troll City. Through the years their Troll City grew and grew.

I never had any interest playing with their Trolls and Barbies. I preferred to play wiffle ball with my friends. Drew, on the other hand, loved playing with Trolls and Barbies. He enjoyed dressing up the Trolls and Barbie's in different outfits. He especially liked dressing up the Barbies. I wouldn't have been surprised if he had a few hidden up in his room. My dad would have killed him if he found them. Karen and Diane eventually got used to him hanging around them and liked that he was helping to build Troll City. Out of all the kids in our neighborhood, Drew gravitated toward Karen and Diane more than anyone else. Girls always seemed more friendly and accepting of him than the boys who constantly bullied and made fun of him.

Every now and then a group of neighborhood kids would gather on our front yard to play games with us. We had one of the larger front yards on our street. The regular games we played were Mother May I and Red Light-Green Light. Drew didn't like being around groups of kids so he stayed in the house. We usually played after dinner at dusk. As dusk turned to dark during those hot summer months, we loved to use old glass jars to catch fireflies, fascinated by their blinking lights.

One evening, Drew decided that he wanted to play Red Light-Green Light with us. That night the majority of the kids who were playing were much younger than Drew. I'm sure this was the reason he was more comfortable playing. During the game, five-year-old Tony from across the street tripped Drew while we were playing. As they both fell to the ground, Tony rubbed his snotty nose all over Drew's shirt. Drew got up and, embarrassed that a five-year-old had knocked him over, spit on Tony's head. Tony's mom, who had been across the street and watching us play, came running across the street and got right into Drew's face. At the time Drew was around fifteen and at least six feet tall. I remember Tony's mom glaring up at Drew, her face now an inch from his face, spewing a slew of swear words I had never heard before at him. She ended her tirade by calling Drew a retard. None of us could stand Tony who was a bratty kid. We were not too thrilled when Dad, upon hearing about the incident, made him go over to Tony's house and apologize to Tony's mom. It was the first and last time Drew ever played any yard games with us.

In the sixties and seventies, we all had our favorite TV shows. Annie was a big fan of *Star Trek, Top Cat, Bewitched*, and *Laugh-In*. Bobby liked *The Monkees, Adam 12*, and *Dragnet*. I loved *Batman, Leave it to Beaver*, and *The Munsters*. Drew wasn't into cartoons so I don't ever remember him being glued to the TV on Saturday mornings. He also didn't seem to like any regular weekly shows. He did enjoy watching old Sci-Fi movies though. His favorites were *Attack of the 50 Foot Woman* and *Dracula* with Bela Lugosi. Most Sundays after praying the Rosary, we watched *The Wonderful World of Disney* as a family. Drew stayed in his room while the rest of us watched TV. He took every chance he could to avoid being in the same room with our dad.

Rock N Roll High School

"STEVE, I'M AMAZED at the level of detail you can remember. I can't remember what I had for lunch yesterday." Wait. Did Dr. Brooks just tell a joke? I must be growing on him I thought as I laughed. He continued. "What was high school like for him?"

After attending numerous grade schools in many different towns, when Drew got to high school, he was able to attend New Providence High School for all of the next four years. They had a program for kids that was labeled at the time as Functioning Special Education. While all the kids in the high school switched classes for each subject, Drew and his special education classmates stayed in the same classroom with the same teacher all day. The only exception was when they went to shop class.

Mr. Errichetto was Drew's teacher for all four years at New Providence and Drew was able to build a trusting relationship with him during those high school years. I don't remember him respecting or enjoying learning more from any teacher other than Mr. Errichetto. He believed in his students and treated them as normal people, which was a completely different experience from Drew's grade school years. Recently, I was able to connect with Mr. Errichetto and thank him for being a mentor to Drew while he attended high school. He remembered Drew this way, "I remember him well. He was tall compared to the other students. He was slender, very quiet, and often struggled to fit in."

In high school, according to his report cards, Drew consistently scored commendable in math, PE, English, organization skills, and shop. He struggled in social studies, science, and history. In shop, he learned woodworking and printing. The education he received in printing helped him get a job at a printing press in New Providence. During his junior and senior years, he worked after school at the Minute Men Printers across the street from the Murray Hill train station. Going to New Providence High was great for Drew because it was centrally located in New Providence and he could walk to school, walk to work after school, and then walk home along the tracks after work.

Going to school at New Providence High School was socially challenging for Drew. The school was small enough that most students knew all the kids in town and what grades and classes they were in. Students in Mr. Errichetto's special education class were frequently labeled "retards" by the neighborhood kids. On a daily basis, Drew was called a retard or told, "Oh, you're in that retard class." During the seventies it was thought to be progressive to mainstream special education kids into the local public schools. The problem was the schools didn't provide any sensitivity and anti-bullying training for all the other students like schools do today.

Bullying was a daily event for him in high school. Drew didn't have any friends during his high school years let alone anyone who could stand up for him. He was afraid to hang out with other classmates from his special education class around school or around town. A few kids from the special education class hanging out together would surely have attracted bullies. During his high school years, he walked to and from school alone. Years later, he told me stories about being bullied by three boys regularly on his walk home from school. About halfway home he'd run into the boys while walking through the woods. One boy pinned him down and sat on his chest, another boy pulled down Drew's pants, and the third boy took a rubber band and stretched it out and flicked it on Drew's testicles and penis. After the encounter was over, Drew ran home and never disclosed to anyone what had happened.

I know Drew liked going to the local high school in contrast to his grade school experience. He was proud to attend a "normal" school. Most adults in our neighborhood and in town knew he went to New Providence Public School, but did not know he was in the special education class. During his junior year, Drew ordered a high school ring that he wore every day. He proudly showed off his ring to anyone who asked about it.

While he was proud to attend New Providence High he never participated in any social events like dances or proms. He didn't go to football or basketball games. He also never dated anyone in high school. He missed out on friendships and the social side of attending high school. For most of us, that would have been unimaginable. For Drew, it was a way to keep his social anxiety down to a minimum.

There are three events that I remember Drew attending while he was in high school. It's hard to believe, but New Providence High School had both Santana and Black Sabbath separately play a concert in their gym. No joke! How Santana was booked to play there after Woodstock is beyond me. I know Drew went by himself to both concerts. The third event Drew attended was called Friday Night Bullring. I know because I went with him that night. Drew was a senior in high school and I was in the eighth grade at the Catholic school. I was ecstatic that my parents let me go with him. I thought I was so cool. I believe the Friday Night Bullring was an attempt by the city to keep the high school kids off the streets in a central location and in an adult supervised and controlled environment.

It was the first and only time I was ever in the high school with Drew. Three memorable things happened that evening. First, it was interesting to hang out with him and walk around his high school. He interacted with no one except me the entire evening. He didn't say "Hi" to anyone as we walked around. Second, I saw for the first time what someone looked and acted like when drunk. One of the students drank too much, stumbled around, spoke incoherently, and eventually threw up all over the cafeteria. I'm sure the kid ended up in detention the next week.

Third, my love for Led Zeppelin began on that crisp, chilly fall night. There was a jukebox in the cafeteria playing music that evening. The jukebox was loud, and played in stereo through two gigantic speakers. "Whole Lotta Love" must have been played over a dozen times that evening. Led Zeppelin connoisseurs know that when you listen to "Whole Lotta Love" you're in for a special treat. The music fades from one speaker into the next and in and out of the left and right speakers. All the potheads were certainly in heaven that evening. Drew and I both went out and bought the *Led Zeppelin II* album the next day.

Drew graduated from high school in four years. He proudly accepted his diploma wearing the green cap and gown. It's one of the rare documented achievements in his life. My parents both seemed so happy and proud of him, probably that night more than any other time in his life. He had never been awarded any blue ribbons or trophies but he cherished his diploma.

Growing up, Dad always told us that we had three options when we turned eighteen. We could go into the Armed Services, get a job, or go to college but we were not going to remain living at home. I knew that when I turned eighteen, I had to be out of my parents' house. For me, college seemed like the best choice. For Drew, my Dad would have to make an exception.

You Better Run

"YOU SAID THAT you and Drew bonded over music. What are some of your early memories around music and Drew? What kind of music did he like?"

As Drew's and my taste in music grew, so did our album collections. I was into rock and pop while his music tastes were much more diverse. He introduced me to soul, R&B, and eventually punk. When he started working at the factory, he had a lot of extra cash to spend on albums, more than I ever had. His album collection quickly doubled and tripled in size as compared to mine. He was always great about lending me his albums to listen to in my room as long as I didn't scratch them. On the occasions when he wouldn't let me borrow one, I would sneak into his room while he was at work and give his records a spin, being careful not to scratch them. One day when he was at work, I borrowed his Isley Brothers album. He never knew that I lost my virginity to "That Lady" by the Isley Brothers.

We had a couple options for shopping for our albums. Since neither of us were driving, we hitchhiked to our closest department stores, either Korvette's or to Two Guys, which were both over five miles from our house. While we had some interesting rides, we never had any issues hitchhiking. Another option for us was to walk the tracks to the Murray Hill train station and take the train into Summit. In Summit there was an independent record store called Scotties that was our favorite record store. They had great record displays and cool band t-shirts and posters. Scotties also let you sample albums on their store sound system to help you decide on your purchase.

One brisk fall afternoon after a trip to Scotties, Drew and I left the Murray Hill station and started walking on the tracks to head home. We couldn't have been walking for more than five minutes when we both heard someone yelling from behind us. We turned our heads to see a grown man running full speed at us wielding a knife in a raised hand and yelling at us in a foreign language. We knew it was time to haul ass.

Drew jetted off leaving me far behind. In no time he was at least twenty-yards ahead of me. I tried my best to keep my distance from the crazy man with a knife. I started crying and yelled at him to not leave me alone as his lead continued to increase. I was freaking out about the crazy man with a knife behind me and pissed at Drew at the same time for leaving me so far behind. I was terrified of losing my balance and falling on the loose rocks below my feet. God, Drew was fast. Once he reached a path deep in the woods that both of us knew really well, he slowed down and let me to catch up to him. Our breath hung in the cool air as we struggled to breathe. We looked back at the tracks and the crazy man was gone. We ran as fast as we could the rest of the way home just in case he was somewhere still behind us. I came to terms with Drew for leaving me behind that day. He did what anyone in the same situation would have done, run as fast as possible.

Another incident that scared the crap out of me happened a block away from our house. Drew and I liked to play and explore the new homes being built down the street that were in the framing stage, before the builders put locks on the doors. We climbed up the stairs, went down into the basements, and hung out on the roofs for an aerial view of our neighborhood. Occasionally, Drew got destructive by throwing rocks at the windows, bending a copper pipe, or pulling wiring out from a wall. Many times, I had to yell at him to stop destroying things or we were going to get caught.

One day, some of my friends and Drew were playing in a house that was being built in a new development. The builders had left a huge pile of sand on the driveway right below the garage roof. We took turns jumping off the roof and into the sand pile. Our hour of fun was interrupted when a police car entered the driveway. Someone yelled, "Cops!" and we all scattered.

Running as fast as I could, I headed up a path behind the house. When I stopped to look back, I saw the police officer putting Drew into his car. "Shit! Dad's going to kill us," I said to myself. I wasn't about to be taken prisoner so I took a very long and unorthodox way home, making sure that my tracks were being covered while constantly looking behind me for that cop car. I stretched a ten-minute walk home into thirty minutes.

When I got home, I checked the driveway to make sure there wasn't police car parked there. I opened the back door not knowing what to expect and there was Drew sitting alone at the kitchen table. Thank God no one was home except us at the time. I asked him, "How the hell did you get home? I saw you sitting in the cop car."

He explained with a smile, "After he put me in the back of his car, the cop left to try to find you guys. He never locked the back door, so I jumped out and ran home as fast as I could." I learned to appreciate Drew's speed, which in this instance helped us to avoid another disaster and what I'm sure what would have been another whipping from Dad if he ever found out.

Take On Me

"YOU'VE TALKED A BIT about your older sister Annie, but we really haven't discussed her too much. Tell me about your sister."

Ann Marie (a nice Catholic name) was born in Newark, New Jersey on June 14, 1954. She was nearly two years younger than Drew. We all called her Annie. I can certainly vouch that Drew and Annie were complete opposites in every possible way. He had that dark "different" look to his face. Annie had the cutest face with golden blonde hair.

While Drew struggled in school and was in special education programs, Annie was a straight A student all through grade school and high school. She received a full ride scholarship to a prestigious all girls' Catholic high school. Annie scored a perfect score of 1600 on her SAT test. Drew didn't even know what the SATs were.

Growing up, Annie was a tomboy. She was not only amazingly smart but she could hold her own playing catch or basketball with me or anyone in our neighborhood. She intimidated most of the boys in the neighborhood with her athletic abilities. Annie was also never one to back down from any competition. The boys in our neighborhood were a bit afraid of her. I remember Annie being in high school and going on a miniature golf date with a guy she'd been seeing for a couple months. When they returned home, her boyfriend was fuming and wouldn't talk to her the rest of the evening because she had kicked his ass.

Annie and I had the usual spats like any brother or sister. We were both competitive and didn't like losing. If the competition had anything to do with intelligence she always won. If it was anything to do with athletics, I had at least a fifty-fifty chance of prevailing. She also had a powerful punch and frequently dug her nails into my skin if she lost at some competition. I hated those nail imprints she left on my arms or thighs. Once I hit puberty, I had enough of her punching and nail digs. After losing a basketball game of HORSE, she dug her nails into my forearm in a fit of rage. I took my left fist and hit her as hard as I could on her arm. At that exact moment, Annie knew it was the changing of the guard. For the first time she backed off and she never hit me or used her nails as a weapon again.

Having to follow Annie in school was no picnic. She was three years ahead of me in school. I was a decent student, mainly As, Bs, and an occasional C. Annie was an exceptional student. She set an extremely high scholastic bar with my Dad and the nuns who were our grade school teachers. I was used to hearing comments from the nuns like, "Steve, you're just not as sharp as Annie," or "Is Annie really your sister?" I knew what they meant. The nuns were very honest, though it would have been nice if they had cared a little more about my feelings.

Annie and Drew never got along. He had to be jealous of her. She was everything he wasn't and she had the full attention of Dad. Annie was the closest thing to perfect—pretty, smart, and popular. She had a huge group of friends and Drew had none. Dad swam and Annie was a competitive swimmer. Dad placed an inordinate value on intelligence and was able to relate to her; they appeared to speak on the same intellectual level. They got the same jokes and had the same sense of humor. Drew never got the joke. Dad taught her chess while he appeared to give up on Drew at an early age. Dad was very proud of Annie's accomplishments through her school years and was embarrassed to be around Drew. If Dad had a favorite child, it certainly was Annie. We were just the boys while Annie was Daddy's little girl. I don't remember Annie ever getting into trouble. After high school, Annie went to college and earned a PhD in chemical engineering and biological sciences. Drew worked in a factory. Today, she is one of the top engineers in the world. She continues to be preeminent in a field that is dominated by men.

Annie and I have always had a great relationship. Out of all my siblings I am closest to her. She played a key role as my big sister, especially since Drew was never able to fulfill the role of big brother for me. I got her jokes. We can spend hours on the phone quoting lines from the last comedy movie we saw or talking politics. My street smarts and her intelligence are a powerful mix and we still love to compete.

One thing I failed to mention earlier was that Drew was very talented at sketching and drawing. When he sat down at our kitchen table for breakfast and lunch, he usually had a pen and pad of paper by his side so he could draw while he ate. His sketches were always of fashionable women modeling a variety of highly colorful fashions.

They looked like the sketches on the covers of McCall's cutout sewing patterns or in the Fashion section in the Sunday New York Times. My parents never seemed to compliment or encourage Drew's talents in art. Dad didn't like the idea of Drew making drawings of women all the time so he hid them from Dad. I always thought he could have been a fashion designer. His sketches were that good. But he had his sister Annie to compete with.

Annie was also a phenomenal artist. She could draw any cartoon or animal character flawlessly. While Drew showed promise at sketching women, Annie was great at animation. Dad recognized her artistic abilities early on in her life and signed her up for all kinds of classes and art competitions. All through grade and high school, Annie took art classes on Saturdays. She placed first in most of the competitions she entered. Drew, on the other hand, was stuck at our kitchen table sketching out beautiful fashionable women. When it came to art he was as talented as Annie, but no one ever gave him any accolades. There were no Saturday art classes for Drew. I still wonder how Mom and Dad produced two children who were so different.

In My Room

"STEVE, YOU LIVED in the same house with Drew for seventeen years. Tell me another memory you have about growing up in the same house with him."

We had two full bathrooms in our house on Crane Circle. One bathroom was in my parents' room and was off limits to us kids. The other bathroom was used by the four of us, three boys and one girl. It seemed like someone was always in the bathroom with the door closed. Drew spent an inordinate amount of time in there, more than anyone else. It's not that he took more baths or showers than the rest of us. He just spent a lot more time in there, doing what I don't know. If we needed to get in there, it was always Drew that we were yelling at to get out.

Drew's time in the bathroom also became a huge issue when we needed to go somewhere as a family. When we headed to church on

Sundays, without fail we sat in the car waiting on him. After about five minutes Dad would reach his breaking point and furiously yell at me, "Steve, go tell your brother we're leaving in a minute and he better get his ass in this car."

I'd run into the house and up the stairs and yell at him through the door, "Drew, Dad says we're leaving in a minute and he's really pissed."

A typical response from him would be something like, "Screw him."

I'd run back to the car and of course Dad wanted a full report. I'd say, "He said he's coming." A couple of minutes later, Drew would climb into the car and put his head down to avoid eye contact with Dad. Dad would hit the accelerator harder than normal all the way to church mumbling under his breath but not saying anything. The rest of us just recited our prayers all the way to church.

It was even worse when we were leaving to go on our two-week vacation to Norfolk. Drew's usual five extra minutes in the bathroom would turn into fifteen or twenty minutes. After about ten minutes, Dad would tell me to go get him. I'd return to the car and report that he was coming. When he didn't show up, Dad instructed Bobby to go get him. Bobby would return to the car with no Drew in sight. Now Dad was really angry. He wanted to beat the traffic by getting on the road by five in the morning and get coffee at Howard Johnson's before we hit the Garden State Parkway. I don't think leaving that early ever made a difference and Drew ruined his strategy every time. And when Drew finally joined us, nothing was ever said. We recited our prayers on the way to the Parkway while Dad mumbled a few select swear words under his breath, directed at Drew.

I don't believe that Drew hung out in the bathroom while we waited in the car to make Dad angry. I also don't think he had hygiene issues he was dealing with. I believe he was anxious and freaking out about leaving the safe environment of our house and his room. Having to go to church for an hour was one thing but going away for two weeks was another. Drew had tremendous social anxiety and fear. He had to psych himself up so he could leave his safe space. His situation could have been handled much better. A little patience and understanding for what Drew was dealing with might have created a better outcome for him.

I Can't Drive 55

"IT'S IMPRESSIVE THAT DREW did so well in high school. Did he ever try to learn how to drive during that time?"

One sunny Sunday afternoon after Drew graduated high school, Mom decided she was going to teach him how to drive. I don't know if she thought that if Drew learned to drive, he could help her cart us kids around or whether he was pushing her to learn. I decided it would be fun to tag along and watch. I promised Mom I'd sit in the backseat and not say a word. I was excited about the idea of Drew driving. If he got his license, we wouldn't have to hitchhike or take the train to go buy albums. This would open up a whole new world of freedom for the two of us.

Mom drove over to the high school parking lot where there was plenty of open space for someone learning how to drive. She parked and she and Drew switched seats. Mom went through the normal pre-drive checklist. She explained how to adjust the sideview mirrors, how to adjust the seat, where to position his hands on the steering wheel, the purpose of the brakes and accelerator, and how to put the car in drive, reverse, neutral, and park. After her detailed review it was time for Drew to practice. He put the car in drive and pressed too hard on the accelerator resulting in Mom's panicked voice yelling at him to brake. He hit the brakes too hard and my body flew forward positioning me halfway between the backseat and the front seat. Mom barely missed hitting her head on the windshield.

Drew gripped the steering wheel to steady himself. The jerk of the car not only scared him but also embarrassed him. He figured he had failed. He put the car into park and said, "Fuck it," and got out of the car. Mom followed him and tried to calm him down. After they spoke for a few minutes, he got into the passenger seat while Mom returned to the driver's side. On the way home Mom kept trying to explain to him that everyone jerks the brakes when they're first learning to drive. Drew would have none of it and didn't say a word the remainder of the ride home. She never pushed him again to learn how to drive and he never expressed any interest. For me and my selfish ways, it was back to trains and hitchhiking. Drew seemed perfectly fine walking everywhere.

You Gotta Fight for Your Rights

"I'VE SENSED FROM some of your earlier comments that your dad was pretty strict. What's another memory of your dad that helps you to form this strong opinion of him?"

Our Sunday dinners as a family were entertaining to say the least. That was the only day we ate as a family at our dining room table. During the week we were all busy with our individual activities— Annie with school, Bobby and me with school and sports, Mom took computer classes in the evenings, and Dad was earning his master's degree and then his PhD. After church on Sunday mornings, Mom started cooking around eleven o'clock. Drew, Bobby, and I watched TV while she cooked. Dad stayed at church helping out at the later masses and got home around one o'clock. By one thirty the aroma of the feast Mom had prepared filled our house and the entire family was sitting at the dinner table in our assigned seats.

Before taking his seat, Dad liked to put music on from his record collection; usually something from a Broadway play—*Oklahoma, An American in Paris*, his favorite *West Side Story*, or my favorite *Damn Yankees*. Mom delivered the mouth-watering dinner that she'd spent hours on—pot roast, meat loaf, Swiss steak, or everyone's favorite, southern fried chicken. Unfortunately for us kids, the meal always included some type of vegetable. We all liked corn and carrots but none of us were fans of Brussels sprouts or lima beans. Bobby frequently got caught hiding his vegetables under his uneaten food or chewing his vegetables and then spitting them into his napkin, and many a Sunday found Bobby sitting at the table by himself after dinner to finish eating his vegetables.

The conversation around the dinner table was fairly light and pleasant stuff. It was nothing like at the home of my Italian friend Jerry, down the street. I'd eaten Sunday dinner at Jerry's house a few times and was amazed by the difference. Dinner with Jerry's family was marked by a lot of yelling, swearing, loud conversation, burping, and farting.

Sunday dinner at our house was quiet and tame, except for the incidents that happened with Drew. Often, out of nowhere Drew would get into some kind of argument. I focused on my plate of food rather than the contents of their argument or what started it. Once in a while, Drew would loudly call Annie a slut or a whore. I didn't know what those words meant at the time. As soon as those words left Drew's mouth, Dad jumped up out of his chair followed by Drew leaping out of his chair and knocking it over and running up the stairs to his bedroom. As I sat in my chair in complete silence, I could hear Dad bust through Drew's door and start hitting him. I knew Drew was on his bed because I could hear his bed creak every time Dad struck him. I heard slaps against skin and sometimes punches. After the punching, Dad's thin belt could be heard whipping through the air and onto Drew. Drew would scream and yell one of his favorite lines, "Get away from me you queer." Hearing that must have incensed Dad to hit him ever harder.

As Drew was getting beaten up, the rest of us continued eating our meal at the dining room table as if nothing was happening. Mom was silent and none of us kids made a peep. I'd lose my appetite and just stare at my plate of food. Sometimes I'd speak up just to cut through the tension saying, "Annie, could you please pass the potatoes?" I felt bad for Drew. When Dad returned to the table looping his belt back on his pants, his face would be bright red and he struggled to catch his breath. He ate his now cold meal in silence. I finished the rest of my meal as fast as I could and asked to be excused.

In my room after dinner, I could hear Drew through the walls that separated our bedrooms, either crying or talking out loud to himself. Once he had to call out for Mom because he had gotten a bloody lip. Whippings were one thing, but I felt punching Drew in the face was very wrong. Embarrassed, many times Drew would stay in his room the rest of that Sunday and not come out until Monday morning.

Every Sunday afternoon, Dad took his regular three-hour nap.

How he was able to sleep was beyond me. Growing up I can remember Drew getting beat up by Dad during Sunday dinner at least a half dozen times. I would eventually learn the meaning of slut and whore but I still don't believe it called for the beatings Drew endured. At Jerry's house, his family would have thought Drew's comments were funny or, at worst, been told to "shut up."

Working For A Living

"AFTER HIGH SCHOOL what did Drew do, Steve?"

Drew had worked at the printing press after school for three years but after graduating high school, he switched jobs. He went to work at a factory called Fablok Mills. I often wondered how he got through the interview process. I can't imagine he would have been able to answer any questions looking directly into the face of his interviewer. He must not have been too bad though as he did get hired.

Drew continued to walk to and from work every day. Fablok Mills was about a half mile closer to our house than the printing press was. Each day was the same for Drew. He got up at seven, ate a couple of toaster waffles, got dressed and walked through the woods to work. He ate lunch from the food truck that came by the factory, known to Drew as the roach mobile because he said he often found cockroaches in ice on the truck. He walked home after work through the woods. He had dinner by himself around ten o'clock, eating whatever Mom had made the rest of us for dinner earlier. He took a shower and was in bed by midnight.

Drew's job at Fablok Mills was to unload trucks that contained huge rolls of fabric and put them in marked bins throughout the factory. He also filled orders from within the factory. An employee would request ten rolls of fabric and Drew would pull the ten rolls from the storage area, put the rolls of fabric onto a dolly, and roll the dolly over to the requesting employee. After the employee dyed the fabric, Drew took the dyed fabric rolls and either loaded the rolls into a holding area or onto a truck. The work was extremely physical. The rolls of fabric were very heavy and awkward to handle. During the summer it was sweltering hot on the factory floor as the building had no A/C.

During those years at Fablok, Drew was in the best shape of his life. He had no body fat and was extremely muscular from lifting those heavy rolls all day long. He also started to build an impressive bank account. Living at home and without friends and a girlfriend to go out with, he was able to start building a nice nest egg.

After I completed my freshman year in college, I came home during that summer to play baseball for the American Legion and to work. It was the last time I ever lived at home. Drew had now been at Fablok Mills for over four years and was able to get me a job there for the summer. It was fascinating working at the factory with Drew and seeing him interact with other employees. He worked hard and fast and wore me out every day that summer. I basically performed all the same job functions as Drew. He could unload trucks three times faster than I could and lift rolls of fabric twice as heavy. The management at Fablok loved Drew. He was the model employee. He showed up every day on time, was never sick, never took a vacation, never caused a problem, and busted his ass the entire eight-hour shift. His mode of operation was to complete every task as fast as he could and wait for the next one. I enjoyed a steadier pace, which caused our boss to nickname me "summer help."

While Drew was the model employee at Fablok, behind the scenes he loved to play practical jokes on some of his coworkers. Our boss, Ron, was his favorite target. Ron was the son of the owner and behaved like the rich, spoiled and privileged kid that he was. Ron always acted like he knew exactly what was going on in the factory but Drew could read right through his bullshit. One day when Ron had gone out to lunch, Drew went to Ron's desk, unscrewed the voice part on the handset of his phone and removed the metal speaker from it. I couldn't believe what he was doing. He went out the side door and threw the metal speaker as far as he could into the bushes. After lunch and throughout the afternoon, Ron was paged to answer his phone. He picked up his headset every time saying, "Hello... Hello..." not realizing that the person on the other end of the line couldn't hear him. After numerous calls Ron got so frustrated, he smashed the headset onto the phone base causing it to break into pieces. Hiding and watching from a distance, Drew and I couldn't stop laughing.

Ron never figured out what happened or that his "model" employee was behind the prank.

At times like these, Drew seemed almost normal to me. He could bust people's balls with the best of them. At work, he was one of the guys. Walking home with Drew that night, he could have been any one of my friends. I always thought he would work at Fablok Mills for the rest of his life. It was the perfect situation for him. He loved the routine, he was saving a lot of money, he never complained about his job, and management at Fablok Mills loved him. Unfortunately, our father's plans would end Drew's employment there.

Flow It, Show It, Long As God Can Grow It, My Hair

"Now you and Drew grew up in the sixties and seventies. I did, too. Your dad sounds a lot like mine. I can only imagine what he thought about long hair. What was that like?"

Drew was working full time and he began to seek more independence. While most teenagers begin to seek independence at fifteen or sixteen, Drew was four or five years behind. At age nineteen, he had the challenge of wanting more autonomy while still under our father's roof. Dad liked to remind us that while we were under his roof we had to play by his rules. If we didn't like his rules we could leave. Drew was now six feet three inches tall and very muscular from lifting all those rolls of fabric. Dad was also six-three but weighed at least seventy-five pounds more than Drew. Annie had gone off to college by now so the verbal disagreements during Sunday dinner had ended.

The major battles for Dad and Drew had now shifted from fights with Annie to the length of Drew's hair. It became almost a daily battle. Dad loathed long hair. He had served in the Navy and had always kept his hair short and cropped, going to the barber every other Saturday. To me, his hair looked the same when he left to get a haircut as it did when he returned after his haircut. He continued going every other week even when his hair was balding and he only had patches of hair on the sides of his head. It seemed like a waste of money to go to the barber every other week, but maybe it was an escape from the family for him.

In the seventies, long hair on men was still in fashion and considered cool. Drew wanted to fit in and didn't want short hair to make him stand out. He also didn't want to look like he was in the military, or worse, look like a "narc." He let his hair grow long and kept a big bushy mustache. Dad hated it. He constantly badgered Drew about it, calling him a dirty hippie, a fairy, or a faggot. As he continued to grow his hair, he tried to conceal it by tucking it behind his ears and under the collar of his shirt. That strategy worked well for him until his shoulder-length hair slipped out from under his collar. Dad, noticing the length of Drew's hair, would demand that he get a haircut tomorrow. Drew never did. Instead, he came up with an excuse that would satisfy Dad until his next encounter with him. Dad knew he couldn't throw Drew out of his house, even if he wanted to.

Later, Drew came up with a different strategy. He started avoiding Dad. I swear he could go weeks without seeing Dad. When Drew was in the family room hanging out with us and heard Dad pull into the driveway he hightailed it through the kitchen, up the stairs, and straight to his bedroom until Dad went to bed, usually by nine o'clock. He would wait until around nine thirty when he was sure the coast was clear, and come out of his room and then stay up until midnight.

The only problem with this strategy was Sunday Mass. We were all supposed to go to Mass together as a family. Drew also had an answer for that. If we went to nine o'clock Mass, he'd get up early, walk to the church, and say he attended the eight o'clock service. He could have hung out in the woods for that hour for all I know. It was the same thing a kid of fifteen would do. Eventually, Dad gave up criticizing him. I was proud that Drew had taken Dad to the mat and had worn him out."

Everybody Must Get Stoned

"CONTINUING ON THE SIXTIES and seventies track, did you and Drew experiment with drugs during that time?"

Oh, yes. During the fall of my sophomore year in high school I wanted to experiment with getting high. I'd never smoked pot before and wanted to try it and see what all the hype was about. My two best friends were not into smoking pot so I had to find another avenue in which to get high. One of my classmates who wasn't someone I hung out with, started to brag about getting stoned on the weekends. I quickly warmed up to Kevin and discussed my desire to get high. We hatched a plan to go down to the Jersey Shore for the weekend with his parents and experiment. Kevin's folks had a house on Long Beach Island. I convinced my parents to let me go down to the Shore with Kevin after school on a Friday.

That Saturday night, Kevin and I told his parents we were going out to walk on the beach. It was late September and no one was out. Kevin taught me how to roll a joint before we left the house, being careful not to include any seeds. We walked down to the dark beach and Kevin lit the joint. I attentively studied how he took a hit, kept the smoke in his mouth, and let it out into the cool ocean air after about ten seconds. When he passed the joint over to me, my hands were shaking and I had to concentrate so I wouldn't drop it in the sand. I took a drag and let the smoke filter into my lungs. I then coughed my head off for the next five minutes. I took two more hits as a burning sensation filled my lungs. I felt a little buzzed and Kevin and I shared some silly laughs for the next two hours. By the time we got back to Kevin's house both his parents were asleep. The orange juice at breakfast the next morning didn't mix very well with the remnants of the pot taste in my mouth. I was raspy and a bit paranoid the entire day.

A few days after my weekend at the Jersey Shore, I nonchalantly mentioned to Drew about getting high with Kevin. His response was, "No big deal. I get high all the time."

"What? You're kidding, right?" I was shocked.

He abruptly went into his room and returned with a plastic bag filled with pot. "See?" I couldn't believe it. He told me that he'd been smoking for about a year. I asked him where he got his pot and he told me he someone at work got it for him. Drew and I made plans to smoke at the next concert we went to together.

For the next two years, Drew and I got high together at every concert we attended. Sometimes on Sunday night after saying our family rosary, both of my parents would retire to their bedroom around eight o'clock. Around eight forty-five, he and I would sneak out to the woods and smoke a joint. After we snuck back into our house, we'd munch on Charlie Potato Chips and watch *Monty Python's Flying Circus* on PBS. We'd laugh and giggle the entire show. My parents never had a clue.

In November of my senior year, the employee Drew bought pot from at work got fired and his weed supply dried up. I mentioned to Drew that there was a freshman at our high school who was rumored to be selling ounce bags of pot. He gave me some money and asked me to buy some for him. The next day, I tracked down the freshman and bought an ounce bag of pot from him and gave it to Drew. He was thrilled and continued giving me money to buy more. He wanted to stock up so he wouldn't run out if the source dried up again. In the next month I probably bought three or four more ounces for him.

Then something weird happened. The day before my school's Christmas break was to start, the entire school had to walk a mile up the street to the Cathedral for a special Mass. After Mass, we walked back to school in the frigid air to get dismissed for the holidays. As we returned to school, a group of us tried to enter through the locker room doors at the back of the building. To our surprise, we found the locker room doors, which were always unlocked, locked. Perplexed, we went to our homeroom to be dismissed. While we were waiting to be released, we could see from the classroom windows that the police, along with a few police dogs, were getting into their cars and leaving. *This was not going to end well,* I thought. I knew they were looking for drugs in our lockers. Numerous times during that Christmas break, my mind was filled with paranoid dreams and thoughts about what was going to happen when we returned to school. My dad was going to kill me. My suspicions were right on target.

Upon returning to school in January, the freshman drug dealer was expelled for what the police had found in his locker. To reduce the charges against him, he provided the police and the school a list of students who had purchased pot from him. Every afternoon after school for the next week, two or three students were individually questioned by the priest about their drug dealings with the freshman. After each student interrogation, the priest called the student's parents to let them know that their child was buying drugs at school. For the next ten days I had a pit in my stomach waiting to be called to the priest's office. I thought maybe the freshman hadn't included my name and I began to feel a sense of relief. On the eleventh day, my name was called to meet with the priest that afternoon. I was an absolute mess. In my four years at that high school, I had never gotten into any trouble; not even a detention. I'm sure the priests were all shocked that my name was on that list. All day I tried to think of what I would say. Should I admit that I was only buying pot for my handicapped brother and not for me, which was ninety percent true?

When it was my turn, I entered the room with the priest and gave my best academy award performance. I acted completely shocked and denied ever buying pot from the freshman, pretending to be outraged that the freshman would single me out. My best line was, "I knew that kid didn't like me. He hates jocks!" I lied my ass off and to a priest no less. I spent a lot of time in the confessional the next week. Following my afternoon meeting with the priest, I waited anxiously each of the next few nights for the phone call from my school. The thought that I was a dead man ran on a loop in my brain. Dad was going to kill me. Through the process I learned something about myself; I could never squeal on Drew, who had endured enough beatings from Dad. Surprisingly, the phone call never came. I guess the priest believed my story. I chalked it up to all the grace I received by going to Mass every day for the last thirteen years. Drew and I had to find a new safer source for buying pot.

Jailbreak

"YOU MENTIONED GETTING STONED and watching Monty Python. I remember watching them. I loved the 'Dead Parrot' sketch. Did your dad ever find out that you two were smoking pot?"

One evening in the spring of my senior year in high school, I arrived home around nine o'clock after being out with a few friends. When I pulled into our driveway, I noticed that my parents' car was missing. This was odd because it was Friday night and my parents rarely went out on a Friday night. As I entered the house, I was greeted by Annie who told me Drew had been busted and was in jail. She said that the police had called our parents and that Mom and Dad had gone downtown to bail him out of jail. Annie didn't have any other details and told me I'd better go hide because Dad was furious when he left the house.

I went directly into the bathroom and splashed cold water on my face to cool myself down. When Annie told me that Drew had been busted, I was sure that I would be brought into the situation. I knew Dad would interrogate him and he would spill the beans that I, too, bought and smoked pot. I was dead. When my parents still weren't home at ten o'clock, I started pacing the floor as my heart beat wildly. After a few minutes of this, I decided to go up to my room, get into bed like a good little boy, pull the covers up over my head, and pretend I was asleep. No matter what time my parents got home I was not going to be able to sleep.

Around twelve-thirty in the morning I heard Dad's car pull into the driveway. I pulled the covers tight over my head and started hyperventilating knowing that in a minute he would be in the house. I hoped that since it was twelve-thirty, Dad would wait until morning to wake me up. Surely, whatever conversation was going to happen could wait until the sun was up. Then I heard, "STEPHEN! COME DOWNSTAIRS!" This was followed by, "NOW!"

I climbed out of bed and with my best "dead man walking" trudge, slowly made my way down the stairs and into our family room. Immediately I could see Dad with his beet red face standing over Drew who was sitting on the couch looking the opposite direction of Dad. Quickly assessing the situation, I was sure that Drew had squealed on me. I was toast! For the next ten minutes Dad informed me what Drew had done to get arrested. He spent the following thirty minutes lecturing me that if I ever did what Drew had done, he would never bail me out and he'd let me rot in jail. He then told me to get to bed... like I was going to be able to sleep after that conversation. I couldn't believe that Drew hadn't ratted me out. I owed him big time!

The next day, Drew told me what happened to get him arrested. After work on Friday, he and a couple of his coworkers decided to drive around town getting high. While they were smoking pot in the car, a police car pulled up beside them, noticed them smoking, and told them to pull over. As they were pulling over, one of the guys gave Drew his two joints and told him to hide them in his socks. He did as he was told. The officers ordered them to get out of the car and stand up against the car with legs and arms spread. They were frisked and patted down individually. Drew was the only one who had marijuana on him and was the only one arrested. He was then thrown into jail and our parents were called.

In New Providence at that time, if you were busted for drugs your name would be printed in the local paper the following week with all the other derelicts. This terrified my father. At the time, Dad was studying to become a deacon in the church and he felt that if his family's name were tarnished in any way, he would lose his opportunity in the church. It quickly became an issue that was more about Dad's reputation than it was about Drew. Dad called the mayor of our town the next morning and Drew's name never did appear in our local paper.

As I tried to go to sleep the evening of his arrest, a few thoughts ran through my mind. First, it sucked that Drew, who never ever went out with anyone from work, got caught up in this. He was taking a big step with his social anxiety issues to create some friendships and the first time he attempts to make friends this happens to him. I'm sure this was another setback for him. Second, I didn't know the people he was out with that evening. I hoped they hadn't set him up by giving him their pot to hold, knowing very well that he would be the one arrested. Finally, even though we never really talked about it, Drew and I had developed a "bro" code. I got caught buying pot from the freshman at school but never mentioned Drew's name in my questioning. He got arrested and never mentioned my name in his interrogation with Dad. For the first time we were creating a tighter relationship built upon some level of trust.

New Kid In Town

"EARLIER YOU TALKED ABOUT Drew not having any friends, but you did say that he had a cousin that he appeared to be close to. Let me look at my notes... I believe his name is Johnny. Tell me about Johnny."

To me, Fonzie from the TV series *Happy Days* defined what cool was supposed to be in the fifties. My cousin Johnny defined what cool was in the sixties. Johnny was the only child of John and Judy, my uncle and aunt. When we were kids, they were the only extended family we ever visited on our summer vacations, or who visited us in New Jersey. I didn't need any other cousins. Johnny was plenty for us to handle. Cousin Johnny was two years older than Drew and seven years old than I.

When we visited Norfolk on those hot August summer vacations, a whole new world opened up for all of us kids. For some inexplicable reason, Dad lightened up a bit and didn't rule us with the clenched fist he did in New Jersey. The drive from New Jersey to Norfolk also exposed me to Stuckey's (that highway convenience store) and fields of cotton. As we drove closer to Norfolk along the eastern seaboard highway, we saw fields of cotton being picked by entire families of African Americans. This was something we didn't see in New Jersey. In ninety-five-degree heat, African Americans of all ages worked barefoot in the cotton fields. It looked like a picture from my history book depicting slavery; and this was the sixties.

Cousin Johnny helped contribute to Drew's and my delinquency. In our early years, Johnny, Drew, and I slept out on their porch. Johnny would sneak food out there, let us read his collection of *MAD* magazines, and teach us to make fart noises with our armpits. We giggled and laughed until Dad came out to the porch and yelled for us to get to sleep. As we got a little older, Johnny taught us how to pick cattails and smoke them. We thought we were so cool.

The summer that Johnny was sixteen, things began to get a little crazier. He now had a big afro and a cool ass red Honda motorcycle. He gave us rides around the neighborhood on the back of it. I knew this drove our Dad nuts. Johnny always called my dad by his first name, which I thought was so ballsy. He was the first kid I'd ever heard do this. Johnny dropped out of high school when he was sixteen and started working as a mechanic at the local gas station. He was a very talented mechanic. The guy could fix any problem and put anything back together. He would have made a phenomenal engineer. Johnny was also the first person I knew who started his own garage band. He loved and turned me onto the Allman Brothers Band. We listened to the "Idlewild South" album that entire summer vacation.

The other thing that made my cousin Johnny "cool" was the way he acted around Drew. When they were together, he treated Drew as if he were his best friend. Johnny included him in everything he did during those vacations. He was the closest thing Drew ever had to a real friend. Here was Johnny, the coolest person on the planet, hanging out with Drew who had visible issues. Drew seemed happiest when he was around Johnny. When they both got into their late teens, eighteen and twenty respectively, Johnny took Drew out to hang with his friends. I watched the two of them get dressed up and slap some cheap cologne on their faces before they left. They stayed out until one or two in the morning drinking at the local bars. After one particular night out, Drew spent the entire morning hugging the toilet and throwing up. It didn't faze Drew much, because the two of them went out again that next night.

Drew and Johnny also hung out at Ocean View Amusement Park at night trying to pick up girls. Once, Drew won a naked cupid doll playing a dart game and brought the Barbie-looking doll back to my uncle and aunt's house. This doll had a special feature I'd never seen on a Barbie before. When the doll was squeezed, its boobs ballooned way out. The next morning at breakfast Dad noticed the doll lying on the counter. He picked it up and asked, "Whose is this?"

Drew replied, "I won it last night."

Johnny jumped into the conversation. "Hey, Bob, give it a good squeeze."

Dad squeezed the doll and the boobs ballooned out and we all burst out laughing. Dad got pissed and took the doll and slammed it on the counter a few times. Every time he hit the doll on the counter the boobs would pop out again. As we surrendered to fits of uncontrollable laugher, Dad grew angrier. He tried ripping the head off the doll but that didn't work. He took the naked cupid doll outside and threw it in the trash can. When he came back into the dining room, we were trying to squelch our laughter because we knew how angry he was. He pointed his finger at Drew and said, "You'll be going to confession tomorrow." He stormed out of the room.

My uncle, aunt, and Johnny visited us several times in New Jersey for Thanksgiving, but one time in particular stands out. Johnny certainly left his mark on New Providence during a visit when he was sixteen. One frosty November day, Drew and I introduced Johnny to our woods and the train tracks. On the tracks, Johnny found two wires and figured out how to make the crossing signals go on and off. Even though the rail crossing was about a hundred fifty yards away, we could hear and watch the cars come to a complete stop every time Johnny connected those two wires. To Drew and me it was the funniest thing ever.

Later that same day, we were playing on a huge pile of dirt behind one of the factories near our house. There was a yellow tractor not far from that pile of dirt and Johnny decided to climb up into the driver's seat. After thirty seconds of playing with some wires, Johnny started the tractor up. He called out to Drew to ride shotgun. Drew climbed up and Johnny drove the tractor around in circles for the next twenty minutes. Drew and I thought it was very cool.

On this same Thanksgiving break, Johnny took a liking to Annie's friend Diane from across the street. Johnny bragged to Drew and me about how he had gotten to second base with her. I didn't understand what that meant, but Drew and I both believed it must be something to be admired. For the next couple of years every time I ran into Diane, she asked me when Johnny was coming back to visit. Yes, to us, Johnny was the epidemy of cool.

Unfortunately, when Johnny was in his early twenties, he became addicted to heavy drugs. Drew told me it was heroin, but I didn't want to believe it. He was arrested on the Norfolk Naval base for selling heroin, which was a major federal offense. He spent the rest of his adult life in and out of prisons. Johnny would spend five years in jail, get out, and then get arrested again in a month for petty larceny to fund his drug habit. Johnny would then end up back in jail. Uncle John passed away while he was in jail. Aunt Judy made up excuses for Johnny's absence when she would visit us for the holidays, never admitting to us he was in jail.

Aunt Judy passed away in 1993. I was living in Colorado at the time and Mom asked me if I would accompany her to Judy's funeral. I told Mom I would fly into Norfolk and meet her at the funeral home the morning of Judy's funeral. When I arrived at the funeral home, Aunt Judy's family were all bickering about who was going to pay for her funeral. The other topic of discussion that morning was whether Johnny was going to be let out of jail to attend his mother's funeral. His uncle had called the governor of Virginia to try and get Johnny out for the funeral. I was asked by her family to be a pallbearer, which was a new experience for me.

Later in the day, we drove over to Holy Trinity Catholic Church for her funeral. This was the same church my parents were married in. After we arrived, I walked over to the hearse to help remove Judy's coffin with the other pallbearers and place it in on the rolling catafalque. As we rolled her coffin toward the front steps of the church, I heard police sirens very faintly in the distance. We lifted the coffin off the catafalque, put the coffin on our shoulders and carried it up the church steps and into the foyer of the church entryway where we were met by the officiating priest. The police sirens grew louder and louder as we entered the church. I turned to the open front doors of the church and in walked cousin Johnny with two exceedingly large armed state troopers behind him. They had let him out. Johnny hugged his mother's coffin and then followed us in the procession line into the church.

The church was full so Mom and I found an open pew about twenty rows from the altar. Johnny decided to sit right between Mom and me. He was now forty-seven and I hadn't seen him in at least twenty-five years. He was much shorter than I remembered, probably five feet four at best, and most of his teeth had rotted out. His hands were cuffed, but he had a jacket over his hands to hide them. When we were all were seated, Johnny looked over to me and asked, "How's it going, Steve?"

I replied, "Obviously, better than you." He laughed. It was extremely awkward having a state trooper in the aisle towering over us with his hand on his revolver for the entire service.

After the service, Johnny's uncle convinced the state troopers to allow Johnny to attend his mom's burial at the cemetery. This time, the state troopers transported Johnny to the cemetery without the sirens. After the burial, Johnny's uncle persuaded the funeral director to let Johnny pay his last respects to his mother. The funeral director walked over to her casket, took a key out, and opened one half of the coffin. When the funeral director looked inside her coffin, he whitened like he had just seen a ghost. Aunt Judy's body must have slid down to the other end of the coffin while we were walking up the church steps. The funeral director quickly grabbed Judy's collar and yanked her body back up to the other end of her coffin. Johnny cried as he paid his last respects. He was then whisked away by the two state troopers. That was the last time I saw cousin Johnny.

New York State Of Mind

I GLANCED AT MY WATCH and realized that Dr. Brooks and I had been at it for over three hours. He noticed me looking at my watch and asked if I needed a break. I said I was good with continuing if he was. He said, "Let's roll. What else did Drew like to do when he wasn't working?"

Norfolk, Virginia created some new opportunities for Drew, but New York City offered him a whole new world of sights, sounds, and filth. New Providence is only twenty-eight miles from New York City, a quick train ride away. After graduating high school, he started regularly going to New York City on Saturdays. It was another way for him to avoid Dad. He walked the tracks to the Murray Hill train station and caught the train for the forty-five-minute trip to Hoboken. From Hoboken he took the PATH and got off at Thirty-Third Street. Drew made the trip by himself until I started tagging along with him two years later when I turned fifteen.

His routine in New York City was always the same. After getting off the PATH, he walked through the dirty, foul smelling subway station until he reached the steps to take him to street level. That train station regularly contained a slew of homeless people sleeping in their own urine and nursing the white bandages covering the sores on their legs. Drew climbed the steps and came out on the street facing Madison

Square Garden. He often grabbed a slice of pizza or went to McDonalds, which had an upstairs eating area. After eating he walked up the nine blocks to Forty-Second Street.

Around 1972 when Drew started going into New York City, Forty-Second Street was one of the seediest places not only in New York City but in the country. He walked that street being propositioned by prostitutes, drug dealers looking to score a deal, and numerous shady people trying to sell merchandise they had recently stolen. He also had to dodge the bible thumping street preachers with their megaphones. He would stop and look at the marquees of the numerous movie houses advertising adult movies. After casing the street, he would decide on the form of entertainment he would take part in. He usually opted to visit one of the many live sex shows, or see a porn movie at one of the several adult movie houses, or if he had extra cash negotiate with a prostitute for oral sex behind one of the buildings.

After his adventures on Forty-Second Street, Drew headed back toward Thirty-Third Street, making two stops along the way. To kill extra time, he sat on a bench and watched the people of NYC hurrying by. He could people watch for hours. He might also stop at a few shops to buy the latest and hippest clothes—clothes he rarely, if ever, wore. Around five, Drew caught the PATH back to Hoboken and then the train back to Murray Hill. He walked along the tracks and through the woods to home. Often, I'd be outside playing ball and see Drew walking home with his purchases. I was always curious to see what he had bought. He'd proudly show me his new platform shoes, a glitter t-shirt, or the cologne he had purchased. He'd run into the house, making sure to avoid Dad on the way to his bedroom so he could hide what he'd bought. Most of the things he bought never saw the light of day. His purchases would be eventually thrown away, offered to me or Bobby years later, or sold at a neighborhood garage sale.

Drew loved going into New York City. It was so different from the colonial, suburban town of New Providence. He always said, "New Providence is boring!" Another reason I believe Drew loved New York City is that he fit in there. No one judged him or thought he looked or acted different. He didn't stand out. New York City was just the right fit for him.

Finding My Religion

"I'M SURE NEW YORK CITY offered all kinds of new sights and opportunities for Drew. Did you all ever go to any concerts in the City? The seventies were such a great time for music."

On July 21, 1973 Drew and I took the train into NYC for my first concert. I will never forget that date or the thrill of that show. Drew had been to numerous concerts by himself in the last few years. He was now twenty and I was fifteen. We had pizza before making our way into Madison Square Garden for the show. Every now and then as we were walking, I noticed people staring at him but I didn't care. I was fifteen and I was at Madison Square Garden to see my first concert— The Allman Brothers. Going with Drew was a small price to pay. None of my friends' parents would have let them go and at fifteen I wasn't going to go alone.

When the Garden's lights dimmed signaling the show was about to begin, the crowd went nuts and my body vibrated with anticipation. The Marshall Tucker Band, the warm-up band, took the stage. The first chord was struck and the orange and red spotlights hit their faces and the song, "Take The Highway" began, flute and all. I was hooked. I'd never seen, heard, or felt anything so beautiful and mind blowing before. After Marshall Tucker's set the Allman Brothers came out and played for the next two and half hours. I recognized a few songs from their Idlewild South album that cousin Johnny had turned me onto. On the late train ride back to Murray Hill my hearing was fuzzy from the concert but I was buzzing with euphoria. Drew told me not to worry and that in a day my hearing would be back to normal.

Not bad for a first concert, but my second was even better. Six days later Drew and I returned back to Madison Square Garden to see Led Zeppelin. I always tell people that I found religion that night. My God, what an experience! That concert was filmed for the movie The Song Remains the Same, which I watch every couple of years to reminisce. If I was hooked after the Allman Brothers, I was addicted after Led Zeppelin. My new goal in life was to be Jimmy Page.

For the next two years, Drew and I went to over fifty concerts. Many times, I had to skip school or Drew would have to miss work to stand in line to buy concert tickets at the closest Bamberger's Department Store. Early on, I noticed how easy it was to smoke pot at these shows. I was paranoid about being arrested until I discovered that the police that were present seemed to not care. He and I would usually sneak in a joint or two and light up as soon as the lights went down. I think the lights, music, and getting high removed a lot of anxiety for Drew and took him to a different place. He loved to stand with hands in his front pockets, bobbing his head up and down to the beat of the music and taking in all the sights and sounds.

We also ventured out to other venues in New York and New Jersey—The Beacon Theater, The Academy of Music, The Felt Forum, The Passaic Theater, and Roosevelt Stadium. Some of our favorite shows were: Yes, David Bowie, Lou Reed, Queen, Mott The Hoople, The Doobie Brothers, Lynyrd Skynyrd, and Iggy Pop. Our all-time favorite concert was on New Year's Eve in 1973 at the Academy of Music. Blue Oyster Cult was the headliner, with Iggy Pop, Teenage Lust, and a new band we had never heard of before, KISS. Gene Simmons actually set his hair on fire that night. After that show Drew and I became huge KISS freaks and followed their careers for years. We must have seen them another twenty times. I didn't have an affinity with any member of the band but Drew loved Ace Frehley—The Spaceman.

Going to all those concerts with Drew and getting high with him continued to strengthen the bond between us. He was five years older than I but his maturity level was on the same level as mine. He was twenty going on fifteen, and I was fifteen and acting like any other fifteen-year-old. All this would change when I left for college.

Sex & Drugs & Rock & Roll

"We've talked about drugs and rock and roll, Steve. You know what's coming next, right?" I nodded, knowing where he was heading. "Enlighten me on Drew's sex life."

Drew was now in his twenties and he had never been on a date or had a girlfriend. There were no girls calling him and he didn't call any girls. He'd never kissed or held the hand of a member of the opposite sex or the same sex for that matter. The only physical contact he'd had by this point was the oral sex he received along Forty-Second Street. It seemed Drew resorted to satisfying his sexual desires and fantasies through magazines.

In his late teens, he started collecting magazines like *Playboy* and *Penthouse*. A year or two later, he moved on to edgier magazines like *Club* and *Hustler*. During this period, he kept his magazines carefully buried in a locked box out in the woods. He wouldn't have dared bringing his private collection of magazines into our house. Dad would have annihilated him. Drew took the train into Summit, the town next to New Providence, to purchase his magazines. There was a newsstand across the street from the Summit train station, which was convenient for him.

When he entered his twenties and was going into New York City on Saturdays, the subject content of his magazines drastically changed. He went from *Hustler* to some quite darker and harder stuff. His magazines were now filled with bondage, S&M, and fetishes. He also started keeping his magazine collection in his room, where he had constructed a new hiding spot. In his closet, a wooden shoe rack had been built into the wall. He removed the nails holding the top of the shoe rack together and made a secret compartment where he stored his magazines. Luckily for him, my parents never discovered his hiding spot or his stash.

Sometimes when Drew was at work or had gone into the city, I pulled out a few of his new magazines to take a look. He never knew I discovered his secret hiding place. At fifteen, I preferred *Playboy*. Drew's new preferred magazine content was, to me—who had never been exposed to this before—some uncomfortable material: leather, whips, chains, ropes, foot fetishes, boots, golden showers, you name it. Every time he added a new magazine to his collection, the content was more shocking. I always took care to return his magazines to his hiding spot so he wouldn't know I had been in his room.

I suspected that those magazines were a turn on for him and that he masturbated to them. I never heard him through the bedroom walls but I'd bet on it. Honestly, his collection of magazines and attraction to pornography, while it wasn't for me, never truly bothered me. I was dating and trying to meet and pick up girls and hoping to round the bases. Drew had no one, just his right hand. He wasn't hurting anyone and if this stuff brought joy and happiness into his life, good for him.

Walk Away

"IN OUR FIRST VISIT, you mentioned that when you went off to college you felt guilty about leaving Drew behind. Talk to me more about that."

This is a tough thing for me to say, but I always thought at some point Drew would kill himself. There were many instances growing up that he got quite down and negative on himself. I know there were times he felt like he was a burden based on comments he made such as, "I'm just a fuck up." I heard him say at least a dozen times, "I might just as well kill myself." The first time I heard him threaten suicide, I was terrified. I thought he'd follow through for sure. I don't think I slept a wink that night. As he continued to make threats, I realized that he was never going to follow through and that it might be his way of seeking attention and wanting us to feel sorry for him. I also realized that Drew wasn't going anywhere.

On the other hand, I couldn't wait to get away and out of the house after graduating high school. Annie had gone to MIT University for college and graduate school. My father wanted me to go locally. Nothing against MIT, but I needed to get further away. To this day, I'm still not sure how I convinced my parents, but I ended up going to school in Florida. Florida State University was eleven hundred miles away, had an excellent baseball team, and the huge palm trees in their brochure seemed to be inviting me to move there. I didn't visit the campus before I applied, but when I was accepted my decision was made. I needed freedom and would have done anything to get out from under the strict rule of my dad.

When I was seventeen, Drew was twenty-two and following his same daily routine. The last couple of years before college we had spent a considerable amount of time together. We had attended over fifty concerts and made many trips into New York City. We'd shared albums and lived together in the same house all our lives.

While he wasn't a "normal" big brother, I did love him and would miss his company when I went away. On the day I left home, Mom and Annie helped me to load my gear into our car that the three of us were going to drive to Tallahassee. Before we pulled out of the driveway, I went upstairs to go say goodbye to Drew. He was in the bathroom, of course, with the door locked, and would not come out to say good-bye. We had to speak through the door to each other. I did most of the talking. I told him goodbye, to smoke a joint for me, and that I'd see him at Christmas break. He didn't answer. I then called out a big and boisterous, "See ya!" and walked out of the house and drove away.

Over the years, I've had several people tell me that I don't take the time to look back in my rearview mirror—meaning that I don't focus on my past, just what's in front of me. I'm not sure this is a good or bad trait but I am sensitive to it. I know I make it hard on others when I move on very quickly from a situation and don't give those around me time to adjust. Selfishly, at the time I left I was only focused on myself and going off to college and the great time I was going to have in Tallahassee. Occasionally during those years, I regretted not looking back at Drew in my rearview mirror and I sometimes felt I wasn't a very good little brother. I had matured and, I hope, grown wiser, but Drew was a fifteen-year-old in the body of a twenty-two-year-old. The good news for Drew was that Bobby was now fourteen and would do just fine taking my place.

I Feel The Earth Move

"WE'LL TALK ABOUT BOBBY and his relationship with Drew in a little bit, but I understand that while you were in college your parents, along with Drew, moved from New Jersey to Greenville, South Carolina. How did he adjust to his new surroundings?"

Horribly! Every winter growing up, Dad said that he was done with the Northeast winters and threatened to move back down south. By springtime he calmed down and it was New Jersey business as usual. He had grown up in the south and hated the snow and ice in Jersey. It's not like he ever had to shovel the driveway. That was Drew's and my responsibility, but he hated driving in the snow.

In 1978, after an extremely brutal winter, Dad made good on his threats. He accepted a job with an engineering firm in Greenville, South Carolina. Annie was finishing up graduate school at Rutgers and I was completing my third year at Florida State so we were not involved in the decision or the move. My parents quickly sold the Jersey house and Dad, Mom, Drew, and Bobby moved to Greenville in the fall of seventy-eight.

If Drew thought New Providence was boring, Greenville was comatose. The town appeared to be ruled by the elders from Bob Jones University. Bob Jones University is a private, non-denominational, and very conservative university that seemed to have a stranglehold on the town. On my first visit to my parents for Thanksgiving that year, three things stood out. All the stores, including the mall, were closed on Sundays. The bars served liquor in mini bottles like the airlines use. The women all wore their hair long and straight and their skirts well below the knee—a rule in the Bob Jones Handbook. After living on a college campus for the last three years in Tallahassee, Greenville seemed like a boring, dead-end place to live.

For Drew, all Greenville offered was misery. There was no true rail or bus system for him to use. There was no New York City for him to visit on Saturdays. He had no place to buy his porn and no one to buy pot from. There were zero concerts for him to attend. He was stuck in the house with Dad. It was no mistake that when they all moved to Greenville, Drew picked the farthest bedroom from my parents.

While these were all negative issues for Drew, the biggest issue was that the move to South Carolina changed his daily routine. He had followed the same routine every day for the last eight years since graduating high school. The elimination of his daily routine set him back and he never really recovered. I often wondered whether my parents took Drew's situation into account when making their decision to move to Greenville. I do believe that no one understood how much the move would affect him in the short and the long term.

Take This Job and Shove It

"I HAVE THE FEELING that a move like that would have been really hard for him. Did Drew get a job when he got to Greenville?"

After the Christmas holiday of seventy-eight, Drew landed a job in a cardboard box factory in January. He was now twenty-six. His job was similar to the one at Fablok. Each shift he unloaded trucks, moved boxes around the factory floor, and then loaded up trucks. While it was difficult for him to make friends working at Fablok, it was impossible at his new job in Greenville. He was in a new town and he spoke very differently from the people in Greenville. Instead of a deep southern drawl, he talked like he was from Jersey. The social anxiety he experienced at work in South Carolina must have been off the charts.

His employment didn't last long, just two months to be exact. One day on a lunch break Drew went outside by himself and smoked a joint. He was scoring his pot from Bobby now, who had made some connections at his new high school in Greenville. A janitor on the factory grounds saw him getting high, told management, and he was fired on the spot.

After six months in Greenville, Dad was loving his new job, the Catholic Church he attended, the weather, and the conservatism of Greenville. Drew, on the other hand, was totally miserable and out of place. After he was terminated from his job, Dad had to make the tough decision on future employment for Drew. Remorse around moving him must have set in for Dad because, surprisingly, he decided that Drew's work career was over. He was not going to make him work ever again. Drew was now a full-time prisoner in his bedroom. Time would tell whether this was a smart decision.

The Boys of Summer

"WE'RE GETTING CLOSE TO OUR time ending here, Steve, but there are a couple of topics I'd like to talk about before we finish up. We haven't discussed your younger brother Bobby yet. Tell me about Bobby."

Robert Edward was born November 22, 1961 in Summit, New Jersey.

He was named after Robert E. Lee, one of Dad's favorite generals in American History. We always called him Bobby. Bobby was four years younger than I and nine years younger than Drew. Bobby was the baby in the family and was treated as such. He struggled out of the gate with school and ended up repeating kindergarten. Drew loved to tease Bobby about it. Many times over the years he was heard saying to Bobby, "Yeah, but you failed kindergarten."

When I discovered Drew's report cards in Mom's basement, I also discovered Bobby's. His grades varied from Bs to Ds. A few issues stood out on Bobby's his report cards though. He struggled with paying attention and staying focused in school. I wonder if he had undiagnosed ADHD. On two report cards it was evident that he had changed a D grade to a B by adding a small line in the middle of the D. He hadn't even used the same ink color.

Bobby and I were never very close. We cared for each other, but being four years younger and five grades behind me meant we had very different interests. Even though we shared the same bedroom and slept in bunk beds, we had entirely different lives and friends. He wasn't able to keep up or play any sports with me. I felt that he never grew out of being the baby of the family. Bobby went to the same grade school and high school that I did until our parents moved and he finished his last two years at Greenville High.

Bobby was extremely extroverted and had no problem making friends at his new high school. He would have made the perfect salesman. Drew was happy because Bobby could now supply him with pot and, at age seventeen, drive him around town.

After high school, Bobby dabbled around at the local technical college but dropped out after only taking a few classes. He would never go back to school. He started working in retail at a few different stores in the local mall, and would later get into the restaurant business. He remained living at home while he was working and continued chauffeuring Drew around town. Drew and Bobby ended up going to several concerts together at the Greenville Auditorium, which was a far, far cry from Madison Garden. Drew now had access to pot and concerts, but I wasn't sure what he was doing to fill his craving for porn. I am thankful and appreciative of Bobby for making such a smooth transition from me to him in becoming a companion to Drew.

I have one story about an adventure that involves both Drew and Bobby. After graduating college with a degree in psychology, I accepted a job with a restaurant company that quickly transferred me from Tallahassee to Daytona Beach, Florida. I had washed dishes and been a waiter in a local restaurant in Tallahassee to earn extra cash my last two years of college. When I graduated, there were no worthwhile job opportunities for someone with a degree in psychology and since I enjoyed the restaurant business so much, I continued down the restaurant path and got into management.

When I lived in Daytona Beach, I had the greatest schedule. As the assistant manager, I was the one who closed the restaurant. I went to work at four in the afternoon, dealt with all the rowdy kids who came in to drink, closed the restaurant down, and was home by two in the morning. I woke up around ten and went to the beach to hang with friends until two when I went home to shower. I was back at work by four. At twenty-two and with no family responsibilities, it was the perfect schedule for me, and I had an unbelievable tan.

When I was in Daytona, Drew and Bobby decided to come visit me. I picked them up at the airport with another friend of Bobby's who tagged along. Drew didn't have the best flight experience, though. It was the first time he'd ever had flown and he threw up for most of the flight. It was obvious to me that he didn't deal with motion well. It made him dizzy and nauseous. He'd never liked that roller coaster at Ocean View and he certainly didn't care for flying. We all squeezed into my car and headed to the house I was renting. I had to go to work that evening, so I gave the three of them a map of Daytona Beach and showed them all the hot spots.

When I got home at two in the morning, I was surprised that Bobby and his friend Jim were still up. "Where's Drew?" I asked, hoping he'd already gone to bed.

"Drew is in jail," Bobby answered as he avoided looking at me.

"What?" I yelled. Bobby explained what happened to them that evening. The three of them had gone around town hitting several bars after which they decided to buy beer at the liquor store and go walk on the beach. While they were walking on the beach and drinking, a police car stopped them (at that time in Daytona you could drive your vehicle on the beach). The police officer asked the three of them for their ID's and confiscated their beer. Drew started shooting off his mouth at the police officer who then put him up against his car and started to frisk him.

As he was being frisked, Drew used his favorite line on the officer, "Get away from me, you queer." The officer handcuffed Drew, put him in his police car, and told Bobby and Jim to leave the area. Bobby and Jim went to the police station to try to explain their situation but the desk officer told them that Drew was going to spend the night in jail and would have to go before the judge at nine o'clock the next morning.

I was very angry for so many reasons, made worse by the fact that I wasn't sure who to direct my anger at. I don't think I slept at all that night waiting for morning to arrive so I could go deal with Drew. I drove to the Daytona Courthouse early so I could speak to the police and understand what was in store for him. I took a seat in the courtroom and watched as one by one all the people who were jailed the night before stood before the judge. About an hour into hearing every sob story imaginable, it was Drew's turn. He walked into the courtroom in handcuffs and stood to face the judge.

The judged explained that he was being held for resisting arrest. The judge asked him if he understood the charge. He nodded, but the judge scolded him telling him to speak up. Drew answered, "Yes." The judge said that since he had no prior arrests (I guess his drug charges in New Jersey were erased) he could pay a fine of $150 and be released. Drew agreed and was led out of the courtroom. I quickly went to the office and paid his fine. The officer gave me his paperwork and directed me to a bench in an open area outside the courtroom to wait for him.

I couldn't have been waiting more than five minutes when a line of prisoners in handcuffs and leg shackles (all connected to each other) walked past me headed to the prison bus to take them to the county jail. As I looked up there was Drew walking in the line. He spotted me and yelled, "Get me out of here!"

I ran back inside to the officer that I had dealt with before. The officer made a quick call on his walkie-talkie and told me, "Go back to the bench. He'll be there shortly." He never apologized for the mix up.

Drew came running around the corner and said, "Let's get the fuck out of here."

The ride back to my house was rather quiet. I lectured Drew about watching his mouth. It kept getting him into trouble. It was the first time that I felt I was the parent. Bobby was his friend and, somehow, I had transitioned into his father. Bobby, Drew, and Jim laid low the rest of their trip. A few days later I dropped them off at the Daytona airport to catch their flight. I felt that if Drew had the same kind of flight going home, it was a small price to pay for getting himself thrown in jail and for my having to bail him out. I'm certain that their Daytona escapades were never shared with Mom and Dad. I drove away from the airport without looking back at him in my rearview mirror.

In My Time of Dying

"STEVE, YOU CERTAINLY HAVE some strong story telling skills. I'm very impressed. One last topic—tell me about your Dad's battle with cancer and the effect it had on Drew."

After living in Greenville, South Carolina for a little over five years Dad was diagnosed with cancer. About eight months before his diagnosis, he complained about not feeling right, saying he just felt "off." His doctor first diagnosed him with a chemical imbalance and had him drastically change his diet. He followed his doctor's recommendations but he never improved. After he continued to struggle, he was finally diagnosed correctly with stage IV cancer in June of 1984. The cancer was in his liver, stomach, and esophagus. The doctor said he had never seen anyone live longer than six months with this type of cancer. His oncologist wanted him to start chemo treatments immediately. Dad struggled with that decision. If he only had six months to live, he didn't understand the need for chemo. He conferred with his parish pastor who convinced him to move forward with chemo treatments.

I knew Dad's cancer was the result of smoking three packs of cigarettes a day for over thirty years. He was a long-time Winston and Marlboro man. Dad swore that he got cancer from drinking water that came out of the Passaic River, was filtered as drinking water and then piped into his engineering office in New Jersey. He decided to take a leave of absence from work and begin his chemo treatments. The chemo never did help and the cancer continued to grow quickly. By December, he had to have a feeding tube inserted into his stomach because he could not pass food through esophagus due to numerous tumors. He lost eighty pounds at this stage.

I was living in Dallas while Dad was battling cancer. Our first-born son, Steve Jr. was only a year old. Mom wanted us all in Greenville for Christmas that year. She never said it, but Annie, who was living in California, and I knew that this was going to be the last time we celebrated the holidays together with our father. When I first laid eyes on Dad, I was shocked by how frail and gaunt he looked. He'd always been a larger-than-life intimidating figure and now he was weak and his clothes just hung off him.

That Christmas trip back to Greenville was very emotional for us as a family. We had some great times and did a lot of crying, but not in front of our sick father. I also spent time with Drew and Bobby, who were still living at home. It was good to see how close Bobby and Drew had become. They had a nightly ritual of leaving the house and going outside to get high. Bobby, I noticed was also better than I was at inviting Drew with him when he hung out with his friends. I wasn't jealous of their relationship. I was just glad to see him doing something other than hanging out in his bedroom. I had been so busy with my job in Dallas, Colleen, and our first born, that Drew wasn't ever on my radar screen.

His behavior around Dad's illness and imminent death was interesting. He still avoided Dad and spent most of his time in his bedroom, only coming out to hang out with Bobby after Dad went to bed. Even though Dad was home all day, Drew still did his best to avoid him. When I brought up the subject of Dad's cancer with Drew, he acted nonchalant about it. He showed no emotion and his attitude was, "Well, everyone has to die sometime." You'd never know that Dad was dying with each passing day just a few feet away from him.

It was the same stone-faced demeanor that I remembered when we found Annie's dead cat on the tracks back in Jersey.

It was difficult leaving Greenville after that Christmas, knowing that it was going to be the last time I saw my father. I offered to stay behind and help but Mom was adamant that I return to Dallas and continue living my own life. She said, "What are you going to do, sit around and stare at your Dad all day? He'd want you to live your life." Knowing Mom was an extremely strong woman did give me some comfort.

Right after the holidays, Dad had a burst of unexpected energy and decided to go back to work. He wasn't able to drive so his colleagues from his office took turns driving him to and from work. After working for one week, Dad passed out walking down the driveway after returning home from work. Mom took him to the hospital where he died a week later on January 17, 1985.

Dad's funeral in Greenville was packed. He had made a great many friends within the church he attended and worked at as a Deacon. I've never seen so many priests in a church at one time. Steve Jr., who was a year old at the time, was a great distractor during the service. He kept things light and in perspective. I had held up pretty well, but lost it leaving the church when the service was finished. Having to walk down the church aisle behind Dad's casket was just too emotional for me. Drew attended both the funeral and the burial with a blank non-emotional look on his face the entire time. I never saw him upset or shedding a tear the entire week. When we got home after the services, his first order of business was to go out into the woods with Bobby and get high.

For Drew, Mom was always his rock and the one person he leaned on. Our father's passing wasn't going to affect him very much and Drew knew it. I felt that Dad had some serious regrets about how he'd handled Drew during those years back in Jersey. Once in Greenville, he just gave up on Drew and stopped continually nagging him about his hair and his strange behavior. Dad discovered that avoidance and noncontact worked well for the two of them. A few years after our father passed away, Drew told me, "You know, I don't blame Dad for all those beatings and whippings. I probably deserved them."

Solsbury Hill

"I'm very sorry to hear about your Dad, Steve," Dr. Brooks said. "I really don't want to end on such a down note today, but our time is just about up. I do want to make sure, though, that you've had every opportunity to share all that you wanted to share before we stop for the day."

I was exhausted. I felt like I'd spoken for the entire five hours, which I pretty much had. I quickly assessed whether I had anything else I wanted to share with Dr. Brooks. "You know Dr. Brooks, I'm honestly spent. I'm sure on the way home I'll think of something that I should have shared, but at the moment I think I'm good."

"Well, Steve, if you think of something, you have my number. Please feel free to call me. I greatly appreciate your honesty and candor today. Not only do you have exceptional recall and an eye for detail, but your insights have been very helpful. Drew is truly blessed to have such a caring brother as you. I realize you're carrying a large amount of guilt on your shoulders, but please keep in mind that in Drew's world, he may be truly happy. We might never really know."

Dr. Brooks continued, "What I'd like to do, Steve, is take a little time to review my notes and think about our conversation today. I'll provide you with a write-up outlining a few of my thoughts and give you with some additional reading materials. After you've had a chance to read them, we can schedule a call to follow up on any of your additional questions."

I thanked Dr. Brooks for his time and told him I looked forward to seeing his report. I wasn't expecting any major breakthroughs today. Having the opportunity to just sit and talk in detail about Drew was worth every penny I was spending with Dr. Brooks today.

As I got in my car to head home, "Solsbury Hill," by Peter Gabriel came on the radio. I needed to sit in quiet before I headed home to the chaos of three children. I wanted to take a few minutes and reflect on the last five hours. I thought to myself that I couldn't have selected a more appropriate song. In my life, any time I've had to a make a major decision or needed some time to think and reflect, there isn't a better song for me.

Today had given me the opportunity to connect a lot of dots. I had never taken the time to evaluate Drew's situation and, step-by-step, put the pieces of his life puzzle together. There were several events in his life that I had never stopped to reflect on. There's that "not ever looking in my rearview mirror" thing again. I was able to take a step back today, and string events together, bringing some clarity for me.

While it would be easy to blame my parents for Drew's current state of mind and situation, that is really not fair. It became evident to me today that my parents were dealt a hand that they didn't know how to handle. Drew came with no instructions. They did the best they could with the information that was available at the time. Dad was obviously frustrated with himself and Drew's behavior. Mom had tried to keep him safe but she was now pretty burned out and just tired.

After my time with Dr. Brooks today, a lot of my feelings of guilt were lifted. I hadn't thought about it before but Bobby filled my void after I left for college and Mom and Dad continued to support Drew financially. He had a roof over his head, food, and a safe environment to live in.

The one thing we all could agree on was that the move to Greenville was catastrophic for him in so many ways. Emotionally and developmentally, it set him back many years. In fact, he was never the same. I wondered what he would be like if he had never left New Jersey. He might have had his own place to live and, who knows, maybe gotten married and had a few kids. It really made me wonder.

I was eager to receive Dr. Brooks' report. I wasn't expecting any major "aha" breakthroughs, but maybe a little help understanding what might go on inside Drew's head. I knew I could never share any of this information with Mom. Our last conversation was sad and painful enough for the two of us and I was never going to go there with her again. It's not in my DNA, but I was just going to "let sleeping dogs lie" as she requested...at least for the time being. I sensed that there would be a time in the future for making things right.

I turned up the volume, put the car in drive, and headed home singing along to the lyrics of "Solsbury Hill."

Part III

Greenville, South Carolina, 1997 – 2010

Part III

Greenville, South Carolina, 1997 – 2010

I TRIED TO VISIT MOM at least once a year. Sometimes we made the long drive from Dallas or from Colorado after Colleen and I had moved there. Other times we flew in for Christmas, which is also my mom's birthday. Many times, we flew into Atlanta on Christmas Day, rented a car, and make the two-hour drive to Greenville. Colleen and I now had three children: Steve Jr.; Valerie, who was two years younger than Steve Jr.; and Mark, who was three years younger than Valerie. When we visited during the summer, we usually went to Kiawah Island for a week at the beach. Drew was never interested in going to the beach, so he stayed home in Greenville. Mom cooked for a week to fill the refrigerator with food that was easy for him to prepare while she was gone.

After Dad passed away, he maintained the same schedule as when Dad was alive. He got up around six at night and came out of his room around ten. He ate at midnight when everyone had gone to sleep and watched TV until he went to bed around six in the morning, when our kids were just waking up. Often during my visits, when he'd come out of his room at night and everyone else had gone to sleep, I'd get to spend an hour or two with him to reminisce about old times back in Jersey. We'd talk about our trips into NYC or the latest KISS album. By now Bobby had moved to Florida for work and had gotten married so it was just Mom and Drew in the house.

When my kids were younger, Drew avoided them when we came to visit. He didn't know them and, frankly, I think he was afraid of them passing judgment on him. Drew had never been around any little kids his entire life. If he did run into my kids at night, he stayed as far away from them as he could. If he found himself in the same room with them, he stayed in the back of the room with the light off so he could remain in the shadows. I noticed that in the rare occasion he did speak, he had picked up a habit of putting his hand in front of his mouth while he was talking. I'd never seen this behavior before. When my kids got a little older, they started to wonder about all the secrecy that surrounded Drew. During the day they knew he was in his room, but his door was always locked. Sometimes they would knock on his door and call out his name, thinking it was funny. They might get Drew to say a word or two, but he quickly said he was going back to sleep and I ushered them away from his door.

On half of our trips to Greenville, I never even saw Drew. Mom's house was awfully quiet when Colleen and the kids were not there. When we all visited, I'm sure Drew could hear our voices and the commotion from three children and two extra adults in the house. We could be there for a week and never see him. Usually, before I left, I talked to him through the door to say goodbye. Sadly, he always had an excuse for not coming out during our stay. On the drive back to the airport I'd get a few choice comments from Colleen about Drew's mental health. She could not understand why Mom was not getting him more help instead of letting him "veg out" in his room. I knew it was a moot point and just listened and nodded my head. There was not a good answer.

Drew also developed another habit during our visits that I was not too happy about. Most time when we visited, Colleen and I would stay in Mom's room. It had a large king-size bed. When our kids were young, all three of them wanted to stay in the room with us at night. We'd put a collection of sleeping bags and blankets down on the floor at the foot of the bed. All five of us would sleep in that one room with the door always open. One early morning around three I was awakened by a noise in our room. I looked up saw Drew standing sheepishly in our room. He couldn't tell I was awake, so I watched him. He stood in the room and stared at all of my kids for about ten minutes before he left the room not knowing I was awake and had seen him. Honestly, it kind of freaked me out. From that night on, I kept our bedroom door closed and locked whenever we visited. I was pretty sure he wouldn't harm my kids, but not having been around him much since college, I didn't want to take any chances. I would never have been able to forgive him or myself if he hurt them. I never did confront him about it or ever mention it to Colleen.

Everything In Its Place

DURING OUR FAMILY VISITS to Greenville, Drew developed another bizarre habit. Like any family with children there is always going to be a trail of toys left behind them. In the evening before we went to bed, Colleen and I usually would try to put all the kids toys in a pile on the floor so they weren't scattered throughout the house. I'm sure we missed a few. The amount and size of kid's toys seemed to increase as they got older. Through the years there were plenty of Barbies, video games, stuffed animals, cars and trucks, and a few balls to name a few of the toys that made the trip with us.

When we'd all awaken in the morning and head to the family room, we'd see the strangest thing that occurred while we slept. All the kid's toys that had been scattered around the house the previous day were magically placed on the floor by Mom's fireplace in the morning, totally organized. I mean, they were lined up in a neat and orderly fashion. It looked like a perfectly symmetrical aisle in a toy store. It was as if someone's housekeeper had come into Mom's house during the night and cleaned up all of their toys. It was like a scene out of the movie Toy Story where all the toys had put themselves back in place so no one would know they had come to life during the night. It even got a little stranger. This occurred every night while we slept in Mom's room. After several visits, I noticed something I hadn't before. Not only were the toys organized, but they were arranged in exactly the same way in the same space, facing the same direction each and every morning of that visit. For example, if the football had the word Spalding on it, the word Spalding faced directly at you. The next day the word Spalding would be staring directly at us the exact same way and place as the day before, just like an expertly aligned and faced grocery aisle.

To be honest, it took me a few years to figure this all out. Drew obviously had developed a bad case of Obsessive-Compulsive Disorder (OCD). I had never noticed this kind of behavior before. In his mind, everything in the house had to be in its proper place and my kids disrupted his perfect world inside our mom's house. In order to deal with his anxiety and OCD, he had to return everything to its right place at night while we all slept. Gathering my kid's toys that were strewn throughout the house and placing them into the same organized area in the exact same place each night must have relieved his anxiety. He could go now go to sleep in the morning before the kids were awake. Drew, it appeared, was most comfortable and could best function when everything was in its place.

As I was having these experiences during our family's visits and observing some of Drew's new behaviors, it was apparent that he was getting worse and more withdrawn. I thought after Dad passed away that he might improve, but he seemed to be falling backwards. In the mental place he was in at that time in Greenville, he would have never been able to go into NYC by himself, like he had in Jersey. He never left the house anymore. The "Jersey" Drew who was strong, in great shape, and confident enough to take the train on his own into the city had now disappeared.

Forty-Five Going on Fifteen

THE YEARS AFTER DAD PASSED AWAY didn't bring any changes for Drew. His world was the four walls of Mom's house and he seemed perfectly fine with this. He kept to his same routine and schedule. For years, other than my family, the only contact he had with another human being was Mom, or when Bobby or Annie would come to visit. Colleen, the kids, and I still tried to make it to Greenville once a year, though it became harder and harder as my kids grew older. They would rather stay at our home with their friends and visit places other than Greenville for vacation. I could understand. I remember how it felt having to travel to Virginia every summer.

When Steve Jr. and Mark were teenagers, Drew started coming out of his room a little more. He wanted to hang out with them when we visited. He was at the same emotional level as they now were and they all shared similar interests. He was now in his late forties but still had the emotional maturity of a kid of fifteen, and it seemed he wanted Steve Jr. and Mark to be his new buddies. Steve Jr. was fifteen both mentally and physically and had been drumming for over ten years and was into all types of music. Drew loved to talk to him about music and got a thrill showing Steve Jr. his record and eight-track collection. Many of Drew's albums were in perfect condition and still had the plastic wrap on them. The kids were fascinated by Drew's eight-track as they had never seen one before.

There were a couple of times during our visits that Drew wanted me to take him out to a store or two. He also wanted Steve Jr. and Mark to come along. There was a local record store in Greenville that the four of us visited and spent hours in. I loved being able to get him out of the house. He would purchase a few albums while Steve Jr. bought a couple of CDs. The two of them would compare their purchases on the way back to Mom's.

Another time, out of the blue, Drew asked to be taken to Kmart. The four of us walked around the store for a while a little confused as to why he wanted to come here and shop. After about ten minutes of browsing, I was growing a little impatient and wanted to leave. Drew headed back to the toy aisle and returned with a Barbie. Taken aback, I asked him why he wanted a Barbie. He didn't answer. He just went to a checkout aisle to buy it. As Steve Jr., Mark, and I waited by the exit door, Steve Jr. asked me why he wanted a Barbie. I stumbled for an answer and responded, "Hey, if it makes him happy, so be it. He doesn't have much happiness in his life."

Another shopping excursion Drew requested was a trip to Best Buy. He was now listening to CDs and wanted us to go check out the new releases. While we were walking around shopping, he floored me with this comment, "I know I'm different and that people stare at me." It was the first time in my life I'd heard him communicate this fact. On the drive home, I continued to think that Mom should get him out in public more. Instead of being a prisoner in his room, maybe a little progress could be made in his life. Any thoughts of progress in Drew's life quickly dissipated as reality sunk in. Mom had no interest in carting him around and was tired of the disappointment she'd experienced. "Let sleeping dogs lie."

As short and as infrequent as our time was, I was glad that both Steve Jr. and Mark were able to develop a relationship with Drew. Even though they continued to think he was odd, both of them also thought he was hilarious. Once, while returning to Mom's house after a few hours at the record store, Def Leppard's "Pour Some Sugar On Me" came on the car radio. Drew said, "You know this song is only good for one thing—stripping." Steve Jr. and Mark laughed the rest of the trip home. They learned that their uncle had quite a sense of humor.

Same As It Ever Was"

BY 2007, THINGS WERE STILL pretty much the same in Drew's world. For him, it was like Groundhog Day every day in Greenville. He was now fifty-five years old and had maintained the same routine since Dad passed away twenty-two years ago. Mom, at age seventy-seven, still went to her job each day at the church. She never wanted to retire. Every time we came to visit her, I asked her why she was still working and not retired yet. She felt that as long as her mind was still sharp, she didn't need or want to retire. She loved her job. The other reason I believe she continued to work for so long is that work gave her a break from Drew every day. The thought of being in the same house with him twenty-four seven wasn't appealing to her, though she would have never admitted it.

I was having growing concerns about him. Some of his taste in movies and music got very disturbing. He became a huge fan of dark horror films—the bloodier and the more screams from tortured women, the better for him. He enjoyed seeing women tied up and tortured. It reminded me of some of the S&M magazines he'd bought in NYC. Over the years, his musical tastes evolved from classic rock, to hard rock and metal (bands like Metallica), to death metal. I wasn't aware of what death metal was until he showed me. A band called Cannibal Corpse was his new favorite band. He also liked other death metal groups that were from Germany. The lyrics of these bands glorified, death, Satan, and going to hell. His days of Led Zeppelin were long over.

Every year for Drew's birthday, I sent him a gift in the mail. One year I forgot to send him a present and received a call the next day from Mom telling me that I had disappointed Drew and how sad she was that none of his siblings remembered his birthday. I never forgot again. I always asked him what he wanted and every year he had the same response, "Porno." I'd find some adult store in my town, pick up a couple of magazines hoping not to run into anyone I knew, go home and wrap them, and mail them to Mom's house without anyone in my family ever finding out. Once I did run into a neighbor in the store. It was quite embarrassing for both of us. I'm certain he would have never of believed me if I'd said, "They're not for me, but only for my brother."

I doubted that anyone would understand that these magazines were the only sexual outlet Drew had. I made Drew promise me that he wouldn't open my gifts in front of Mom, or I'd never send him porn again. He'd also wanted the same thing every year for Christmas. I always felt a little weird sending him porn as a gift for Christmas. Mercifully, he never opened my gifts in front of Mom. If he had, the latest editions of *Hustler* and *Juggs* would be in full display for her. Thank God that never happened.

On later visits to Greenville, Drew asked me to take him to a magazine store in town that he had discovered sold adult magazines in a back room. I waited in the car while he shopped because the store was disgusting. Not only did they sell magazines, but there were always four or five of Greenville's "finest" citizens smoking up a storm and playing video poker there. After spending about thirty minutes in the store, Drew would exit with his brown paper bag stuffed with magazines. The store didn't sell anything as hard as the stuff he bought in NYC but I guess still it worked for him. I always reminded myself that taking him was the least I could do. I seemed to make him happy.

Bobby visited Greenville about once a year, bringing pot for Drew on each trip. It was the only way Drew could score any weed. I believe he was getting high three to four times a week. He'd wait until Mom went to bed around ten and go outside in the backyard to get high. He always seemed to have pot on him so either he was a master at rationing or Bobby was bringing him a quite a few ounces on each visit.

Drew's eating habits had also changed. He now only ate one meal a day, always at midnight after Mom or any out-of-town visitors went to bed. He filled the largest bowl from the kitchen cabinet with a huge mound of food. He could have been Jethro in *The Beverly Hillbillies*. His meal consisted of whatever Mom had cooked that night for dinner. After he filled his bowl, he poured gravy on top of everything. On one visit, I was up late and made my way to the kitchen. Trying to be inconspicuous, I glanced at his bowl, amazed at the amount of food that he had mixed together.

He'd place his bowl in the microwave to heat it up and then sit and eat his dinner by himself while watching TV. His usual viewing fare was anything on HBO or Showtime; he hated commercials. After his meal, he went to the freezer for his favorite vice—ice cream. I always wondered why Mom kept at least five half-gallons of Breyer's ice cream in the freezer at all times. When I witnessed Drew eating his midnight meal, I understood why. He could go through about three quarters of a half-gallon at a sitting. I had no idea how someone who was six three and maybe a hundred sixty pounds could pack away that much food at one time.

By 2007 I was also growing concerned about Drew's health. He never went to a doctor and only saw a dentist if he needed to have a tooth pulled. Mom tried to get him to go but he was hard headed and refused. At the rate he was going, he'd end up with no teeth. The only time Drew got fresh air was in the backyard at night getting high. Like a vampire, he never saw the light of the day. He was tall, very pale, gaunt in his face, and extremely skinny. To me, he looked like he might be bulimic or anorexic. I wondered how someone could eat that much food and be so thin. It wasn't like he was hitting the gym every day or running marathons. How was he burning off all of those calories he was consuming?

I never heard him vomiting but he was binging. Since he ate by himself in the middle of the night, I doubt anyone who was sleeping would have heard him purging. I also wondered what eating only one huge meal a day was doing to his body and digestive system. In Jersey, when he was thriving, he ate three meals a day and was in tremendous shape. His body transformation from Jersey to Greenville was dramatic. We all noticed it, but no one would raise the subject. Mom had the responsibility for his care and we all knew that she didn't want any feedback or any ideas on how improve his life. Greenville had not been kind to Drew.

I've learned and I strongly believe that all that matters in life are our relationships and our happiness. Drew was never capable of building relationships. He was afraid of being around people he didn't know. He was anxious about people looking at him and passing judgment on him. He was aware that something was wrong with him and that he was "different." I never knew whether he had any real moments of happiness. He didn't express any emotion and always wore the same blank look on his face no matter what the situation. I couldn't tell if he was happy or sad. I had seen him frustrated, like the time he was learning to drive, but I never saw him angry or really pissed off. Any time he had something positive happen in his life, his facial expression remained neutral.

He was fifty-five, lived with and was dependent on his mother, didn't work, never had female companionship, and stayed primarily within the four walls of my mother's house. Anyone else would have been miserable and, at best, last a week under those circumstances. I think about the happiest times in my life—hitting a homerun, my first kiss, learning that the girl I wanted to date liked me, my first car, getting married, buying my first house, the birth of my children, the incredible feeling of an orgasm while making love, the smiles on my children's faces, my wife and kids telling me they love me. Drew never got to experience any of these special moments. All he had was sticking to his daily routine to keep his social anxiety to a manageable level. Maybe he was happy deep inside. I would find out soon enough.

"Ch-Ch-Ch-Ch- Changes"

AFTER MY DISASTROUS CALL WITH MOM in 1996 about my new-found discovery of Asperger's Syndrome, I didn't broach the topic with her again until 2007. The pain and agony I had experienced on that call cried to me that she never wanted to go down that road again. She was seventy-seven and understandably tired. Drew was in a stable, safe environment and she didn't want to make any changes that would add stress to her life. I thought of all she'd had deal with throughout his life—his troubles all through school, the diagnosis from the psychologist in Morristown, his inability to make friends and need to avoid human contact, the fights with Dad, and the move to Greenville. She was reconciled to the fact that he was safe in her house and that he would live with her for the rest of her life.

Annie and Bobby and I frequently discussed Drew's situation and we all agreed that trying to make any forward progress in his quality of life was too much for Mom to handle. The three of us were occupied with our jobs and families and none of us lived in Greenville. Annie and I were more than half-way across the country. While it sounded like a great idea to try and improve his life, at the end of the day the burden would have fallen on Mom.

In May of 2007, Mom came out to Colorado for Mark's high school graduation. After developing some needed study habits through his work with Dr. Brooks back in second grade, Mark's grades continued to improve through grade school and he was an honor student throughout high school. He received a full academic scholarship to the University of Missouri, and was to start in the fall majoring in journalism.

We all had a great weekend celebrating Mark's graduation as a family. I felt so blessed that Mom was still mobile and able to fly in for my family's celebrations. She was my children's only living grandparent and it was important to me that we all made time to gather and share memories as often as we could. After the graduation weekend, Mom's return flight was early on Monday morning so I offered to drive her to the airport before heading into work.

About half-way through our drive to the airport Mom said, "Steve,

I need to talk to you about something." By the seriousness of her tone, I could tell she had something important she needed to share. "I've been dealing with an issue for about six months now and I need to fill you in on what's been going on. Six months ago, they discovered a lump in my breast during one of my mammograms. They did a biopsy and the results came back that the tumor was cancerous. My doctor wants me to have a half mastectomy and then start radiation."

My face grew flushed and I began to feel so nauseous that I had to pull my car over onto the shoulder of the highway. I asked, "What? When do they want you to have this procedure?"

"At the end of next week."

I didn't know what to say at first. A mixture of emotions flooded through me. I felt sad for her. I didn't want to see her upset. I didn't want her to suffer. I was dumbfounded that she waited six months to have this procedure. Having known many people who had cancer, I knew how important it was to deal with it as fast as possible after diagnosis. The six months she waited might have allowed the cancer to spread to other organs in her body. If only she'd brought this up earlier in the visit. Why did she wait until we were thirty minutes from the airport to tell me?

Now, looking back, I kick myself for remaining so quiet and not trying to comfort her by hugging her right there on the side of the road. True to the Wilson way of dealing with uncomfortable topics, I took the traditional non-emotional, business-like approach to the situation. I had to get back on the highway so she wouldn't miss her flight. I peppered her with tactical questions during the rest of our drive. Where would she have the procedure done? Who would be there to help her? What is the recovery like? Do Annie, Bobby and Drew know? How much time would she take off from work? Did she need or want some help? Just like all of our past conversations when drama is involved, she downplayed the entire situation. She really didn't want any help. She had friends in Greenville who would be there if she needed anyone. She hadn't told Drew yet. She was only going to take two weeks off from work. As usual she had everything planned and under control. She just hadn't told anyone.

I was still numb by the time I walked her into the airport, got her boarding pass, and accompanied her to security. At security I hugged her and told her I loved her. I told her I'd call her later that night to make sure she got home safely. She asked me not to tell my kids about our conversation yet. She didn't want to upset them. I had to think about that one. I watched her go through security and waved good-bye to her. I wondered what the future held.

On the way back to my car, I digested the events of the last hour. I felt like I'd had the wind knocked out of me again. A jumble of thoughts flew through my head bouncing off each other. I got into my car and backed out of my parking space without looking in my rearview mirror and that's the exact moment when the tears began to flow. I was a sobbing mess by the time I approached the parking attendant. The attendant asked me if I was okay. I answered, "I'm not sure." I paid for parking and headed down the highway the same way I had come this morning. I was going home. I would not be going into work today.

Cancer Sucks

A FEW WEEKS LATER, Mom had her surgery. She spent the first week of her recuperation at home with friends who were taking turns helping her. Drew knew she'd had surgery but didn't know or understand that it was for cancer. She told him she was just having a "female procedure." When she returned home after her operation, he was curious about her condition, but spent the majority of the time in his room like always. He also didn't want to run into any of Mom's friends who were in the house to help her.

Mom decided for her second week of recovery that she wanted to spend it at the beach. Annie flew in to drive Mom down to Kiawah Island and spent the week with her at the beach. Mom made sure Drew had enough food for the week and her cell number if he needed anything while she was gone. Annie was a great help and companion for Mom during that week at the beach. They spent the majority of the time working on crossword puzzles, jigsaw puzzles, and taking walks on the beach.

After two weeks of recuperation Mom felt she was ready to go back to work as the manager of the church office. I think they needed her as much as she needed them. From the way she talked, there was a fair amount of incompetence in the office. The priests were not knowledgeable about running a business like a church and the pastor liked to spend the church's money foolishly on the latest Apple products. Mom felt it was her responsibility to help curb his spendthrift ways. She always felt that the parish was counting on her.

Two weeks after the mastectomy surgery things were back to normal in Greenville. Mom started radiation treatments that could be done during her lunch hour so Drew never had a clue what she was going through. Other than being a little more tired than usual, everything was back to normal at the house. Drew was not one to say, "Let me help you with that. You've been sick." I wished he knew how to be more helpful. He never understood people's feelings or how to anticipate someone's needs. If she asked him to do a chore like feed the cat, he'd do it but he had to be told, just like a teenager.

I called Mom at least once a week to check in and see how she was feeling. I never once heard her complain. She always painted a picture that everything was just "fine."

Colleen and I decided that we'd all go to Greenville for Christmas that year. Mom was very eager to see her grandkids. We had a great time playing cards, laughing, watching movies, and just being around each other. Drew did come out of his room a little more than normal on this trip but, true to his form, he stayed in the back of the room with the light off to hide himself. He must have had trouble sleeping with all of our laughter filling the house. I observed how Mom's cancer and the radiation treatments had slowed her down. She walked a bit slower and had a little trouble with her balance. She looked a little washed out and had started sleeping until nine in the morning, when all her life she'd been up by seven. She was in her late seventies and still working full time. She deserved to sleep in as long as she wanted as far as I was concerned.

Mom told us that Christmas that she was thinking about reducing her hours at the church. She planned to talk to the pastor about moving from forty to twenty-five hours a week. This was a huge step for her. Cancer had informed her body that it was time to slow down, that she wasn't infallible. There was no need for her to be superwoman anymore. I was happy and relieved that she had made this decision but I wished she would just retire. I understood that working made her feel needed and that she also had to have a daily break from Drew. In January, she followed through and started working her reduced hours.

F@#* Cancer

WHEN DAD PASSED AWAY, I was certainly upset and sad. In the end, cancer robbed him of any quality of life. His last couple of months he couldn't even swallow food. He lost a tremendous amount of weight and was weak and nauseous from the chemo. Instinctively though, he acted like the macho-man he had always projected. He'd been brought up in a generation of men who were supposed to be tough as nails. He had fought for his country during WWII. A "real" man never complained about being in pain. Up to the day he died, he never complained or wanted anyone to feel sorry for him. I knew that at the time of his death, his deep Catholic faith would see him through.

It was different with Mom. I couldn't bear to see her struggle with pain. The feeling I had in dealing with Mom's cancer was much different from my experience with Dad's cancer. Mom called in the first week of April and said that her cancer had metastasized and spread to her liver and lymph nodes. I was gutted. Dad smoked three packs of cigarettes a day for thirty years. I understood how he could have gotten cancer. My mother—a saint, in my eyes—never smoked or drank and always ate a healthy diet. No one that I was aware of in our family had ever had breast cancer. It just didn't make any sense and certainly did not seem very fair.

Mom decided against any chemo treatments. Her attitude was that whatever God's plan was for her should just happen naturally. She had witnessed what chemo had done to her husband and she wanted no part of it. As she hid her fatal condition from Drew, she also kept Annie, Bobby and me in the dark as to her true prognosis. The three of us wanted to speak to her doctor to get a clearer picture of her situation because she wasn't sharing much information with us. After much convincing and long conversations with Mom, Annie finally was permitted to speak to her oncologist. After Annie's conversation with the oncologist, Bobby and I got on a conference call with her. Mom was now in Stage IV of her cancer. The oncologist told Annie that he'd never seen anyone live longer than three months with her kind of cancer. I was devastated. This was so much worse than Mom had let on.

Knowing Mom's condition was going to continue to deteriorate, Annie, Bobby and I made a plan that for the foreseeable future, one of us would be in Greenville with her during every week. We would rotate our schedules so that each of us could care for her every third week. We all had ample unused vacation time from work that we could use. Mom wasn't too thrilled with our plan initially and continued to downplay the severity of her condition. But the three of us carried on a united front this time and were not going to have it any other way.

Through April and May, the three of us each took our turn every three weeks. Mom continued to work through April and shared very little with her co-workers regarding her condition. They must have known that things weren't heading in the right direction for her. She had slowed down considerably. None of us, including Mom, brought up the subject of death during our visits in April. Drew was curious about why the three of us were visiting that month. We told him that we were helping out Mom while she continued to recover. By the end of April, he had grown suspicious. I could tell he was nervous. He was out of his room more frequently and being more social. He asked a lot of questions. We couldn't hold him off much longer and would have to share her prognosis with him soon.

The month of May was a different story. Mom never complained that she was experiencing any pain, but we could see that her body was starting to shut down. She also was growing very frustrated. Her brain was perfectly fine but her body was failing. The cancer in her liver caused her legs to retain fluid and she struggled to walk. She finally had to quit her job.

I took her to an oncologist's appointment that month and the oncologist wanted her to have a blood transfusion. I took her to the medical center downtown to a large room where there were patients of all ages receiving chemo and fluid treatments. I sat next to Mom with that needle in her arm for the next three hours observing the steady flow of cancer patients in and out of the clinic. Even with everything going on around us she still maintained her positive outlook. On the way home I had to pull the car over twice so she could throw up. I got the feeling this wasn't the first time this had happened. She had brought a few plastic bags along with her in light of the past results of her treatments. The medicine from her transfusion and the motion from the car didn't agree with her. She never once complained and kept apologizing to me for having to watch her get sick in the car.

On one of my trips in early May I was able to overlap with Bobby for a day. We decided to tell Drew what was happening with Mom. Bobby felt it would be best to talk to him while he was getting high. I had mixed emotions about talking to Drew while he was smoking pot. I left the decision up to Bobby since he had spent more time with him recently. The three of us went out in the woods behind Mom's house that night and let Drew light up his joint. I had no intention of smoking. I hadn't smoked pot since college and couldn't take the risk with my job. They regularly tested us for drugs. Bobby and Drew had smoked about half of the joint when I spoke up.

I told him that Mom was very sick and was not going to recover. Acting like he was already aware, he said he knew she was sick. I explained that the doctors believed that Mom wouldn't live longer than a month most likely. I was expecting him to show some form of emotion, but he stoically replied, "I know. Everyone has to die." No tears, no sorrow, no change in his facial expression, so matter of fact. I also told him that Mom wanted to die at home and not in the hospital like Dad. Drew took the joint from Bobby and finished smoking the rest. Before we went back into the house, I asked him if he had any questions. "Not really," he said. He acted like he understood the process of dying and that it was no big deal. We returned to the house without Bobby having said much of anything the entire time we'd been outside.

During that same trip, Mom went over all her papers with me for the first time. She knew that her time was growing short and she needed to review her will with me. I knew that I was the executor but we had never spoken about her financial accounts, deeds, and life insurance paperwork. She was very serious and business-like, going over all the information while I was a total wreck. The sense of finality hit me like a punch in the gut and I couldn't focus on much of what Mom told me. At least I knew where everything was kept.

That night was Bobby's last night of his trip. Mom pulled the two of us into her office and said, "I want to talk about Drew and who is going to care for him." In order for her to have some piece of mind, she needed to have this issue settled. I was dreading this conversation and, again, the finality of the situation was overwhelming. Bobby and I both knew that Drew would not live with Annie. First, she lived far away, and second, she traveled for months at a time for her job.

Everyone, including Mom, always believed it would be Bobby who would take responsibility for Drew. Bobby lived two hours from Greenville in Atlanta. He and his wife had no children and he had remained closest to Drew over the years. As soon as Mom brought the subject up, Bobby jumped into the conversation and spoke up. He understood that everyone thought he'd be Drew's caregiver but he said he just couldn't do it. He said that his wife felt uncomfortable around Drew and that Drew would never be able live under the same roof with them. It seemed to me that he had rehearsed his lines and prepared for the conversation well in advance. My first thought was, "Are you kidding me? This was not in the plan." We had all been led down the path that Drew would live with him when Mom passed. And now, in Mom's hour of need, he was backing out? And using his wife as an excuse? I was absolutely floored.

Prior to Bobby getting close to Drew after I went away to college, I thought that the long-term responsibility for Drew would fall on my shoulders. That all changed as Bobby developed a close relationship with Drew, plus Bobby didn't have the responsibility of children to support. Sitting there stunned, the ball seemed like it was back in my court. Here were Bobby and I, front and center with Mom in her last days, and we were out of options. Mom needed closure quickly and I couldn't disappoint her in her last hours of need. The only choice I had was to speak up. I said, "I'll take him. He can come live in Colorado." The relief on Mom's face was plain to see. I couldn't look at Bobby, I was so pissed at him. All of our lives were about to change.

The End And The Beginning

I HAD THE FIRST WEEK IN JUNE for my rotation to be with Mom. I arrived on the afternoon of June 1 and relieved Bobby's wife who'd had the week prior. Bobby knew I was very angry at him for abandoning Drew and sent his wife to help out to avoid running into me. Honestly, I was still a little pissed at him, but I'd have to deal with those emotions at a later time.

I was startled when I saw how much Mom's condition had worsened since the last time I was there. Her legs now were retaining so much fluid that she could not get out of bed or off the toilet without help. We had been in contact with Greenville Hospice throughout the last month and they had been fantastic in helping us with Mom's care, comfort, and quality of life as she approached the end. I called them that afternoon and described her current condition. They offered to send a hospital bed and a device for her toilet to help her stand up.

The next day, as promised, the Hospice nurse arrived in the morning and set up a hospital bed in her room and installed a device for toilet assistance and safety. Both would help her to lift herself up without help. The nurse also spent time alone with Mom in her bedroom. Mom continued to be very frustrated that her mind was working fine but her body was shouting down. Still, she never complained of having any pain. The nurse pulled me aside before she left and told me that Mom was in her final days and that they would send a full-time nurse to the house tomorrow to provide around the clock care. I called Bobby and Annie and told them that they should make plans to come to Greenville sooner rather than later.

Mom was very reluctant to get into that hospital bed. She understood it moved up and down and would help her get in and out of bed but there was something about that bed that bothered her. I decided to sleep in her regular bed that evening so she wouldn't have to be alone. Every now and then Drew would emerge from his bedroom and stand in her doorway watching us. He occasionally interjected some strange comment that didn't fit into our conversation. It was his own way of dealing with his anxiety. Mom and I had some wonderful conversations that evening. We talked about her childhood, raising her family in Jersey, and about Dad. We shared many great laughs. The only time Mom cried was when she told me a couple of stories about how Drew was bullied growing up. She felt guilty that she was unaware of how some kids treated him and wished that she could have prevented it. She asked me to take care of Drew and make sure he was as happy as he could be. Several times that evening she asked me to come hold and rub her hand. She fell asleep fairly early that night. I remember having some very vivid dreams about Dad that night.

The Hospice nurse arrived early on the morning of June 3. She was an elderly woman, close to the age of Mom. She was a great help and I know Mom enjoyed having another woman to help her get dressed and go to the bathroom instead of her son. Early in the morning, Mom and the nurse had a long talk about the process of dying. I had left the room to make breakfast and when I returned, they were in a very deep emotional conversation. I set one foot in her bedroom and quickly turned and left, shutting her door.

With the nurse there I could go to the grocery store, hang with Drew a little, and make some needed work-related phone calls. Annie arrived later that afternoon and spent the rest of the night with Mom before Mom drifted off to sleep.

Earlier in the day another nurse had come to the house and hooked Mom up to an IV and inserted a catheter. Everyone knew her time was short. Again, that night Mom did not want to get into that hospital bed and kept stalling. It was as if she knew that if she got in that bed, she might never get out of it. Mom was always right.

On the morning of June 4, Mom woke up early and complained of pain for the first time. She said she felt like the pain was shooting right though her bones. She was now unable to get out of bed. For the first time the hospice nurse administered morphine through Mom's IV for the pain. Mom was in and out of consciousness the rest of the morning.

The Hospice nurse, who had slept in the same room as Mom the night before, informed me that she probably wouldn't make it through the entire day. I took her at her word since I'd never had seen anyone die before. I called Bobby again and told him that he needed to get to Greenville. The hospice nurse also shared with me that in the night

Mom was talking to her mother—my grandmother—in her sleep. Sixteen years of Catholic education, going to Mass every day, and my Catholic faith had taught me that when you die, you are greeted in heaven by all your family and friends who have passed before you. Was Mom talking to people on the other side last night?

Through the rest of the morning and into the early afternoon, Mom's breathing got slower and heavier. I could hear that rattle in her chest that I've always read about. She was sedated so she wasn't truly conscious anymore. Bobby finally made it around two o'clock. When he arrived, Drew came out of his room and I could tell he was extremely nervous due to the fact that all three of us were here at the house. I told Drew that Mom was probably not going to make it through the day. He started pacing the hallway floor. He returned to his room for about a half hour and then return to pacing again.

Around three o'clock I realized that I hadn't called the church to request last rites for Mom. Mom and I had never discussed last rites and I had been completely caught up in what was happening around us. I frantically called the church and spoke to the pastor, Mom's boss. He arrived at our house in twenty minutes. Father Looney administered last rites to Mom and cried the entire time he was conducting the sacrament. Father Looney loved Mom and was obviously agonized by her imminent death. She was like a mother to him. I had never seen last rights given to anyone before but I would have thought that the family of the dying could look to the priest for strength and comfort. Today, it was the priest who needed comfort. I said a silent prayer of thanks that I remembered to call Father about the last rites. I would never have forgiven myself if I hadn't called Father Looney. Mom loved to use the phase, "A little birdie told me," when she had information to share but didn't want to reveal her source. I truly believe the she was my little birdie that day, reminding me to call him.

After Father Looney left, Annie, Bobby and I sat round Mom's hospital bed. It was the first time all three of us had been together since we started coming to Greenville to work different shifts. We could tell she was struggling to breath and the nurse reassured us that she wasn't in any pain and that this was part of the normal process. For the next hour, the three of us shared stories about growing up, our family vacations, and about our mom and dad. Then Mom's breathing began to change and her breaths grew farther and farther apart. Drew eventually joined us in the room and sat down to complete the circle around Mom. It was the first time that the four of us had been in the same room together in many years. Drew also joined in adding his commentary to some of our stories. It was now the four of us sitting around our mother laughing and sharing stories while Mom's breathing pattern became more uneven.

For the rest of my life, I will remember the moment of Mom's passing. Annie was in the middle of telling a story and all four of us were laughing out loud. Suddenly, time seemed to stand still. Mom's lack of a breath caused Annie to stop in mid-sentence. We all gazed at each other in silence. Mom took one more breath and we waited, and waited, and waited for her next breath. It never came. The four of us grew frightened and looked at the Hospice nurse who was sitting in the corner of the room. She confirmed that Mom had just passed.

It was so peaceful. It was nothing like I had expected. I feel certain that once Mom felt the four of us were around her and she could hear all of us, including Drew, laughing, she knew she could go. It was very surreal and something I will never forget.

The four of us stayed in the room around her for a while. Each of us took turns holding her hand. Stories and laughter were replaced with silence and reverence, each of us dealing with what we had witnessed in our own way. Hospice sent their nurse supervisor who officially and legally confirmed Mom's passing. After a while, all but Drew left the bedroom. He didn't want to leave Mom's side.

An hour later, an employee from the funeral home came to the house. He asked if anyone wanted to stay in the room while he prepared Mom's body for transportation. All of us declined except for Drew. He wanted to witness the entire proceeding. Annie, Bobby, and I had no desire to watch. I had to go outside in the backyard and get some air. I wanted to call Colleen and the kids. Drew stayed with Mom until she taken from the house on the gurney and put into the funeral home's van.

The house was rather quiet that evening. No one knew what to say. The realization hit us that for the first time in our lives, we had no parents. We all went to bed early, though I doubt anyone slept much. I noticed that several times during the evening, Drew went into Mom's room and walked around staring at the articles in her room. I believe he was making sure everything was in its right place, just the way he thought Mom would have wanted it. For the rest of the evening, Drew followed his usual routine, eating his huge meal at midnight and watching TV until he went to bed around six in the morning. I would bet that he also made numerous trips into Mom's bedroom that night while we were all asleep. It was the only way to relieve his anxiety. He knew he was about to face some major changes in his life.

Rain In Greenville

IF YOU LISTENED TO THE CALLS Mom and I had every Monday evening, you would swear that it never rained in Greenville. Well, Mom must have gone straight up to heaven and had a conversation with the powers that be. It poured the day of her funeral and burial. We got soaked leaving the church after the service. I hadn't seen Father Looney since he'd been at our house to administer Mom's last rights. He gave a beautiful eulogy and was able to remain composed throughout the entire service.

After the funeral Mass we all went to Woodlawn Cemetery for the burial in the pouring rain. Only Drew refused an umbrella to stay dry. He preferred to stand in the cemetery in the soaking rain. Mom was entombed next to Dad. We were each given a red rose by the funeral home to lay on her casket as we departed the service. Drew was emphatic that he would lay the last rose on her coffin and no one was about to argue with him. We waited in the limo while he stood over her coffin for several minutes, laid his rose down, made the sign of the cross, and walked back to the car. I wish I knew what was going through his head that day.

Having Steve Jr. and Mark around for the week was a great distraction for Drew. He stayed close by them during the funeral and burial. When we got home from both services, Drew tried to convince them to take him to the record store. We had a family dinner planned for that evening and no one was in the mood to go to the store that night. We never had the chance to all go to that record store again.

Annie, Bobby, and I thought it would be great to take all of our families out to dinner later that evening. It was rare for all of us to be in Greenville at the same time. It was also extremely rare to get Drew to go out with us, but having Steve Jr. and Mark there helped to convince him to go. We chose to go to Mom's favorite restaurant, The Peddler. Not wanting the evening to ever end, Bobby and I decided to get champagne for everyone before we left and went our separate ways. While the bottles of champagne were chilling in ice buckets on our tables, everyone took turns telling their favorite story about Mom. The wonderful stories that were told that night lifted our spirits and made us all laugh. Even Drew shared a story about a time in Jersey when he stole a chocolate cake from the kitchen that Mom had baked for desert that evening. He took the cake up to his bedroom and ate the whole thing. Mom never found out what had happened to that cake even though she had her strong suspicions.

While Bobby was in the middle of sharing his story, the cork from one of the champagne bottles exploded. The cork hit the ceiling, bounced off the floor, and landed right in Mark's lap. I mentioned before that Mark always had a special place in Mom's heart. We all swore that Mom was present in the room that night. She must have wanted to give Mark a special treat to remember her. That was a once in a lifetime evening. After our champagne toasts, we hugged each other and said our goodbyes, not knowing when some of us would see each other again.

Bobby and I went back to Mom's house with Drew. The two of them went outside in the backyard and burned a joint. I stayed inside and started to make a list of all the things that needed to get done tomorrow. Bobby and I had taken a lot of time off from work and needed to get back to our respective homes. We had only a few days to empty the house and get it ready to sell and get Drew packed up. The next few days were going to be interesting in so many ways.

Packing Up

BOBBY AND I DEVELOPED a strategy to get Mom's house ready to sell and prepare Drew for the move to Colorado. We had three days to get everything accomplished. Our team of Bobby, Drew, Steve Jr., Mark, and I created three piles for Mom's possessions: one for Goodwill, one for the junkyard, and one for Colorado. Mom wanted all of her furniture donated to the church. It was difficult deciding what was going where and into which pile and Drew didn't make it any easier. I got it. The house he'd lived in for twenty-one years was being torn apart. When he moved from New Jersey to Greenville, it didn't go very well for him. He was very vocal and opinionated when it came to what was being kept and what was being thrown away. He wanted nearly everything that had been in the family for years to go to Colorado. He wanted to keep all the dishes, Christmas ornaments, and many of the pictures that hung on the walls. He had no issue donating things that were new and that he wasn't attached to.

I went through every piece of paper Mom had saved. I went through all her files in her office and up in the attic. I cleaned out every box. I found receipts and tax returns for the last thirty years and box after box of cancelled checks. I found some cool items such as Dad's dog tags from his time in the Navy. There was one thing that I was hoping to find that I never could locate. I hoped Mom had kept a note, a file, anything about Drew. I was so hoping to find some answers, but I came up empty handed. I found nothing other than those old report cards of his that I had seen before. I guess it was too painful for her to keep anything regarding his mental state. She must have wanted no records of those trips to the psychologist in Morristown. It would have helped me now as Drew's caregiver. I was extremely disappointed and a little scared.

Bobby's truck was a huge help in taking four full loads to Goodwill. Drew had no interest going to Goodwill but he went on every trip to the junkyard. He loved taking items and throwing them into the landfill. Not only did he throw the items into the landfill but he made sure that each item was shattered into a million pieces. He seemed to enjoy the sound of broken glass and smashing of breakable items.

It reminded me of walking to the A&P back in New Providence as kids when Drew and I would walk the mile to the grocery store and hang out. On our way, we walked through the woods and past the factories and a few fairly large greenhouses. Next to one of the greenhouses was an old broken-down wooden shed that we liked to go in and explore. It was filled with thousands of clay flowerpots of all different sizes. Drew liked destroying the pots by smashing them into a million pieces. I'd yell at him to stop and get out, thinking we were certain to get caught. I'd have to physically yank him out of the shed. We were lucky that we never got caught.

Clearing out Mom's house was fairly straightforward and we ended up finishing ahead of schedule. The church came and took all the large items and our "pile" strategy worked perfectly. We got most of the house cleared out in one day.

Packing Drew up though, was another story. Other than his furniture, all of his belongings were stored in Ziploc bags, tall kitchen trash bags, or thirty-gallon black trash bags. It's not that he packed this way for the move; his stuff had always been stored this way in his bedroom. Strangely, quite frequently he would change out the bags so Mom always needed to have an assortment of plastic bags available for him. I was never sure what his reasoning was, but it could have been connected to the same reason he always had a paper towel in his hand to pick up things. He didn't like any object to touch his skin directly.

We loaded Drew's plastic bags into the U-Haul truck we had rented to get us to Colorado. We had no idea what was in all of those bags other than the large collection of toiletries he hoarded, such as mouthwash, lotion, toothpaste, and razors, some of which must have been over twenty years old.

During the twenty-one years Drew had lived in Greenville I had never been in his bedroom there. When I visited, he was usually in his room with the door locked. Even when he was out of his room, it was off-limits. When it was time to load his furniture onto the truck, I went into his room for the first time. I was surprised by how simple and sparse his room looked. His furniture dated back to when he was in high school. At six-three, his feet must have hung off that small twin-size bed. He had a matching dresser and small student desk with a little student lamp on it. I calculated that he'd had this same furniture for over forty years. The walls of his room were bare. His room was plain and somewhat sterile.

One thing in his room was very odd. On his bedroom wall, at least six feet high, by the wooden doorframe, was a large round greasy spot on the wall. After we emptied his room, I stood there for a while trying to figure out what caused that greasy spot. I tried to remove the spot with Lysol cleaner and a rag. As I was cleaning his wall, I realized that the spot on the wall was the same height as Drew's head. For twenty-one years, he must have stood by his door with his head against the wall trying to hear what was going on outside his room. He must have been desperate to hear what was going on in a world where he didn't feel comfortable inserting himself. I cleaned the wall and never said anything to him or anyone else.

Bobby had to get back to Atlanta for work so he couldn't make the trip to Colorado. The plan was for me to drive the U-Haul to Colorado with Drew as my wingman. Steve Jr. and Mark would follow us in Mom's car. Greenville had developed into a cosmopolitan town with a great downtown area but I never did feel like it was home. My parents had loved the town but I had always felt like a visitor. I had no trouble pulling out of Mom's driveway knowing that I'd probably never return. I did not look back in my rearview mirror. I focused only on the fifteen hundred miles ahead of us. The long drive to Colorado would give me plenty of time to share my big news with Drew.

I Have The Feeling We're Not In Greenville Anymore

YOU KNOW THE SCENE in *The Wizard of Oz* where Dorothy opens the door of her house that has just crashed back to earth from the tornado? The movie was filmed in black and white but when she opens that door, vivid technicolor greets us. As a kid, those bright colors represented an entirely new and beautiful world.

Drew's previous life's experiences had been New Jersey, trips to NYC, the move to Greenville, and one trip to Daytona Beach. There were many sights and sounds during our drive to Colorado that he had never experienced before and it made me realize how much we take for granted. When we drove across the Mississippi River, he was amazed at how wide it was. He had never seen a river that large before. The huge farms and highways lined with cornfields for miles and miles in Kansas surprised him. He saw herds of farm animals along the way that he had only seen on TV before. He was astonished by the size of the Rocky Mountains. His awe reminded me that I needed to stop and smell the roses more frequently. I live in Colorado and have an unbelievable mountain view to experience every day. Sometimes I have to remind myself just how lucky I am to be surrounded by such beauty.

I hadn't anticipated some of the issues that Drew would face on our travels. On our first day of the trip, Steve Jr. and Mark wanted to stop at a Steak and Shake for lunch. As we climbed out of our vehicles to go into the restaurant, Drew stayed in the truck. When I asked him what was wrong, he said he didn't want to go in. I wasn't going to force him but I said that's a problem. He asked why and I told him that it was a sit-down restaurant. "How are you going to eat? You don't even know what's on the menu."

He replied, "Just get me whatever you're eating—to go." *Good answer*, I thought. I don't think he had actually been to a sit-down restaurant since he left Jersey. As the three of us were eating our delicious steak burgers, I periodically looked out the restaurant window to check on Drew. I had to explain to Steve Jr. and Mark why he wouldn't eat inside. Much to their chagrin, we went to drive thru restaurants the rest of the trip.

Hotels and sleeping arrangements were something else I hadn't anticipated. I knew we would have to spend two nights in hotels along the drive but I hadn't thought about how that might impact Drew. The first night, I figured it would best to get two hotel rooms. I thought Steve Jr. and Mark would enjoy a break from me and Drew. Surprisingly, Drew felt comfortable and safe within the four walls of the hotel room he shared with me. If I had let him, he would have slept in the bathtub and not the bed. He liked the privacy of that small bathroom and spent a lot of time in there. I was able to lure him out of the bathroom by telling him that the TV had HBO. I have no idea how long he stayed up watching HBO. I fell asleep once my head hit the pillow. We were on two totally opposite time clocks.

Traveling through St. Louis was funny. Nothing against St. Louis, but every time I've driven through that town, my goal has been to get out of that city as fast as possible. No stops! Out of all the cities we drove through on our fifteen-hundred-mile trek across the country, Drew liked St. Louis the best. We hit St. Louis just as the sun went down. It was June, so Gay Pride month was being celebrated. Many buildings were lit up with rainbow-colored spotlights. The city was very colorful as we drove along. Drew thought that was the greatest. Since he had never seen Gay Pride lights before, he thought St. Louis was a very progressive city. I don't think Bob Jones University would ever have allowed Gay Pride lights in Greenville. Drew has always been accepting of protecting people's LGBTQ rights. I never thought Drew was gay but had always felt that he could have been bisexual. While he never told me, I always had my suspicions that he had some homosexual experiences on some of his visits to NYC.

Another set of lights attracted Drew's attention as we drove through St. Louis. From his window, Drew could see bright red lights on a building we were approaching. As we got closer, I could make out the words spelled out in the flashing red lights. It was the Larry Flint's Hustler Strip Club. Larry Flint was the founder of *Hustler* Magazine. Drew, being a long-time connoisseur of *Hustler*, thought that was just greatest—a Hustler strip club with live dancers. As we drove down the highway past the club he said, "You know, I think I could live here."

I nodded my head and just kept driving. It had gotten dark as we drove through the city and Drew asked, "Why don't we just spend the night here in St. Louis?" Next, he would ask me to take him to Larry's club.

I quickly said, "Our plan is to keep driving until we get to Kansas City tonight." I had to chuckle when I thought that most people make decisions on where to live based on a job or the schools they want their kids to attend. Drew made his decision on where to live based on the quality of the strip clubs.

The next morning, we left early so we could make the eight-hour drive from Kansas City to arrive in Denver by nightfall. We had already driven a total of sixteen hours and I was getting a little antsy. At least Drew and I had listened to some great tunes along the way. We alternated from classic rock to punk rock to Drew's death metal. I struggled with the death metal but sucked it up by reminding myself that I wouldn't have many chances to drive cross-country with my older brother.

I had been holding off telling Drew my news, but with four hours left in the drive I needed to bring it up. I also wanted to give him some time to digest what I was about to talk to him about. I waited until there was a crappy song on the radio. I believe it was "We Built This City," by Starship. Just kidding; I don't remember what the song actually was. I turned down the radio and said, "Drew I need to talk to you about something that's really important. You know that our plan all along has been that you would move to Colorado and live with Colleen and me. We figured it would work perfectly since the kids are now gone and you could take the entire basement that is completely finished. The problem is, that plan is not going to work anymore." Drew looked surprise and somewhat worried.

I continued, "Colleen and I have decided to separate for six months and most likely we'll be getting divorced. Colleen is going to stay in the house and I've rented an apartment in Boulder for you and me. We'll be living together in Boulder. I know this is different from what we talked about but I think it will be best for you and me."

Drew asked the obvious question, "Why are you getting divorced?"

My simple answer was, "We just fell out of love."

The longer story was that we did just fall out of love. I distinctly remember waking up one Saturday morning after twenty-five years of marriage and looking over at Colleen and thinking, *And you are?* It was as if I didn't know the woman who I shared a bed with and was married to anymore. For twenty-five years we'd had our kids' activities to go to every weekend. Between baseball games, soccer games and cheerleading competitions, we were busy every weekend. We forgot about each other along the journey. We were so wrapped up in our kids' activities that we failed to take care of our relationship. We were too tired, or that was the excuse we used, to go on dates anymore. There was no infidelity in our relationship, just twenty-five years of drifting apart a little each day. Then that weekend arrived when there were no kid-related activities. I rolled over in bed that Saturday morning and looked at my partner and wondered who this person was next to me. She didn't seem at all like the same person I married years ago. Her interests were now different from mine. Her values were not the same as mine. She didn't even look like the person I married. The flame of passion had burned out.

I wish that someone had advised me years ago pay attention to my marriage and my partner and continue to develop our relationship. Every chance I get now, I tell young married couples to continue to go on dates throughout their marriage. By the time Colleen and I came to the same conclusion it was too late. The train had already left the station. For the past seven years we had been miserable around each other. We went to several sessions with a marriage counselor but it was quickly evident that our relationship was "dead on arrival." Sadly, both of us were tired and had no deep desire or energy to work on it. With the kids out of the house now and Drew coming into town, it was as good a time as ever to make the break. At the end of the day, life is all about being happy. Colleen and I were just fifty years old and we both agreed that we had a lot of life left to live and didn't want to remain miserable living it. Telling Drew was one thing. It didn't matter a whole lot to him, he wasn't that close to Colleen. I was really dreading having to let our kids know. Not that they would be that surprised but I understood that at any age, the reality of their parents divorcing would be very painful.

I asked Drew if he had any questions, but he had none. Looking at his usual stoic face I couldn't tell if he was upset or even cared. I would imagine he was more concerned about his new home. What did the apartment look like? Was there HBO? Where could he score pot? And where could he buy porn in Boulder.

Over the last month, my life had been an overwhelming combination of dealing with Mom's illness and death, her funeral, vacating her house, packing Drew up, and my job and impending divorce. I hadn't spent a second thinking about what it is was going to be like living with Drew. We hadn't lived under the same roof for over thirty years. Both of us were very different from the long-haired teenagers we were back in Jersey. I spent the last two hours of our drive thinking about what life might be like for the two of us. The positive side of me thought that this reunion of brothers could be good for both of us. Drew would be a great distraction for me going through a divorce and

I knew I could help him adjust to his new living arrangement. I had learned a few things seeing him go through his move to Greenville and thought I could help him.

On our way into Denver, we stopped at DIA (Denver International Airport) to drop Steve Jr. off so he could catch his flight back to San Diego. I gave him a huge hug and thanked him for all of his help. Drew gave him the "bro" hug—a hug and a few hard slaps on the back. On the drive from DIA to Boulder two thoughts crossed my mind. One, I remembered that Steve Jr., being the last person to place a load in the U-Haul and secure the lock, had the key for the lock. It was too late to reach him because I was sure he had already cleared security. Drew started to freak out but I told him that I had tools that could cut through the lock and not to worry.

The other thought that entertained me for the rest of the drive to our new digs in Boulder was that I was now Drew's caregiver. I was going to have to morph from Drew's little brother into his parent. Having raised three kids, I felt like I was up for the task. Honestly, I really didn't have a choice. I still vividly remembered that day in Dr. Brooks' office discovering what Autism is. I equally remembered that call with Mom and how she wanted to "let sleeping dogs lie." Drew's life was about to change and neither of us had any idea what was to come. The one thing I did know was that my time had arrived and I was going to do the right thing for Drew.

Part IV

Boulder, Colorado, 2008

Part IV

Boulder, Colorado, 2008

DURING MY SENIOR YEAR at Florida State University, I took part in a psychological experiment hosted by the Psychology Department. I was majoring in psychology and was leaving the Psychology Building after my last class for the day when I noticed a sign on the exit door. The sign advertised free rent for helping with a departmental experiment. The only requirement was a full year commitment. The idea of free rent was very attractive for this poor college student, so I called the next day to inquire. My phone call led me to the head of the Psychology Department. After answering a couple of simple questions, I was invited to a meeting the following evening.

The head of the Psychology Department, Dr. Collins, and his assistant Joan, led the meeting. While Dr. Collins was the head of the department, he also maintained a private practice outside of the university. One of his patients was a twenty-two-year-old man named Howard. Howard was described to us at the meeting as a schizophrenic with the maturity of a fifteen-year-old. Howard was an only child whose father had passed away six months prior. Howard's mother and Dr. Collins were looking for two male seniors around the same age as Howard, to live with him for a year. They wanted these two seniors to model the appropriate behavior and maturity level of a twenty-two-year-old. In exchange for living with Howard, the rent and other utilities would be paid for by Howard's mother.

My first response was, "Where do I sign up?" There were ten other students at the meeting that evening who expressed an interest but in the end Darren and I were selected to be Howard's roommates for our senior year. Darren, who was also a male cheerleader for the football team, had more dates during the year than anyone I'd ever seen during college. He certainly would be able to role model how to score with the women for Howard. I wasn't sure what benefit I could offer Howard but I would give it my best effort.

I was a little nervous about living with a schizophrenic, mainly because I had no idea what to expect. I thought schizophrenics were all like Sally Field's character in the movie Sybil but in reality, Howard was great guy. Yes, he was twenty-two and acted much younger, but he ended up being a lot of fun and a great roommate for that entire year. He did have a few strange quirks or what I would call "obsessions." His mother had bought him a brand-new car when the year started and he was obsessed with it. He washed it a few times a week and took thousands of pictures of it. He loved to show me the pictures of his car, but after looking at a few hundred from every possible angle I explained to him that he didn't need to show people dozens of photos of his car; pulling out just a few to show would be more effective. He was also obsessed with his cat. He spent hours touching and smelling it and, again, taking a thousand pictures of it. Other than his few obsessions and a low level of maturity, he was not a bad roommate.

Darren and I lasted the entire year with Howard and left him in much better shape than when the school year began. We role modeled appropriate behavior and provided weekly written progress reports to Dr. Collins, Joan, and Howard's mom. We were all sad when the school year ended and we had to go our separate ways. Our sadness at knowing we would not see each other and the excitement we were feeling for our futures were also the appropriate emotions for us to role model for Howard.

As Drew and I were about to begin the next chapter in our lives in Boulder, I knew I would call upon my past experiences with Howard to help prepare me for our new adventure. Drew and I were both older and hadn't lived together in thirty-three years, but there was a lot of life left for us to live. I had no idea what the future held for me, but I was excited about our potential. It wasn't Jersey, but it was Boulder, Colorado. "The boys were back in town."

Our House

AFTER COLLEEN AND I decided to separate for a six-month period, I had a short amount of time to find a place for Drew and me to live. I looked at a few places in downtown Denver thinking that living in a downtown area could benefit Drew. While it wasn't NYC, living in downtown Denver would offer him the opportunity to walk around the city. He'd fit in fairly well and would have access to a lot of shops. I just could never find the perfect apartment for us in Denver. With time running out I decided to focus on Boulder as another option. While Boulder's downtown area was nowhere near the size of Denver, it offered many of the same opportunities. Boulder has always been very friendly to people who walk and ride bikes, which was also a plus. The University of Colorado is right in the middle of the downtown area. Boulder also rests up against the foothills and offers some of the best views of the foothills in Colorado.

After looking at few apartments in Boulder I stumbled upon the perfect one. It was a two bedroom on the north side of Boulder. The apartment had three levels. The first level had the garage and a storage closet. The second floor was perfect for Drew with a bedroom, bathroom and sitting area to watch TV. He would have his own private space and if he kept the same hours as he had in Greenville, his late-night escapades wouldn't keep me awake. The third level had a living room, a full kitchen, a half bathroom, a bedroom with a private bathroom, and a deck off the living room with a great view of the foothills. This would be the perfect floor for me. Outside of our apartment were numerous trails leading into the foothills or downtown Boulder. The apartment was next to the bus stop, shopping, restaurants, and my bank. Drew was very excited that there was also a "head" shop that sold marijuana paraphernalia across the street. He'd have easy access to all his accessories he needed for smoking pot.

The only possible negative was a huge homeless shelter north of our apartment less than half a mile away. In the morning all the homeless people who had spent the night at the shelter walked down our street heading to downtown Boulder to hang out for the day. In the evening they would make their way back up the street to the shelter. While it was an eye sore for the neighborhood, in a funny way Drew would fit right in with the homeless crowd. He kept his greying hair long and wore a fairly good-sized beard, and still liked to wear his torn and tattered clothes just like Dr. Brooks had described.

Mark, Drew, and I moved all Drew's belongings into our apartment. Drew had lost so much muscle tone living in Greenville that he struggled to help moving the heavier items up the two or three flights of stairs. I knew the higher altitude would also be difficult for him until he adjusted to it. While he took lots of breaks and complained that his wrist hurt, Mark and I kept on unpacking the U-Haul. Many more items made the trip from Greenville to Boulder than I had anticipated. Drew had been adamant about keeping several of Mom's possessions that I would have donated. I would store them in our garage until I could convince him to part with them.

My personal situation was certainly different. I hadn't taken any furniture from my house, only my clothes. I didn't know what the future held for Colleen and me after our six-month separation. I thought it made more sense to just keep everything at our house. I needed to buy some furniture as soon as we moved in and I wanted Drew to go to the furniture store with me. We set up his teenage bedroom furniture that we had moved from Greenville in his new room but I wanted him to have new furniture. I worked my best magic to convince him to go with me but he wouldn't budge. He said he was tired from the move and that his wrist still hurt—all excuses to avoid his social anxiety. I gave him a pass this time, but I did get him to commit to talking about it again when he wasn't so tired. Maybe this was progress. Time would tell.

Groceries, Target, and Wax Trax

ON OUR FIRST DAY in the new apartment, Drew and I made a list of groceries and other items that we needed. Drew was more than willing to go shopping. It hit me as we were driving to the store that he probably hadn't been in a grocery store since Jersey. I was certain that the Boulder Safeway was a bit different from the A&P where we'd shopped thirty years ago in Jersey. As we started to move through the store, I realized that he also might not be capable of cooking. Mom had made all his meals for him in Greenville and there was no way I would take on that burden. My life was busy with work and my kids. He was going to have to take some responsibility or he was going to go hungry. I had no issue preparing meals that we could share a few nights a week, but I wasn't going to be cooking for him daily.

It was interesting walking up and down the grocery aisles with him. Many times, I felt like I was the adult pulling my kid away from items that we were not going to purchase. It reminded me of walking through the cereal aisle with my kids when they were younger. I didn't want to get too judgmental with Drew yet regarding his eating habits. At first, I wanted to maintain a world pretty close to the one he had in Greenville so he could get comfortable with his new living arrangements. Once I had accomplished that goal, I'd begin making needed changes.

What do you buy when you only eat one meal a day? For starters, Drew had no interest in any breakfast foods. I guess that makes sense if you eat at midnight every day. I had to move him quickly through the candy aisle because he would have bought enough candy to hand out on Halloween. His other favorite aisles were the ice cream aisle and the dessert section. He was amazed at the selection of ice creams the store carried. While he was enthralled by the numerous brands, he went with his standard brand of Breyers. I was willing to buy only three half-gallons and had to convince him that if we ran out, I could always come back. He also loved the bakery area. We loaded up on doughnuts, a few pies, cakes, and cupcakes. My God, he had such a sweet tooth. This was going to have to change in the future.

I knew Drew was capable of using the microwave so I took him down the frozen foods aisle. I loaded him up on a variety of healthy frozen meals and some not so healthy meals. He was most excited about the frozen potpies. We also went to the prepared foods section and selected some entrées from the deli cases. He had no interest in the produce section, but I was able to convince him that he needed to select one fruit. He picked bananas. It wasn't a diet that Oprah would recommend, but it was a decent start. He wasn't going to go hungry anytime soon.

I hadn't given a whole lot of thought to Drew's financial situation with everything else I'd had to take care of since Mom's passing. After Mom and I had reviewed her financial papers back in May, I quickly calculated how much money Drew had. I estimated that between what he had saved up from New Jersey and what Mom was able to leave him, he had enough money to get him through roughly the next ten years. After that, Annie, Bobby and I would need to have a conversation.

In the checkout aisle, it became apparent to me that Drew didn't have a clue about money or how the groceries would be paid for. He didn't understand how much money he had, where his money was, or how to get access to it. He also didn't know how to pay for things, let alone the value ratio between his money and what he was buying. He just expected that there was money to buy whatever he wanted and that I would pay for it. I decided that I would need to document every single dollar he was spending. From now on, any bill, expense, and discretionary spending would be recorded.

Target was our next stop and I wasn't sure he would want to go in with me, but he had no issues with it. As we walked through Target, I could see how surprised he was by how large the store was and how many items they carried. I don't think he'd ever been in a superstore before. Just like in Safeway, I had to constantly tell him, "No, Drew," as he picked up items that I wasn't going to buy. I took him to the men's clothing section to replace his worn and tattered clothing. I let him go wild. He picked out new underwear, socks, a few cool band T-shirts, and a couple pairs of jeans. I discovered it's not easy finding pants for him with his waist size of thirty-two and leg length of thirty-six. I had to search deep into many stacks of pants to find one pair that had such a small waist and a long length.

Leaving Target, I felt good that we had made a small bit of progress on the clothes front with what we had purchased. I also felt good that Drew seemed to be comfortable shopping and getting out and around in Boulder. Not once did I notice anyone staring at him as we made our way through both stores. I felt selecting Boulder as our home was going to be a good decision.

We went back to our apartment and as we unpacked our purchases, Drew asked where the record stores were. I wasn't familiar with any record shops in Boulder (no comments from you *Mork and Mindy* fans) but I knew a great one in Denver. He was shocked by the Denver skyline while we drove into downtown. He had imagined that Denver was just a little bigger than New Providence. We had a great time visiting Wax Trax Records, which still carried a fair number of CDs, which was Drew's choice for playing music. They also had a large death metal section. He picked out four CDs and a KISS poster. Wax Trax also purchases used albums. On the way back to Boulder, he talked about how he wanted to come back and sell a few of his old albums. I promise you that if he brought his albums back to the store to sell, they would be the most perfectly kept used albums the store staff had ever seen.

We had a great day shopping together. I had many déjà vu moments during the day. It had been a good thirty-three years since we shopped in NYC, but it felt like we picked up right where we had left off. All day I waited for Drew to ask where he could buy porn in Boulder, but he never mentioned it. I knew that topic was going to come up soon and I needed to quickly figure out what my response was going to be.

Rocky Mountain High

WHEN DREW FIRST MOVED to Colorado in 2008, medical marijuana had been legal for a few years already. I had no idea how much pot he had stashed in Greenville but he kept talking about wanting to go to a dispensary. I wasn't aware of what the laws were about purchasing medical marijuana but I was growing tired of his endless questions so I decided to stop by a dispensary on my way home from work one night to get educated.

The intense smell of weed hit me when I entered the dispensary. It smelled a great deal stronger than the weed we had back in Jersey. I spoke to an employee in the store who gave me the lowdown on how the medical marijuana system worked. I learned that Drew would have to go to a doctor for an examination to determine if he qualified for a medical marijuana card. If he did, then once he had his card, he could visit a dispensary and buy pot. This seemed like a pretty simple process. I asked the employee how to find a doctor for this and was told there was a doctor's office next door where Drew could get his examination. *That was convenient*, I thought. I learned that the fee for the examination was a hundred fifty dollars and that the doctor who signs the medical marijuana card receives twenty percent of each future purchase that Drew would make. Someone was making a ton of money.

When I got home and told Drew about the process, he was excited and asked me to make an appointment as soon as I could. This was coming from someone who hadn't been to a doctor in decades. I made an appointment for him the following day. Getting his card was easy. At the doctor's office they wouldn't allow me to go into to the doctor's examination room with Drew, so I sat out in the waiting area. He came out several minutes later with his card in hand. Drew said the doctor asked him if he had any lingering pain and why he thought marijuana would help him manage that pain. Whatever he told the doctor worked. I paid the receptionist in cash as they didn't take credit cards. Now we were ready to go next door and make a purchase, at least that's what I thought.

Drew and I entered the dispensary next door and were asked immediately for our IDs. I pulled out my driver's license and handed it to the employee. I looked at Drew and said, "Oh, shit." Drew had no ID. The only forms of ID he had were his social security card and birth certificate. He had no valid ID—no driver's license, passport, or any other form of ID. He would never go to down to the government office in Greenville to get one because he refused to have his picture taken. I knew mom and Bobby had tried numerous times to get him to go but he refused to leave the house. I also remembered that he hated pictures of himself. Through the years, if he found a picture of himself stored in the basement, he ripped it to shreds. Other than a few baby pictures, there are very few pictures of him floating around the universe.

We were told that we would have to leave because Drew didn't have

ID and I didn't have a medical marijuana card. Back in the car we tried to figure out our next step. Now wasn't the time to berate him for not getting an ID in Greenville, but this was going to have to change. It would be quicker for me to try to get a medical marijuana card than for him to get an ID. I told Drew to wait in the car while I went in. I walked backed into the doctor's office and was able to see the doctor right away. He asked me a set of similar questions that he had asked Drew. I made up a story that my back had been bothering me for years and that marijuana helped in my pain management. I was given a card and paid another hundred fifty dollars in cash to the receptionist. Drew was going to have to pay me back for this one. Hurdle one was accomplished, now it was back to the dispensary.

With Drew waiting in the car, I entered the dispensary, showed my new medical card and ID, and was told to stay in the waiting area until they called me to go into the back room. I felt like I was in some mafia movie having to wait to go speak with the Godfather or, better yet, a Cheech and Chong movie. Another employee who called himself a "budtender," came out and escorted me into the back room. The room was filled with many labeled containers with a variety of strains of pot. When the budtender asked me if I preferred sativa or indica, I had to ask what that meant. I went with sativa because it was supposed to be more energizing and uplifting. I thought Drew needed that verses indica which was supposed to be more sedating. I felt he could use a little excitement in his life. I paid in cash and I left the dispensary with my paper bag in hand. My drug deal was now complete and I was done shopping for the day. This excursion had cost me over five hundred dollars in cash.

In the car, Drew was anxiously awaiting my return. I handed him the bag and said, "You're welcome." He had a huge smile on his face just like a little kid on Christmas morning. I told him on the way home that he was going to have to step up and get an ID so that in the future he could make his own pot purchases. He kept saying, "I know, I know." I had heard "I know" from him so many times before. I knew I would have to push him in order to see him make any changes in his behavior.

The pot in from the dispensary was so much stronger than the junk he had smoked in Greenville and New Jersey. I had to remind him to take it easy on the amount he was smoking until his body adjusted. When I asked him how was the pot was, his response was always the same, "Real stoner stuff." When I asked him why he liked to get high so much he gave a response I would never have expected, but made all the sense in the world. He said, "It makes me feel normal."

Fascinations

APARTMENT? CHECK. CABLE TV? Check. Food? Check. Pot? Check. Porn? I felt Drew had a great start getting all the basics taken care of so his transition to living in Boulder was as smooth as possible. It was only a matter of time though until he would ask me about how he could get his hands on some new magazines.

I can always tell when Drew wants to ask me for something. I'll be sitting at my desk working and he'll casually stroll into the room and look around. He'll act like he's lost something and is looking for it. He won't say a word and then he'll leave the room. He'll repeat this process two or three more times while he's building up the courage to tell me what's on his mind. After we had been living together for about a week, he approached me while I was working on my computer and finally asked, "Are there any places in Boulder to buy porno?"

I told him I didn't know but that I'd check the Internet. While he was in the room, I searched for adult stores in Boulder on my computer and saw one that might work. Drew was interested at looking at their ad on my computer. He was fascinated that you could look up that kind of information. Keep in mind that he had never used a computer before. The only computer screen he had ever seen was Mom's, who I'm certain wasn't looking at any adult sites. I told Drew that we could go check out the store on Saturday.

On Saturday morning Drew was up, dressed, and ready to go by nine. It was amazing what a motivator porn was for him. I told him that this wasn't NYC where the stores are open twenty-four hours and that the store didn't open until ten. It was a quick ten-minute drive from our apartment to the store. I parked in the back of the store of, course. I never felt comfortable going in an adult store. I was always paranoid that I was going to run into someone I knew. The store carried the regular supply of stripper clothes, adult novelties, and a large variety of DVDs. Drew never had any interest in adult videos or DVDs, just magazines. We made two full rounds around the store and never found any magazines. When I asked an employee where the magazines were located, she replied, "We don't carry magazines anymore. We haven't had them in here for over five years." Drew's face looked like a boy who had just lost his dog.

Drew was quite bummed as we drove back to our apartment. He just hadn't progressed through the years from magazines, to videos, to DVDs like the porn industry. I told him I had an idea. When we got home, I pulled out my laptop and asked him what his favorite magazine was. When he answered, "That's easy, *Hustler*." I searched and found their website. Fortunately for Drew they still offered subscriptions by mail. He didn't have a credit card so I had to sign him up using my information. I was not too thrilled about it. Between my new medical marijuana card and now a subscription to *Hustler*, I hoped that none of this would come back and bite me.

Drew's fascination with my laptop and the ease of downloading porn continued as I ordered his *Hustler* magazines. He said, "Maybe for my next birthday I can get a laptop."

I replied, "We'll see, Drew," knowing there was no way in hell I was going to get him a laptop and open him up to a world of online porn. He was just like a kid of fifteen.

One evening before the arrival of his first *Hustler* magazine, Drew asked me about a building he had seen on our drive into Boulder during the move. He asked, "What's the Bus Stop?"

I knew the answer to his question, but wasn't sure I really wanted to get into it with him. I told him it was a strip club. The Bus Stop was a five-minute walk from our apartment. I had been there for a bachelor party years ago and had never had a reason to go back. If I understood their history correctly, the Bus Stop is at the edge of Boulder city limits and where the Boulder bus route begins. There are always plenty of buses parked on the street beside the building waiting to start their routes. The inside of the club has the décor of a fifties' whorehouse. It reeks of stale cigarettes and bar rot. All of Boulder's finest strippers dance there—just kidding. Drew said that he would like to check it out sometime. I honestly didn't feel like that was ever going to happen. I guess I should have been happy that he wanted to get out and not be stuck in his bedroom like he had been in Greenville. I said to him, "We'll see."

On Schedule

I THOUGHT IT WAS IMPORTANT for Drew to establish his own schedule within his first six months in Boulder. I was well aware of the schedule he kept in Greenville, but I didn't know if that schedule had been built around Dad or Mom, or if it was just a daily schedule that Drew created. I also wanted to learn more about him and how he made decisions around his activities. Was there a method to his madness? I preferred not to push him too much during our first six months of living together. I didn't want him to revolt because he really had no other options within our family. I wanted to remain sensitive to what he was going through with Mom's passing and his move across the country. These two events would be traumatic for anyone, let alone Drew.

After three months of living in Boulder, Drew settled into a routine that was similar to the schedule he kept while living in Greenville. He woke up around six at night and washed his hands for an inordinate amount of time in the kitchen sink. He walked around the apartment checking things out. If he felt something was not in the right place, he put it exactly where he thought it should be. Around seven o'clock, he'd ask me what my plans were for the evening because he was going to be in the bathroom for a while to, in his words, "take a dump." I didn't want to know the timing of his bowel movements, but for some reason he thought it was important for me to know.

At eight, he'd let me know he was going to get high before heading back into his bathroom to smoke. I never understood why he didn't go outside and smoke. Maybe he got a stronger high in the smoke-filled room. After he got stoned, he would sit in the same spot every night and watch TV in his sitting room outside his bedroom. I would be upstairs either eating dinner or working at my desk and periodically I'd hear him talking at the TV. Drew had a tendency to comment and sometimes yell out loud to the people on the TV screen.

I usually went to bed by eleven, especially when I had to work the next day. Drew would make his way upstairs to the kitchen around midnight. Because we went grocery shopping on Sundays, I was well aware of how much food he was consuming. He was still in the habit of eating once a day. He was intermittent fasting well before it became popular. He had kept the bowl he'd used every night at Mom's and still filled it up the same way he had for years. Just as he'd done at Mom's, he microwaved whatever was in his bowl and returned downstairs to continue watching TV. After he finished eating, he would come back upstairs, rinse his bowl and put it in the dishwasher. Drew had no clue how to turn on the dishwasher. Mom had always taken care of the dishwasher and never taught him how to use it. In our apartment, that was certainly going to change.

With his dinner bowl in the dishwasher, he would then take another bowl and fill it with ice cream. I'm not exaggerating—he polished off three to four half gallons of ice cream a week. I didn't understand how someone could eat that much ice cream. He'd return downstairs and would watch TV until six in the morning. During the workweek, I usually got up around five-thirty and hit the gym down the street. Returning from the gym some mornings I would run into him heading to his bedroom to sleep. I'd always ask him if he'd watched anything good on TV the prior evening and he always mentioned some show on HBO that I had never heard of.

On Sundays before we went grocery shopping, we cleaned the apartment. I did the kitchen while he mopped and vacuumed our entire apartment. I also made him clean his own bathroom each week. I learned that he had never vacuumed or cleaned a bathroom in his entire life. As I gathered the cleaning supplies every Sunday, I would call down to him to come upstairs to help clean. He said the same thing every week in response. "Again?"

During our first six months of living together, I often wondered if he was happy with all the changes. With Drew, you could never tell. I know he was sad that Mom had passed away but he was able to maintain the same schedule that he had in Greenville, with very few exceptions. He had more independence and was getting out into public more than he had in the last twenty-five years. I had a good friend who was a physician with whom I had worked. One day he asked me how it was going with my brother. He knew that my mom had passed away and I would seek his counsel regularly about Drew's autism. I said to my friend, "As long as Drew has food, cable TV, weed, and porn he's good." My friend responded that Drew had it right. He had food, someone to take care of him, cable, weed, porn, and no stress in his life. He would probably live to be a hundred. Great!

TV Time

I ONCE CALCULATED that in his thirty years in Greenville, Drew had watched over ninety thousand hours of TV. For him or anyone watching that much TV, I'm sure that what he watched heavily influenced his view of the world and his social and political opinions. He had never left Mom's house so he had no other outside influences, such as friends or reading the newspaper. His daily routine of TV viewing consisted of the local news including sports and weather, CNN, HBO and Showtime. The only exception was watching Saturday Night Live on Saturday evenings. I came to learn that he liked SNL so much because the show always made fun of people. Drew's experience of being made fun of was soothed by watching other people being made fun of for a change.

Watching so much TV meant that Drew was always up on current events. He constantly surprised me with some of his comments. For example, like his mother, he was always informed about the upcoming weather. He'd say things like, "I heard it's going to rain later in the week." I never knew Drew to follow any sports but he was well aware of what was going on with the Broncos due to watching the sports report every evening. In Denver, the Broncos dominated the sports coverage. He knew whether the Broncos were home or away or if they won their game last Sunday. He was so much better informed than I was.

Drew's favorite channels were HBO and Showtime. He disliked commercials and he didn't know how to use the remote to fast-forward through them. He limited his use of the remote to turning the TV off and on and changing the channels. Once I came home from work and he told me that the TV was broken. I quickly figured out that the batteries were dead in the remote. He had no idea how to resolve a simple issue like dead batteries or resetting the cable box. His all-time favorite show on HBO was *The Sopranos*. Then again, who's favorite show wasn't *The Sopranos*? Drew enjoyed crime dramas, but I think the real reason he like that show so much was because of the girls from Bada Bing! But I also think he could relate to the show because it took place in New Jersey.

After living with Drew for a few months his political views became very evident. He definitely leaned to the left. He was prochoice and was very vocal about the potential legalization of marijuana. He was also vocal about any issue involving gay and lesbian rights. He struggled with the ideals of the religious right. It didn't take much for him to yell his political views at politicians on TV. He got extremely animated when he felt his freedoms around pot and sex were being restricted by the Republicans. He felt it no one had the right to tell him how to live his life when it came to sexual orientation.

It's a shame that with such strong opinions around politics, that Drew had never voted. We never had a discussion about it, nor did he ever express any interest in voting, but it seemed like it would be easy to fix. The only problem was that I was sure he'd have to get that elusive ID. I had started to keep a running list of things I'd like to see change in his life. It wasn't time yet to start tackling the list, but his six-month transition was coming to an end. My list was starting to get a little long, but getting an ID was still at the top of my list. I knew that if I could convince him to get his picture taken for that ID so many doors would open up for him. In those six months we had made some progress, but there was so much more to get done.

Healthy Habits

ONE OF MY BIGGEST CONCERNS about Drew continued to be his health. I had no idea what a physical would reveal. He might have had cancer for all I knew. High blood pressure runs in our family. I know Mom had taken meds to control her blood pressure as did Bobby and I. My specific concern was his weight. It made no sense to me that he could eat a huge bowl of food and almost an entire half-gallon of ice cream every evening and stay so thin. He only ate one meal a day but he also got zero exercise. I didn't know a lot about anorexia nervosa or bulimia but I did know he was binge eating and not gaining a pound. He was very thin and his pants hung loosely on him.

After a few months I noticed that after Drew ate his meal and ice cream, he'd spend a good amount of time in the bathroom. I could hear him run the water in the bathroom through my bedroom walls as I was trying to sleep. I felt that if he was eating his food and then throwing it up, I'd be able to hear him through my wall. The problem was that he didn't finish eating and head into the bathroom until around one in the morning. I considered putting a mini recorder in the bathroom in order to learn once and for all whether he was purging after he ate. I decided against it. It seemed too deceptive to me and knowing that Drew knew every inch of our apartment he probably would have discovered it. I took a more old-fashion approach. I set my alarm for twelve forty-five waited for him to go to the bathroom and listened through my bedroom wall. I did this for about a week and, even though the water was running, I never heard anything that sounded like someone vomiting. I was somewhat relieved, but I still couldn't understand his metabolism.

Doctor Visit

ONE SATURDAY MORNING after living in Boulder for six months, Drew told me that he needed to go to the doctor. Now he hadn't been to a doctor in over thirty years, so for him to tell me that he needed to see one was pretty remarkable. I asked him what was the matter and he told me that when he woke up half his face was swollen. I took a quick glance and could see the swelling. I told him to get dressed and we would find an emergency clinic that was open on a Saturday.

I said I'd wait in the car for him. Fifteen minutes later he climbed in the car. He was a sight to behold. He was dressed like he was out of an eighties men's magazine. I guess he thought a t-shirt and jeans were unacceptable to go see a doctor. He wore a wide-stripped button-down dress shirt, a pair of thin corduroy pants, and a suit coat. His pants stopped at his ankles because of the high heeled eighties dingo boots he was wearing. I felt bad, but all I could do was laugh as he got in the car. He asked me what was so funny. I couldn't tell the truth for fear that he'd run back into our apartment. I told him I'd been listening to a comedian on the radio.

I signed in at the front desk when we got to the clinic. Then I remembered one other minor detail. Drew had no health insurance. Mom had told me that she paid the full amount of the visit when he needed any medical or dental attention. I'd have to add this to my list. When they called Drew's name, I told him to wait in the waiting room so I could speak to the doctor first. I explained to the doctor that Drew was autistic and hadn't been to a doctor in thirty years. I also mentioned that our mom had recently passed away and I had only been his caregiver for a few months. I went back to the waiting room and got Drew. For someone who hadn't been to a doctor in ages, he seemed pretty calm.

The doctor was so good in handling him. She took his blood pressure and all of his vitals. While she was examining him, she commented on how much she liked his stylish boots. Drew smiled. After she finished examining him, she asked him to wait in the waiting room. The doctor told me that she believed that Drew needed to go to a dentist to resolve the reason for the swelling in his face. She said something was going on in his mouth. She also told me that for someone who had not been to a doctor in years he was in pretty decent shape. She mentioned that all his vitals were good but that his blood pressure was slightly elevated. She thought this might have been due to him being nervous. She also thought it might be good for him to get his blood checked out sometime in the near future.

Drew and I got back into the car and I explained to him that everything was cool with the doctor but that we needed to go find a dentist. He wasn't too happy about that news, but I could tell he was in pain and wanted to get the issue resolved. I got on my phone and was able to find a dentist who could take him in an hour. Amazing. As we were driving to the dentist, Drew told me he really liked that doctor. I think her comment about his boots won him over.

Time For The Dentist

AT THE DENTAL CLINIC, I took the same approach and had Drew sit in the waiting room while I went to speak to the dentist. This time I stayed in the waiting room while Drew was alone with the dentist and the hygienist. I was expecting the worst. I thought the dentist would come out and tell me that Drew needed to have a dozen cavities filled or numerous teeth pulled. After about thirty minutes, the dentist came out and told me that Drew had a blocked saliva gland in his mouth that was causing his face to swell. He said he'd prescribe an antibiotic, which would clear it up. The dentist also said that for someone who hadn't been to a dentist in years his mouth was in pretty decent shape. He said it would be beneficial to bring Drew back at a later date and have his teeth cleaned and x-rayed.

Well, that was an eventful Saturday. I thought I'd have to drug Drew to get him to a doctor or dentist. Who knew that a minor saliva gland would get him to the doctor and dentist, and on the same day? The good news was that the swelling would respond to antibiotics. I was also relieved that he was in, as they said, decent shape. I would have to work on him to get him scheduled to have blood work done and a teeth cleaning. Overall, it looked like nothing serious was going on. On the way home from the dentist, I spoke to Drew about going back and having the additional work done. He said, "Let me get my face back to normal first and then I'll think about it." I knew what that meant. It was Drew's way of saying, "Good luck with that ever happening."

OCD

I ALWAYS KNEW that Drew had social interaction and anxiety issues. Growing up in New Jersey for my first seventeen years with him I never noticed any OCD tendencies though. Somehow while living in Greenville, he developed many habits that, on deeper observation, you'd classify as someone with obsessive-compulsive disorder.

Every time I turned around we were in need of paper towels. We went through at least two extra-large rolls a week. When I say we, I really mean Drew. I probably used ten sheets a week while he used up the rest. I had noticed that Mom had always kept a twelve-pack of rolls in her pantry. I had never understood why two people needed so many rolls. Now I got it. Drew had a habit of always walking around with a folded paper towel in his hands. If he picked up an object there was always a paper towel between the object and the skin of his hand. He didn't want that object touching his hand.

The other items that we quickly ran out of included Ziploc bags, white tall kitchen bags, and large black trash bags. He wasn't putting food in the Ziploc bags or using the trash bags for trash. We stored all the plastic bags in the pantry but he used them in his bedroom. In the process of moving Drew from Greenville, I became aware that everything he owned was either inside of or wrapped in a Ziploc bag or a trash bag. I believe he was trying to keep germs from touching anything he owned. His system for rotating and changing out his bags explained why we went through so many plastic bags.

Our pantry also became the most interesting closet in our apartment. After shopping, I usually put the items away in our pantry. After I put the items on the shelves of the pantry Drew would anxiously stand in front of the pantry. At first, I didn't pay attention to what he was doing. After a few weeks, I noticed that after I finished putting items in the pantry, he came in behind me and organized and faced all the items' labels as if they were displayed on a grocery shelf in the store. Everything was in its place, at least in his head. After I discovered that he was reorganizing the pantry every time we returned from the grocery store, I smartened up and stopped putting the groceries away. I simply put the bagged groceries on the counter and told Drew to put them away. I wasn't going to waste my time when he had all the time in the world.

I didn't know a lot about OCD but was familiar with the depictions in movies of OCD characters obsessively scrubbing their hands. Another of Drew's habits began his daily routine. When he got up around six in the evening, he made his way into the kitchen where he stood in front of the kitchen sink and washed his hands for a good twenty minutes. Once the water was scalding hot, he soaped up and scrubbed his hands and under his nails better than any surgeon could. You'd think his hands would be horribly chapped in the dry Colorado air but they never were. That must have been the reason we were always buying moisturizing lotion. I thought all those moisturizers might be for something else.

Another strange habit of Drew's was around locks and doors. Again, I didn't notice it at first but after a couple of months, I noticed that occasionally he would stand in front of the front door for several minutes, opening and closing the door at least a hundred times. He'd wait until he heard the lock catch and click and then repeat it again, again, and again. He opened and closed the door slowly and then repeated it very fast. This was one behavior I had no explanation for but would have loved to speak with a psychologist about.

In the movie *Sleeping with the Enemy*, Julia Roberts' character fakes her death in order to flee her violent husband. She leaves Cape Cod and moves to a small town in Iowa. She adopts a new identity and starts dating a local teacher. When her husband discovers that she's alive, he tracks her to Iowa. In one scene, she steps out of the shower and reaches for a towel and notices that all the towels on the towel bar are perfectly lined up with each other. In a scene earlier in the movie her abusive husband chastised her for not having the bathroom towels perfectly aligned on the towel bar. The suspenseful music lets us know that she now realizes that her husband has been in her house and knows she is not dead.

I had a similar heart-jumping moment after living with Drew for six months. I was cooking in the kitchen and opened a drawer to grab a large spoon. We all have that kitchen drawer full of a variety of kitchen utensils and gadgets. If your drawer is like mine, it is totally unorganized. As I opened the drawer and started searching for the spoon, I saw something strange that I hadn't noticed in the six months prior. Remember, I've been told that I'm not the most focused and detailed person. It wasn't that the drawer was orderly and organized. It was that every item was in the exact same spot as the last time I opened that drawer. If that spoon was face up in the top left-hand corner, it was now in that exact same spot. Not one bit different from the last time. In that heart jumping moment, I knew that Drew painstakingly arranged that drawer every day. He needed to make sure everything was in its place.

Rather than confront him and cause him to be embarrassed or to deny it, I thought I'd try an experiment. I moved the spoon about two inches to the right of its current spot and waited to see what happened. The next morning after Drew had gone to bed, I open that kitchen drawer and, low and behold, the spoon had been moved back those two inches to its exact previous spot. All I could do was laugh and think, "This is absolutely nuts! I'm living in a crazy house." For the next week, every night before I went to bed, I moved one item in that drawer. In the morning, sure enough every item was always back in its original place. I don't think Drew could relax and go to bed until he was satisfied that everything was in its proper place.

Drew Knows

For someone who struggled in school, I discovered that Drew had an incredible memory. One day after we had been living together for only a short period of time, he asked me, "Isn't Steve Jr.'s birthday coming up this week?"

"Yes. How did you know?" Steve Jr.'s birthday was later in the week.

He answered, "I don't know. I just remember that it's around this time in September." Drew made sure that we got him a birthday card the next time we went to the grocery store. Back home, he asked me when it needed it be put it in the mail. He signed the card at the bottom in large letters: *Love Drew*. On the envelope he wrote Steve Jr.'s name in the proper place for addressing an envelope. He then added his name in the proper spot for the return address. Not knowing anyone's address, including his own, he left it to me to fill in the addresses and put a stamp on it and mail it. He probably thought the cost of a stamp was still thirteen cents, as it was in 1978.

I knew Drew didn't have a calendar but he remembered all of his siblings, their significant others, and my kid's birthdays and wedding anniversaries. He might not know the exact date but he was aware of the exact month and week. I don't how he remembered. He also had me put ten dollars in every card that he sent. Mind you, he never gave me the ten dollars to put in, he just expected me to make it happen.

While Drew never missed sending a birthday or anniversary card to Annie and Bobby and their spouses, I always felt sad for Drew on his birthday. Rarely did Annie or Bobby reciprocate by sending him a card. On his birthday, he would ask me if I had checked the mailbox to see if anyone had sent him a card. I usually had to tell him that I had checked and hadn't seen anything. It pissed me off. Drew, with all of his issues, could remember their and their spouse's birthdays and anniversaries but they couldn't drop a card in the mail to him. Honestly, there were a few times when he gave me their cards to mail that I wanted to throw them in the trash. Nevertheless, I took the high road and begrudgingly addressed them, enclosed ten dollars, added the stamps, and mailed them. I truly didn't care if they arrived on time.

Birthdays and Holidays

DREW'S BIRTHDAY WAS IN AUGUST. He was turning fifty-six years old. This was going to be his first birthday without Mom and living in Boulder. I had no idea what to expect but I wanted to remain sensitive to his emotions during this time. I was a little rusty on the rituals he and Mom had developed through the years for his birthday. The last birthday of his that I was present for was over thirty-three years ago.

About a month out I asked Drew what he wanted for his birthday. I should have expected the answer I received. He said he wanted a new marijuana pipe, fudge candy and, of course, porn. Drew made it easy to shop for him. I also asked him what he wanted for his birthday dinner. I did remember that for our birthdays, Mom cooked us whatever we wanted. He told me that Mom always made him chicken, stuffing, mashed potatoes, gravy, and corn. This was the first time I heard the "Mom always" phrase. It was a phrase I would hear many times in the following years.

I bought all of the gifts he had requested along with a few pairs of pants. I painstakingly wrapped his presents. I'm the world's worst when it comes to wrapping gifts—just ask my kids. I fixed all of the dinner items he wanted. I made the mistake of having everything ready by six that evening. While he appreciated my efforts, he said he'd wait and eat at his normal time around midnight. With some coaxing I did get him to open his gifts. He couldn't open his presents in silence. He needed noise in the background. I could tell he was uncomfortable being the center of attention, even though it was just the two of us. He asked me to watch the *Three Stooges* on TV, hoping that I would be distracted from observing him open his presents. He didn't like people, including me, staring at him. I got high marks because he loved all of his gifts.

As I expected, after he opened his presents, he asked me if Annie or Bobby had sent anything. I truthfully replied that they hadn't. I mentioned before how I'd forgotten to send Drew a birthday gift once and that Mom had called me to say how disappointed he was. This time I got to see up close what a disappointed Drew looked like. I wondered if Mom had ever called Annie and Bobby.

I never thought I'd ever say this in my lifetime but Christmas sucked, for so many reasons. The biggest reason was that in the first week in December Colleen and I decided to officially divorce. We gave it the six months we had committed to but our relationship just never got back on track. We had drifted so far apart that by the time we realized it, it was much too late. We had been married for twenty-six years and miserable for the last five of them. During the last six months, we met monthly to discuss where we were in our relationship and it was very apparent that our flame had burned out. There was no desire on the part of either of us to rekindle it. Neither of us would claim to be perfect in our relationship, but I'd always thought it would take some traumatic event to be the cause for our downfall such as an affair. In reality, it was a slow sad death by growing apart, which led to many personal differences. There were many small disagreements that became large arguments. We both agreed that it was best to wait until after the holidays to tell Steve Jr., Valerie, and Mark. I hadn't failed at much in my life before, but this was certainly going to go down as my greatest failure.

As Christmas approached, I needed to quickly get in the Christmas spirit in spite of our impending divorce. I was in a pretty shitty mood. Christmas had always been my favorite time of year but this year held so many unknowns. Colleen wanted the kids for Christmas Eve and Christmas Day so I took them the day after Christmas. This was also Drew's and my first Christmas without our mom. We had donated some of Mom's decorations to Goodwill back in Greenville but Drew had saved a few of the old family tree ornaments. I bought a small Christmas tree and put it in our family room. Drew was very happy to decorate it with his ornaments.

He wanted the same gifts for Christmas and the same Christmas meal that he had asked for on his birthday. I heard the "Mom always" phrase from him again.

My day consisted of watching my two favorite Christmas movies *A Christmas Carol* with Alastair Sims and *Home Alone* but I spent the majority of the day in my bed being weepy and feeling alone. I haven't experienced that kind of pain in a long time. Christmas had always been such fun. The kids came home every year and we just hung out together, enjoying great food, a few drinks, and a ton of laughs. We played pool. We went bowling. And sometimes we went skiing. This year was nothing like that and it was tremendously depressing. A friend of mine who had been divorced for a while, gave me some great advice before the holidays. He told me that when I didn't have the kids for the holidays I should travel. "Getting out of town is such a great distraction," he said. I should have taken his advice. I made a mental note for next year; I would not do this again. In the words of Clark Griswold, "We're gonna to press on, and we're gonna have the hap, hap, happiest Christmas since Bing Crosby tap-danced with Danny fucking Kay."

Every now and then one of my kids would come and visit me at the apartment in Boulder. Sometimes they would even spend a night or two. Since my separation from their mother, it was always pretty awkward when they visited. I loved my kids to death, but I felt like such a loser. I know it was equally, if not more, awkward for them. They had never seen me living in an apartment before, let alone living with my brother and not their mother.

I tried to make their visits as enjoyable as I could and show them around Boulder. Both Steve Jr. and Valerie had dogs and would bring them when they visited. Drew really took to both dogs. He loved making them run up and down the stairs. I'd often find the dogs sitting with him while he watched TV late at night. He swore that he wasn't giving them any treats, but I wasn't so sure. Valerie had a long talk with him about the dangers of giving dogs chocolate. We all knew how much Drew loved his chocolate. He promised her that he'd never give them any. I still wasn't convinced that he wasn't slipping them a little of his dinner every time they came to visit. Whether it was the food or not, he connected with those two dogs better than I ever did.

I always looked forward to the holidays, but this year they couldn't end fast enough. Like most people, I've always used the New Year and January as a time to refocus and develop a new set of goals. With a divorce and six months of living with Drew under my belt, I couldn't think of a year in my past where this would have been more important. Our lives were now entangled. Change for Drew was imminent.

Forward But Never Backward

IT COULD HAVE BEEN that I was having a really bad day. It might have been that I was going through a divorce. Maybe it was because my company had been sold and my new employer was starting to lay people off. Perhaps it was that I had been so busy for the last year that I never had the opportunity to properly grieve my mother's death. It could have been that I was pissed at Bobby and Annie for not offering some support in taking care of Drew. Whatever it was I was a time bomb waiting to go off.

And go off I did. Unfortunately, Drew caught the brunt of my anger and rage. One Sunday evening after living with him for over nine months, I returned from the grocery store and completely lost it. I had carried all the groceries up the three flights of stairs on a very hot day in Boulder and I was drenched in sweat. As I passed the second floor, there was Drew sitting on the couch, watching TV and laughing, obviously stoned. I put the groceries on the kitchen counter and started to put them away. Then it hit me. What is wrong with this picture? I'm busting my ass trying to make everything right to provide a safe environment for him and he's just sitting there stoned watching TV.

I had recently begun to feel like Drew was starting to slide backward into his old world in Greenville. I found it much easier and faster to do the grocery shopping by myself. He appeared to have no interest in going to Target or downtown to the record store anymore. He never asked to go anywhere. He was perfectly happy to just live within the four walls of that apartment and repeat his daily routine. He absolutely let me do everything for him just the way Mom had. He was taking no initiative. If I needed anything or help around the apartment, I had to ask him. If he needed something he'd just tell me. "I'll be needing pot soon."

I enabled him by making a point to go to the dispensary the next day. I felt like saying, "Fuck you. You go get it. You don't do shit around here." I knew all too well he had no way to make that happen. His life started to look like that drug commercial from the seventies that said, "A mind is a terrible thing to waste."

That particular day, I stopped putting the groceries away and ran downstairs. I was pissed! I shut off the TV, threw the remote up against the wall, and got in his face and yelled, "What is your problem? You're a total waste. All you do is eat, shit, sleep, and get high. What kind of life is that? You contribute nothing! You add no value! All you do is sit around and watch the fucking TV all night. You don't work. You can barely take care of yourself. If you died tomorrow, no one would give a shit about you! Is this really what makes you happy? Are you really happy, Drew? Please tell me, because I'm dying to know. Is this all there is for you? Goddammit, you're a total waste of a human being."

I was so angry with him that I couldn't talk anymore. I just stood there shaking. I didn't even know if I was finished saying everything I wanted to say. I took a second to catch my breath and waited for some kind of response from him. He just stared out the window and said nothing. "You got anything to say?" I asked.

He responded with one word. "What?"

I said, "I'm not done with you. What I do know is that I'm not going to put up with this shit anymore. We're going to be making some changes. Big changes! Your life is going to be changing big time and you don't even know it. Just wait." I stared back at him and this time he barely made eye contact with me.

Again, he responded, "What?"

I stormed upstairs and finished putting away our groceries. Then I quickly started feeling like shit. My Catholic guilt was starting to set in. I had just sounded like our Dad yelling at him back in New Jersey. I started to rationalize our conversation to myself. I had finally released some of my pent-up anger but probably should have handled it better. I knew that with Drew having such low self-esteem, he didn't take negative feedback very well. He was never going to accept it, let alone truly hear what I had said.

I went back downstairs and apologized to him. I told him that I had just had a really bad day and was sorry I had taken it out on him. Before I left his room, I did say to him, "I'm not sorry for what I said, but for how I said it. But we are going to be making some changes." He just stared out the window and said nothing.

Drew and I were at a fork in the road. I could let him slide back and be very comfortable as he was in Greenville or I could push him out of his comfort zone and see if he was capable of contributing something to the world. He hadn't been pushed to accomplish anything in many years, but I could not, as Mom would say, "Let sleeping dogs lie." I could not just sit there and watch him slowly waste away. It was time to make some changes. I would find Drew a psychologist tomorrow.

A Needle In The Haystack

I THOUGHT FINDING A PSYCHOLOGIST who worked with autistic patients would be easy. One out of fifty-nine children in the United States are on the autism spectrum. I found a few potential psychologists in Boulder, but a whole lot more in Denver. I really wanted to find someone close so that eventually Drew could find his own transportation. I made a list of all the Boulder psychologists who listed autism as one of their areas of specialty. I started calling them one by one, but kept running into the same problem. No one wanted to work with a fifty-seven-year-old patient with autism. Most said that they would only take on a patient under twenty-five years of age. It became evident that if you're autistic and over twenty-five, the psychiatric world isn't interested in helping you.

I wasn't going to give Drew a choice about seeing to see a psychologist. I was through allowing him to back down and give me multiple excuses for why he wouldn't go. I explained that it would be good to talk with someone about Mom dying and his move to Boulder. I also told him that I was meeting with a psychologist weekly and that it was really helping me. That was a lie, of course, but I was in the "take no prisoners" frame of mind. Drew had only one request. He said he would go, but it would have to be with a woman. I was happy to try to meet his request. I remembered those days back in our neighborhood in New Providence. He always connected with females better than he did with males. Males bullied him and those fears obviously ran deep.

My search was narrowing now. I needed to find a female psychologist based in Boulder who specialized in autism, who would take a fifty-seven-year-old patient, and who would let me pay in cash because Drew had no insurance. Over a three-day span I called over twenty offices, all to be rejected because of Drew's age. I even started asking if they could recommend someone, only to be told they didn't know anyone who would work with someone of that age. It would have been easier to just throw in the towel and let him slid backwards. With no other names on my Boulder list and starting to get desperate, I had an idea.

The University of Colorado is in Boulder. I was sure they had a great Psychology Department and would know someone who could help Drew. They may even have a graduate student who would take him on. I thought I might have better luck if I went there in person and that it would be much harder to tell me "no" to my face than over the phone. I was desperate. It was already late Friday, so I decided I would take the weekend and develop a "can't lose—can't tell me no" strategy for my visit to the CU campus on Monday.

I took Monday off so that I could to be as focused as possible with no distractions. I didn't want to be stressed about time and having to get back to work. I would take the entire day if that's what it took to get this nailed down. I knew I lived in casual Boulder where no one gets dressed up, but I put on my best suit and tie. I was going to make this as hard as possible for them to say they couldn't help me. At nine o'clock, I made my way onto campus. The University of Colorado is considered one of the most beautiful campuses in the country. It is set at the base of the foothills and its sandstone buildings were designed to blend in with the mountains. I parked my car and walked into the

Muenzinger Psychology building. A receptionist who looked like she was a current student, met me. She asked me who I there to see. That was a very good question, because I had no idea.

"Is there someone I can talk with who teaches classes on the subject of autism?" I asked.

She replied, "I'm currently majoring in adolescent psychology. I've had a few classes that focused on autism. Let me think about which professor might be able to could help you. Dr. Alexander was very good when I took her class. She might be someone. She's the only one I can think of right now. I don't know if she has office hours today, but I know her office is on the second floor." I asked the receptionist if I could check to see if she was in and she said, "No worries."

I took the elevator to the second floor and quickly found Dr. Alexander's office. I knocked a few times but got no response. Then I noticed a sign on her door that said her office hours were on Tuesdays and Thursdays. As I headed back to the elevator, I heard a faint voice ask, "Can I help you?" It came from an open office near the elevator.

I slowly stuck my head in the office and said, "Hello." I could see that the office was stacked with moving boxes from the floor to the ceiling. Out from behind the boxes came an elderly woman dressed like she had just left Woodstock on the third day in jeans with patches, a tie-dyed t-shirt, a headband made of beads, and Birkenstocks. I didn't know if she was with a moving company, or was a janitor, or just lost. She introduced herself to me as Dr. Cohen.

I asked her if she was moving out. She said that after thirty years of teaching at the University she was retiring. I asked her what she taught and she answered, "Applied Behavior Analysis and Autism studies." She then said to me, "You're a little older than our regular students. I heard you knocking at Dr. Alexander's office. Is there something I can help you with?"

I said, "I don't know, but if you can spare five minutes, I promise I won't take any more of your time." I gave her my best one-minute elevator pitch. I told her about growing up with Drew, his relationship with our Dad, moving and living in Greenville, my visit with Dr. Brooks, our Mom passing away, my moving in with Drew, and some of the behaviors I had observed. I then told her I was looking for a female psychologist in Boulder who might be able to help. I spoke as fast as I could, New Jersey style, to get it all out in the five minutes she had granted me.

"When you say 'help,' what do you mean?" she asked.

I wasn't prepared to answer that question, but I tried my best. "You know, help… I guess I want Drew to be more independent. I want him to be able to take care of himself. I came up here today to see if anyone would know someone who could help. I have not had any luck finding someone who will work with a fifty-seven-year-old."

"Interesting," she said.

I then realized I had never introduced myself. "By the way, my name is Steve. Steve Wilson.

She smiled and said, "Well, Steve, as you can see, I am in the process of moving out today. If you can help bring a box down to my car, I'll get your phone number and email. Give me a day or two and I'll think about what you said and see who I might be able to recommend."

I grabbed the largest box I could find and walked with her down to her car. I gave Dr. Cohen my cell number and email address and thanked her for listening.

"No worries. I'll be in touch soon," Dr. Cohen said as she sped off in her yellow VW bug.

The Waiting (Is The Hardest Part)

I WAS FEELING PRETTY GOOD as I headed back to my apartment. I hadn't nailed down a psychologist yet, but I felt like I was on the right path. As soon as I had a chance, I jumped on my computer and started looking for everything I could find on Dr. Alexander and Dr. Cohen. While Dr. Alexander's background was quite impressive, she was very young. She had only been out of graduate school for five years. I was blown away by Dr. Angie Cohen's background. I had been speaking to royalty within the psychology community today and I hadn't known it. I thought I was talking to a Boulder hippie at first. Dr. Cohen not only had taught at CU for over thirty years, but also had been awarded the Grawemeyer Award in Psychology for her research and impact in

Autistic disorders. She was a superstar in her field. I felt even better now because she was so well connected and believed she would be able to recommend someone who could help Drew.

I had no other options for Drew in Boulder, so I spent the following days looking for someone in Denver. I was not looking forward to making the forty-five-minute drive each way every week, but if that's what it took so be it. I was in the middle of a call with an office in Denver when Dr. Cohen called.

She did the majority of the talking and I just listened. "Steve, I wanted to get back with you regarding our conversation the other day. If you can spare five minutes, I promise I won't take up anymore of your time. I think that's how you like to work. Right? You caught me on Monday on my last day at CU. My head was in another place that day, to be honest. I've given some thought about your situation with your brother. My current situation is, I'm seventy years old and, as of last Friday, officially retired after thirty years of teaching. I'm a widow. My husband passed away three years ago and now it's just me and my Australian Shepherd, Margot. We love Boulder and plan on being here forever. My husband and I never had any children because I was married to my work and research. My husband Bob was also a professor at the University and with our busy schedules we just didn't think it would be right to bring children into this world. I feel your pain about your brother. You might have better luck trying to win the lottery than finding a psychologist who will take on a new fifty-seven-year-old patient with autism. Steve, do you believe in divine intervention?"

I answered, "Having lived sixteen years of Catholic education, yes."

"Good," she said. "When you stuck your head in my office on Monday, you caught me in the middle of my mid-life crisis. I had been so busy tying up loose ends with the university the last few months and preparing to retire, I hadn't given any thought to what I was going to do next with my life. While I was packing up my office, I was having a major anxiety attack. It was the first time that I didn't know what I was going to do the next day. I'm not one to sit around and do nothing. My brain won't allow it. On Tuesday, I started thinking about our conversation. I don't want to work full time. I've been there and done that, but I could use a part-time side project to keep my mind fresh and active. I'm not ready to be farmed out to the old folks' home and play cards all day with the ladies. I believe life always opens up new doors for you if you allow it. I don't know if you'll have me but if you're game, I'd like to spend some time with you and your brother. I have no idea where this will lead, but most of my life I've taken chances. If you look at my background, you'll see that has served me well. Okay, that's my five minutes. Any thoughts?"

I wanted to jump through the phone and kiss her! I never thought that she'd have any interest in our situation. I was just looking for a recommendation. I said, "Dr. Cohen, yes, yes, yes!"

She laughed and said, "Steve, please call me Angie."

Making Things Happen!

GROWING UP, I was ever the eternal optimist. When I got a little too far out there, Mom was always there to ground me with comments like, "Don't count your chickens until they're hatched." I was incredibly pumped after my conversation with Angie and my mother was not around to bring me down to earth, which was fine with me. Not that I had ever asked for it before, but I was finally going to get some help for Drew. I still had a lot of work to do to pull this all off.

Dr. Cohen and I agreed that, initially, I would meet with her first for two sessions to discuss everything I knew about Drew. He would then meet with her weekly for one month. After our sessions, she would then reconnect with me and discuss the potential next steps and strategy.

I didn't tell Drew about any of this until he was a few days out from meeting Angie for the first time. I knew if I gave him more time to think and fret about it, he'd have more time to come up with excuses for not going. I've never had to drag him anywhere physically before, but there was always a first time.

I met Angie for my first session at a park in Boulder. We sat on a park bench on a beautiful sunny spring Colorado day. There was still plenty of snow on the mountain peaks, which was the perfect backdrop for me to open up about Drew's history. We decided that in my first session, I would give her a data dump on everything I knew about him.

On our second session, she would ask me questions to clarify what I had told her in our first session. She wouldn't share with me any of her thoughts and opinions until we met after her four sessions with Drew. Speaking with Angie in a park setting put me at ease and was so much more relaxing than meeting in an office. It felt like having a conversation with a good friend.

On the day Drew was to meet with Angie for the first time, he wore the same outfit he'd worn to the doctor's office, dingo boots and all. Dr. Cohen wanted to meet him in the park as she and I had. I introduced Drew to Dr. Cohen and hung around for a bit small talk before I left to take a long walk. After forty-five minutes I headed back to the park bench where I had left the two of them. I was keeping my fingers crossed as I approached, hoping the two of them were hitting it off. As I got closer, I could see the two of them laughing. This had to be a good sign. Drew didn't seem like he was ready to leave the conversation yet but I wanted to be respectful of Angie's time. Angie stood up and shook his hand as we were leaving. I thanked Angie for her time and headed to the car with Drew.

The normal me would have been asking him hundreds of questions on the way home, but I wanted to take a different approach this time. I wanted to down play the entire situation and not pry too much. I only asked him one question. "How'd it go with Angie?"

His simple reply was, "She's cool. She even likes KISS." I left it at that. I hoped we would get into a little more detail in the future because two hundred fifty dollars an hour was not cheap.

Drew and I followed the same routine for the next three weeks. I dropped him off in the park with Angie, went for a walk, and returned to pick him up. On the way back to our apartment I asked him my one question, usually generating a similar response. As he opened up more about his time with Angie, I learned that she also liked Led Zeppelin but that she was more of a Deadhead. She was for the legalization of marijuana and was also a fan of *The Sopranos*. I couldn't wait to see what my next session would bring. I knew Dr. Cohan was more than qualified, but I wasn't looking for someone to take him to a concert at Red Rocks. I couldn't wait for my next session to get her opinion about Drew.

The next Sunday, I decided to do something that I hadn't done in a few years. I went to Mass. If there was one thing Dad drilled into my head it was the power of prayer. He was all about praying. If I was mad at someone who had done me wrong, he would say, "You should pray for him." I remember one of my baseball games that he attended when I was in the eighth grade. I can count on one hand the number of times he came to one of my games.

I was playing shortstop and fielded a grounder. It was a force-out if I could run to third and step on the base before the runner got there. Just as I went to step on the base the runner spiked me in the back of my heel. After I stepped on third base, I looked at the back of my foot. I was missing a large chunk of skin from my heel and it was bleeding profusely. I had to leave the game early and Dad drove me home. On the way home I was very pissed at the kid who spiked me. Dad said, "You should pray for him." That was the last thing I wanted to do. I would have loved to punch that kid in the face.

So, I went to church that Sunday and prayed that Dr. Cohen could ease some of my pain and, more importantly, help Drew. I thanked God for bringing her into our lives. I prayed even harder that God would grant him mental health and provide for him in the future. I turned over every stone I could to help Drew find success in his journey.

Day of Reckoning

I HAD BEEN WAITING for this day for a long, long time. Finally, I was going to get a full diagnosis on the extent of Drew's autism. I decided to meet Dr. Cohen at her office this time. Even though Angie taught at CU for thirty years, she had maintained a private practice and had an office for her patients in Boulder. In the last year she had farmed out her patients to other psychologists in Boulder so she could retire. She told me that she also used her office to conduct her research. I think Drew might have been the only patient that she was seeing at the time.

Dr. Cohen's office was decorated in a Moroccan and African motif. She had quite a collection of African facemasks on her walls. There were pillows in circles on the floor and a lot of beads hanging on the walls. It reminded me of a Moroccan restaurant in Boulder called the Mataam Fez. When I entered her office, I asked when the belly dancers were going to show up. She laughed, which highlighted the difference between her and Dr. Brooks. Angie asked me to remove my shoes and take a seat on one of the pillows on the floor. The strong smell of incense filled her office. We exchanged the normal pleasantries but I was fairly quiet, wanting to get into the reason we were meeting today.

Angie started. "Steve, first I want to say how much I've enjoyed my time with you and Drew. He's quite a fascinating individual. You should be very proud of where he is in his journey. I want to talk about three things today. First, I want to talk about expectations. Second, I'll share with you my observations and analysis. And last, let's talk about a potential plan of action and potential next steps for Drew.

Anxiously awaiting her analysis, I just nodded and said, "Okay."

She continued, "Let me start with expectations. Let's remember that Drew is fifty-seven years old. The behaviors he currently exhibits are from over fifty-seven years of learned behaviors and experiences. Not to be disrespectful, but I'm sure you've heard the phrase about teaching an "old dog new tricks." No amount of behavioral training or medication is going to instantly convert Drew into what we would call a normal human being. If our goal is to help him to become an independently functioning member of society, then there is hope. Let's keep in mind, though, that in order to make progress in this area, it's going to take years. It will take years of focus, reinforcement of desired behaviors, and positive role modeling. Rome wasn't built in a day, and neither will Drew's independence. I believe Drew is a beautiful human being with a brother who obviously loves him. He has the potential and, with help, he can improve his quality of life. Any questions before I get into my observations and analysis?"

Again, wanting to get to the meat of the conversation I answered, "No, not now."

Angie said, "Steve, you seem like a bottom-line kind of guy, so I'm not going to beat around the bush. Let's hit this head on. Drew has got quite a bit going on. Clinically, I would diagnose him with the following: he is absolutely on the autistic disorder spectrum, suffers from social anxiety disorder, has acute Obsessive Compulsive Disorder issues, and mild depression. I know that's a lot to take in all at once. What are your thoughts about what I just said?"

"Angie, give me a second to try and collect my thoughts before I answer that. I'm feeling a little confused at the moment." I had so many thoughts running through my head. Angie walked over to the fridge and grabbed two bottles of water. I continued sitting there in silence not really sure what to say next. I finally spoke up. "I have such mixed emotions, Angie. On one hand, I'm not surprised by what you just said. I've lived with Drew now for a year and have seen these things first hand. I'm a little surprised about the mild depression comment though. I'm happy that I finally have a professional opinion. It confirms many of my suspicions. On the other hand, I feel like a parent who just found out his child has an incurable illness. I feel a little angry at the moment but I don't understand why. Why is it Drew who has to deal with all of this?"

Angie responded, "Understandable, Steve. Why? That's such a great question. That's the reason people like me have dedicated our lives to conducting research to answer that question. While a great deal of progress has been made in the last thirty years, there is still so much work to do in this area. In Drew's case, he was most likely born with these tendencies. But he also could have been exposed to some traumatic event. His tendencies have been reinforced for the last fifty-seven years of his life. What currently makes Drew feel most safe and comfortable is to be in his own space, which in his world are the four walls of your apartment. While we can't always answer why, psychologists like me can help through applied behavior analysis, developing behavioral-based training treatments and, in some cases, medication. Steve, are you comfortable with me moving on to a possible plan?"

Feeling a bit numb at the moment, I said, "Sure, let's do it."

Dr. Cohen continued, "As I mentioned earlier, this is going to be a journey and not a destination. It will constantly be a work in progress. It's going to take extreme focus and lot of positive reinforcement. You currently living with Drew and serving as a role model for him will surely be a huge benefit. After giving this considerable thought, and if our goal is independence and an improved quality of life for Drew, here are my thoughts." Angie took out a sheet of paper from a folder on her desk and handed it to me. It was entitled *John Andrew Wilson's Ten-*

Point Independence Plan. Angie said, "Think of this as a combination of Maslow's hierarchy of needs and a plan for independence." Next, she reviewed, at a high level, Drew's ten-point plan:

1. *Goal Setting – Establish tangible goals for each of the ten points of the plan.*
2. *Emergencies – Teach Drew how to handle and function in an emergency setting.*
3. *Household Management – Help Drew to learn proper eating, cleaning, and laundry habits.*
4. *Personal Care – Teach Drew proper hygiene including hair and clothes.*
5. *Transportation – Teach Drew the life skills needed to get from point A to B.*
6. *Communication – Provide Drew with a cell phone and teach him its functionality.*
7. *Living on his own – Move Drew into his own apartment.*
8. *Employment – Secure employment for Drew.*
9. *Financial Skills – Open a bank account for Drew to manage. Teach Drew how to pay his own bills.*
10. *Companionship – Let's discuss this one at a later date.*

"I also want to discuss with you the idea of putting Drew on a couple of prescriptions. I think prescribing a mild antidepressant along with something to help him with his anxiety would really help him. I know this is a ton of information, Steve. If you're truly serious about improving Drew's quality of life, I'd be willing to work with you under one condition, well really two conditions. First, this has to be a team commitment. We each have a role, you, Drew, and I. You won't see much change if I'm in this by myself. Second, I will do this pro bono. I don't need the money and I don't want a penny of yours. I was planning on retiring anyway and had already developed a plan to handle all my finances. Taking in any more money at this time would just screw things up. And you even showed up to campus wearing a suit. That was so cute." She smiled. "I can see that your eyes are glazing over and I've done all the talking today so what do you think?"

"Angie, when you first said you would work with us, I just wanted to kiss you right through the phone. Now that we're here in person, can I just hug you?" She smiled and stood up. I gave her a huge hug. Then, I started to cry uncontrollably. I couldn't stop. I hadn't cried that hard since the call from Mom telling me that Dad had died. She walked over to desk and grabbed a box of Kleenex for me. I was so embarrassed. I didn't know what to say. "Dr. Cohen, thank you, thank you! I can't thank you enough."

"Well, does that mean you're in? That you're a member of Team Drew?"

"Absolutely" I said. "I'm pretty emotional right now and not thinking very straight. Let's do this. You've covered so much information today that I'd like to take a few days to digest it and maybe talk more specifics next week. You've been such a big help and I can't thank you enough. This truly is divine intervention."

When I got to my car, I was a complete wreck. My eyes were red and swollen. On Sunday, I'd been motivated to go to church. Right now, I was motivated to go have a drink. I adjusted my rearview mirror, put the car in drive and headed to the closest bar I could find.

Team Drew

FOR THE ENTIRE WEEKEND all I could focus on was that fork in the road. I truly felt that Drew was in a much better place than he had been in Greenville. He was getting outside of his four walls and going shopping with me. He was taking responsibility for cleaning his living area in our apartment. The easy road would be just to let him settle in and maintain his old Greenville schedule. He wouldn't really have to interact with anyone and he could sit back, get high, and watch his ten hours of TV all night. The harder road would be to develop strategies and tactics and put in the time and hard work to help him move from being dependent to interdependent and then to independent. I felt like I owed it to him to help him try to discover independence.

Dad instilled in us that if you work hard at something, good things will follow. I knew Dad had struggled with what to do about Drew. I felt Drew's situation must have been heartbreaking for Mom and that she had valid reasons to just let him be and not push him. He was fifty-seven and the world had changed. Much more is known today about how a person can function with autism and fifty-seven is not that old anymore. At the end of the day, I had to go with my gut. I was willing to put in the hard work and at the very least try to improve his quality of life. Team Drew was going to move forward. I realized it was not what my mother would have done, but I knew it was the right thing to do.

Getting aligned with Dr. Cohen meant a commitment. She told me that this was going to take a team and that Drew and I needed to commit to being on time and not missing any appointments. She established that both Drew and I would meet with her individually for one hour a week for at least the first six months and then we could move to every other week. She prescribed two medications for Drew. One to deal with his acute anxiety and another to help with his mild depression. She said it was imperative for Drew to take his meds as prescribed and not to miss one dose. She would help monitor his progress under his meds and make adjustments, if necessary, down the road.

During the next three months Angie and I developed specific goals and objectives around all ten points of Drew's Independence Plan. We dedicated the majority of our weekly time together discussing specific behaviors that Drew should demonstrate during the week. She also gave me numerous tips on how to role model those desired behaviors. She was developing into more of a personal coach for me than a psychologist.

In the beginning, I feared Drew would strongly resist meeting weekly with Angie. Dr. Cohen was a great help in this area. The three of us met one Saturday morning and we spoke to Drew about the longer-term benefits of building a strong relationship. We also described some of the cooler things that we could work toward. He seemed enthusiastic about the prospect of getting his own smart phone and eventually his own apartment. Drew reminded me that when he was working in New Jersey after graduating high school, our parents' plan was always to get him into his own apartment. I wondered why that never had materialized.

Drew has always been all about habits and routine. Having a solid routine kept his anxiety levels down to a minimum. Adding a weekly meeting with Dr. Cohen each week was not going to be easy for him. In the beginning I had to remind him that we were going to live up to the commitment we made with Angie. I'm sure he got tired of the word commitment. He was the master of making excuses. A few things helped him to get over the hump. I thought if I could get him to go for a solid two months, he'd develop the habit we needed. It certainly helped that I was going to meeting with Angie weekly. For the first couple of weeks, I had to reinforce his willingness to go with some enticements. It would have been easy to do that with porn by dangling a visit to an adult store after the appointment. I just couldn't bring myself to use porn as a form of reward so for those first two months I used pot, marijuana paraphernalia, and food as a motivator. All of those worked well and he never missed an appointment.

Weaning Drew

WHEN DREW AND I were in our first couple of months of appointments with Dr. Cohen, I picked up additional responsibility at my current job. The additional responsibility required me to be out of town every other weekend for trainings. I would have to leave on Friday morning and return Sunday evening, two nights away from Boulder. Angie thought that these weekends away would be a great test for Drew. I wasn't too concerned because twice a year Mom went away for an entire week to the beach. She prepared enough food to get Drew through that week and left her phone number in case he needed to reach her.

By now, Drew was more than capable of feeding himself. He had plenty of microwavable food and there were always leftovers from the meals I had made for myself. He was never going to go hungry. When I signed him up for cable service, I included a landline in our package. I had to teach and practice with Drew about how to get a dial tone and how to dial my cell number. He got pretty frustrated in the beginning but after practicing dialing my number over and over, he finally got it.

Being gone for those two nights every other weekend taught me a few things about Drew. I came home one Sunday evening and the apartment was blazing hot. It was May and the daytime temperature went from forth-five degrees in the morning to ninety-two degrees by afternoon. I hadn't moved the thermostat setting to cool yet so it was still on the heat setting. Drew didn't know how to adjust the thermostat so he just baked in the apartment all day until I got home. Another time, I came home to find the sink full of dirty dishes. When I left on Friday, the dishwasher was full and I had forgotten to turn it on. He didn't know how to turn it on, so he just loaded up the dishes in the sink.

I arrived home one Sunday to hear the fire alarm chirping. I asked Drew how long the chirping had been going on and he said it had started Friday afternoon. He didn't know to replace the battery. I don't know about you, but I find that chirping to be the most annoying noise. I can't take it for more than a few minutes. How he lasted for two and a half days with that chirping is beyond me. I also didn't understand why he just didn't just call me to ask how to fix it. I would have taken a baseball bat and smashed it if I'd been him.

It puzzled me that Drew could remember birthdays and anniversaries but he didn't know how to turn on a dishwasher. So many little things that you and I take for granted he just didn't understand. Not wanting to blame or yell at Drew, I just kept a running list of all those little tasks to work with him on. Sooner or later, he was going to catch up and become more independent.

During those weekends away I only received a call from Drew once. Well, it wasn't a call from Drew but from our neighbor. One Saturday night when I was in my hotel room prepping for my meeting the next day, my cell phone rang. The gentleman on the other end introduced himself as my neighbor. Drew and I had never met him. That night, Drew had come over to his apartment and was worried about some water in our apartment. My neighbor went into our place and found water dripping down the walls in Drew's area of the apartment. I asked him to put Drew on the phone. Drew said the amount of water had slowed down and he thought he'd be okay. I told him that he had done the right thing by calling me.

When I got back into town, I made a beeline to our apartment to check on things. We had an ice storm the day I left and the ice collected on the roof of our apartment. When the ice began to melt the water had seeped through a crack in the roof and down our inside walls. For Drew to leave our apartment and go next door to our neighbors was a huge step for him. He would never have been able to do that in the past. He would have been petrified to go speak with someone he didn't know. I told him again how proud I was of him for taking the right steps, the same steps I would have taken. I could feel that progress was being made. It had to be a combination of his meds and our work with Dr. Cohen. I couldn't wait to tell her. I also couldn't wait to tell her that Drew wanted a cat.

911

OUR FIRST ORDER OF BUSINESS was to get Drew an ID. No one in our family could ever get this accomplished before. He had used every excuse he could ever think of to avoid it. His refusal to go in the past centered around one thing: he hated having his picture taken. Mom had tried. Bobby had tried. I had tried and we all had failed. We would not get very far with our plan for Drew's independence if he didn't have an ID. Without it, there would be no bank account or phone and an apartment would have been out of the question. I worried about returning from a business trip to an empty apartment and find him missing. He might go out for a walk and somehow get arrested or worse, injured. He could either be in jail or in a hospital documented as John Doe. The only form of identification he possessed was a birth certificate and a social security card and he didn't carry those around with him. This time none of his excuses were going to work. I had a plan.

Usually, when I picked Drew up from his weekly meeting with Dr. Cohen, we went back to the apartment. This day, I told him I needed to run a few errands. I pulled into the Boulder DMV parking lot. I turned the engine off and just sat there. He asked, "What do you need to do?"

I answered, "We need to get your ID." When he said he wasn't going in, I gave my best impassioned speech. "Drew, here's the deal. You know all those things Dr. Cohen talked about, the phone, your own apartment? Well, if you don't get an ID none of that will happen. It will take five minutes. They even don't want you to smile when your picture is taken anymore. It will be so quick, I promise." Little did he know I had already made an appointment so we didn't need to wait in line. I then hit him where I knew it would hurt. "I really can't be the one anymore to go and buy your pot. I'm so busy with work and the divorce that I just don't have the time anymore. If I can't buy it for you anymore, you'll just have to go without."

I could tell that my last point got him thinking. He said, "Okay, I'll go in but if I'm not comfortable, I'm leaving."

"That's fair. Let's do it."

Drew said he needed a minute to get ready. He didn't have his bathroom to hide in so I waited outside the car while he played with his hair in the rearview mirror. A few minutes later, he got out of the car and whipped his hair around saying, "Let's go." As we entered the DMV, I could tell how much he hated this but we just kept moving. I signed in and we took our chairs. He had never been to a DMV before. He took a look around and figured out quickly that he didn't stand out at all among the slice of Boulder's finer citizens.

When I called to set up our appointment, I explained Drew's situation and that it would best if we could meet with an elderly "mom-like" employee who could coddle him and not intimidate him. They delivered exactly what he needed. He was certainly awkward getting his picture taken and was adamant about approving of his picture before it was laminated on his ID. We were in and out of the DMV in ten minutes. Mission accomplished!

In the months that followed, once a week I worked with Drew on some form of how to handle an emergency. It was critical that he learn how to be safe. I was certain that he had been taught all of these things in school, but he graduated high school forty years ago. There had always been someone around him to ensure his safety and I believed he'd forgotten most of what he had learned in school. Or had he? Thank God for the Internet because I found all kinds of materials with pictures to use when I was explaining things to him. We went over what to do in case of a fire, how to use a fire extinguisher, when and how to call 911, how to call me, what to do when a smoke alarm goes off, how to properly use the microwave and dishwasher, and when and how to use the first aid kit, to just name a few.

As I was reviewing these items with him, he constantly acted like a defensive kid and said, "I know that already." For all I knew, maybe he did know. Maybe he knew a lot more than he let on but preferred to let everyone else do all the work for him. I just pressed on because I had to validate that he was truly capable of handling himself in an emergency. I needed to be convinced that he was safe before we could move onto our next goal.

Household Management

Team Drew had now been up and functioning for a year. Drew had certainly made progress but, honestly, I wished things could move a little faster. Dr. Cohen had to keep reminding me that we were changing behaviors that he had developed now for over fifty-eight years. I felt great that he had obtained his ID and that he was educated on being safe. Going out of town every other weekend gave me hope that he would eventually be able to live on his own.

I noticed slight changes in Drew's level of anxiety. He didn't seem to get as nervous and worked up when we went out in public. Little by little, some of his OCD tendencies started to subside. The pantry wasn't as organized as it once was and neither were the kitchen drawers. He appeared to lose his obsession with the locks on the doors. Dr. Cohen and I both believed that the anti-anxiety medicine was working but I still wasn't so sure about the anti-depressant. I never thought that Drew had been depressed in the past, but I left that decision up to Angie. Maybe the combination of the two was the trick.

The next set of goals were going to take a lot of work and positive reinforcement. I wasn't too concerned about teaching Drew to do laundry and clean the apartment. He was already doing his laundry and cleaning his share of the apartment. What concerned me was changing his routine to being awake during the day and changing his eating habits from having one huge meal to having three meals a day. He hadn't lived on schedule like that since leaving New Jersey thirty-two years ago. He lived the hours of a vampire but for him to eventually get a job he was going to have to move from the night shift to the day shift. I spent some time with Dr. Cohen strategizing the best methods to make these changes. We both came up with the same solution.

For the past year, Drew had bugged me about getting a cat. I had mixed emotions because he struggled taking care of himself. Mom had had a cat when they lived in Greenville. I don't think he ever feed the cat or changed its litter box but had certainly seen Mom do it numerous times. During my visits to Greenville, I observed Drew spending a lot of time playing, and many times taunting, Mom's cat. Valerie had a friend in town who was moving overseas and needed to find a home for her cat. Pickles, was a four-year-old male tabby that was very low maintenance and litter box trained. Perfect!

I told Drew that I would be willing to bring the cat into the apartment under two conditions. First, he would be responsible for feeding him and changing out his litter box. Second, he'd have to change his schedule to day hours just like he'd had in New Jersey. I told him that he wouldn't be able to manage a cat when he kept the current hours that he did. It was a little bit of a fib but I needed him to take this big step. As he thought about it, I added, "Let's do it for Pickles."

Drew said, "Okay. I really want that cat." Pickles became the third member of our household.

I worked with him on the proper way to do his laundry. He was currently washing his clothes but I'd never checked on how he was doing it. I assumed since he ran the washer and dryer, he knew what he was doing. One should never assume with Drew. I discovered he was washing his clothes all right, except he wasn't using any detergent and only putting his clothes on the rinse cycle. No wonder doing laundry only took him ten minutes. This was an easy fix.

Drew and I had been cleaning our apartment together for over a year now so we were in pretty good shape there, except in a few areas. Again, I hadn't paid much attention to how he cleaned his bathroom or his bedroom. Like with most everything else, there were some opportunities for improvement. When we moved in, I bought him his own vacuum to use for his bedroom. Well, he'd never emptied the bag so it was completely clogged and just moving the same dirt around.

I had also purchased a toilet bowl brush for him. As he was showing me how he cleaned his toilet he pulled out the toilet brush. All I could do was shake my head and laugh hysterically. I'm not sure whether I was laughing was because what I saw was so funny or because I realized how much farther we had to go with him. I don't know what the hell happened to the brush, but it looked like someone had burned off all the bristles and melted it. Eighty percent of the brush was gone and all that remained was a thin plastic stick. I picked up the plastic stick and asked him what had happened to it. Like a guilty little kid, he mumbled that he didn't know. Honestly, I really didn't want to know. We still had a way to go for him to gain his independence.

It took me a good six months of work and reinforcement to get Drew on a daytime schedule. I think he was afraid that he was going to miss a show on HBO that played at three in the morning. I showed him how to record a show if he thought he was going to miss something. For the first couple of months, I had to wake him up before I headed off to work. In the beginning, I made him breakfast. Later on, he learned to make his own breakfast. Every day, I left him a list of tasks that needed to done around the apartment. Some days it was a bullshit list, like organizing the garage when I knew it didn't need it. I just didn't want him watching TV all day.

When I got home from work, I asked him what he'd had for lunch. I'd check to make sure he wasn't lying to me. Most evenings I tried my best to get him involved in making dinner with me. He wasn't too good with a knife but he could boil a mean pot of water. He was able to learn some cooking skills, which opened the door for him to eat healthier dinners than the ones he just microwaved. After six months of working with him, Drew was in much better place. The daytime air improved the color of his skin and eating three meals a day allowed him to actually gain a little bit of weight. Unbelievable!

I am very proud to say that Drew did a fantastic job with Pickles. He fed Pickles twice a day and regularly cleaned out his litter box. Drew's definition of regularly was three times a week. I was at work so I never saw him actually empty and refill it. What I did notice was that every week we had to buy a huge container of kitty litter at the grocery store. I never questioned Drew about it. My feeling was that if he was taking care of changing the litter box, that was good enough for me. Who was

I to judge? I reported back to Dr. Cohen that the addition of Pickles to our household was a great success toward getting Drew to move to the day shift. His vampire hours were no more.

Queer Eye For The Straight Guy

THE NEXT COUPLE OF MONTHS could have been an episode of *Queer Eye for the Straight Guy*. Drew's newest goal was working on his personal hygiene. Let's start with his hair. He had worn his hair long since high school. When he moved to Greenville and Dad stopped harassing him about it, he just let it grow out. During my visits to Greenville over the years, I noticed that his hair was shoulder length or longer. Back then his hair was black, long and straight. I know that in his twenty-one years in Greenville, he never once went to a barber or hair salon. He cut his own hair. By the time he got to Boulder, his hair was still at least shoulder length but the color was now salt and pepper—a lot more salt than pepper. His hair had also thinned out considerably. Honestly, it was pretty scraggly looking.

My plan was to take Drew to get a haircut. At first, like every other change we were working on, he wasn't too keen on the idea. Sitting in a barber chair for half an hour and having someone he didn't know so close to him cutting his hair was not very appealing to him. One day I took out my computer and showed him several pictures of today's hairstyles for men. Then I selected a series of rock stars that I knew he liked from the seventies and eighties and presented their pictures from that era and compared them to photos of their current hair styles. In every instance, I made sure that their hair was considerably shorter today. After viewing the images of different rock stars, he finally got the message. I remembered that when we were living in New Jersey and he was still going to a barber, he took a picture of a rock star to show the barber. He would tell the barber that he wanted his hair to look exactly like the rock star in the picture. I specifically remember him trying to get his hair cut like Ace Frehley and Jimmy Page. I told him to pick a current hairstyle from my computer screen and we could print it off and take it with us. Drew picked Mick Jagger's picture.

I told Drew that he could go with me to my barbershop. This was perfect because I had a woman barber who regularly cut my hair. Again, I thought he'd do best with a female. Floyd's barbershop was also perfect because they had pictures of rock stars plastered all over their walls. I made an appointment for the two of us for a Saturday morning. I didn't want him to try and back out so I booked the first open appointment in the morning. I had Drew go first. I knew that my going first would give him time to getting nervous and anxious. He sat in the barber chair and showed Erin his picture of Mick Jagger. Occasionally I looked up from my magazine and saw him in full conversation with Erin. When he was finished, I smiled and said, "Damn, you look great...Mick." On the way home I asked him what he was talking to Erin about, and he said he named every rock star picture on their walls for her.

Next on our Queer Eye adventure, were Drew's clothes. We started by going through his laundry. Anything that had a hole in it or that was frayed I wanted thrown away. He was adamant that everything be donated to Goodwill and not put in the trash. I felt sorry for the folks at Goodwill. We ended up with two full trash bags of clothes. For some reason, Drew had always liked to look at GQ magazine. He not only liked to look at the pictures, but he enjoyed smelling the cologne ads. I bought the most recent copy for him and we sat on the couch and made a list of the clothes he needed. Then we hit the mall.

It was an expensive trip but necessary. We chose several jeans in a variety of colors when we found ones that would fit him. His waist size had increased from thirty-two to thirty-four, which was a positive sign. We also selected various retro band t-shirts. After we had made a dent in all the casual clothes he needed, we had one other item to buy. He needed a suit for when it was time to go interview for a job.

We shopped around at a couple of different department stores until I found one that had a female employee who worked in the suit department. As he was getting fitted and measured, it struck me that he had never owned a suit in his life. I had him try on the entire ensemble—dark blue suit, white cotton shirt, red power tie, and black and brown shoes. I wanted to make sure everything fit just right. I had no idea how long it would be before he would need it. He looked like he could have worked at IBM. Damn, Mick Jagger looked pretty good. On our way out of the department store, Drew asked to stop at the men's fragrance counter. He knew exactly what he wanted. He wanted the cologne that had the half-naked female model in its ad that he'd seen in GQ. After he'd survived four hours in the mall and buying everything on his list, purchasing cologne for him was a well-earned reward.

We were heading toward completion of the personal hygiene goal when one morning Drew asked me a shocking question. He had seen me heading to the gym every morning, Monday through Friday, for the last couple of years. He asked if he could check out the gym with me. I had to pick myself up off the floor. I said, "Sure, but let's do it tomorrow."

There was a gym right down the street from our apartment and I'd never seen more than one other person working out at the same time I did each morning. The next morning, I took Drew down to the gym with me at six-thirty. He played around with a few weights and asked me to show him how to work the treadmill. After a few weeks of experimenting with different types of equipment at the gym, Drew started joining me three days a week. He mainly ran on the treadmill each morning. After a couple of months of running on the treadmill he moved to running outside. He did his run while I worked out at the gym in the morning. His would run for forty-five minutes, averaging an eight-minute mile, better than I could have done. He grew to really love running outside along the beautiful foothills of Boulder. It was the perfect activity for the introvert that he was and most likely always would be.

Under My Wheels

Our next task was to get Drew mobile. We had now been living together for over three years and he had depended on me to cart him around for way too long. We had a bus stop less than seventy-five yards from our apartment. We could see it from our deck. The bus went to downtown Boulder, where a change of buses would take you to downtown Denver if needed. We printed off a bus schedule and posted it in our kitchen. Because of the many trains we'd taken in New Jersey, I knew Drew was capable of reading a schedule. I bought him a Boulder bus pass so he wouldn't have to fumble around for money each trip. For a couple of weekends, we took the bus together to downtown Boulder, hung out for a few hours, and caught a return bus back to our apartment.

When I felt he was ready, I let him go downtown by himself. I didn't want to be like an overprotected parent so I had him leave the apartment and head to the bus stop by himself. I'm not going to lie, I watched him get on the bus from my deck. I gave him a few hours to hang out on Pearl Street Mall and told him to catch the four-thirty bus back to our apartment. When it was close to time for him to return, I watched for him from my deck. He got off the bus exactly on time. I felt like an eager parent waiting for his child to return from there the first day of school. I pretended to be reading the newspaper when he came in. I didn't want him to think I was spying on him. I asked him how it went and he asked, "You were watching me get off the bus weren't you?"

I couldn't lie this time. "Okay, I'm busted. You got me. Guilty as charged." I think he was starting to catch onto me.

Around that same time on a Sunday afternoon on our way to the grocery store, I had an idea. As we passed Boulder High School, I pulled into their parking lot and put the car in park. I sat there for a moment and Drew asked what I was doing. Instead of answering, I got out and walked to his side of the car. He rolled down his window and I said, "I want you to try driving again. Come on, it's been a long time but things have changed. Give it a try Drew. Come on." He didn't budge from his seat. I said, "Well, I'm not leaving until you at least give it a try." I then went over to the curb, sat down, and started checking my messages on my phone. Every now and then, I'd look up from my phone and see him in his seat staring straight ahead. Who was going to blink first?

After about fifteen minutes I yelled out, "Drew, it's Sunday. I've got all day." In another ten minutes, I finally heard his door click. He got out of the car and walked over to me.

"I'll try it once and then we're leaving," he said. After giving him a few instructions while he was sitting in the driver's seat, it was time for him to make something happen. It had been forty-two years since he'd last touched a steering wheel. He put the car into drive and pressed on the accelerator. We went about fifty feet before he slammed on the brakes…hard. So hard, he hit his face on the steering wheel. He put the car in park and got out. He walked over to my side of the car and yelled, "Get out!" Maybe it wasn't such a great idea.

Drew didn't say a word on the way to the grocery store. I tried to lighten things up by cracking a few jokes such as, "Well, Drew, at least you're consistent." He found no humor in my jokes and was silent the entire time we shopped. When we got home, I apologized for making him drive and for my crappy jokes. He didn't talk to me for two days. He never touched a steering wheel again.

London's Calling

WITH DREW NOW LEAVING our apartment to go downtown Boulder regularly, I needed to have the ability to communicate with him. It was time to make the big leap and get him a cell phone. At first, he didn't seem to think he needed one. He thought he could use a pay phone. He was surprised to learn that pay phones didn't exist anymore. We took the bus downtown and went to a phone store. I figured it would be easiest to add him to my plan. He didn't have any credit history so he wouldn't have been able to get one in his name.

My big decision was whether I should let him have a smart phone and give him access to the Internet. The same dreadful decision we all have to make as parents with our kids. I decided against it. He hadn't asked and I didn't want to open him up to the world of porn on his phone. I might not be able to ever get him off his phone if I gave him access. I made sure to get the insurance, knowing that there would be a very good chance of him losing it. Before we left the store, he found a KISS protective case for his phone. He was pumped.

Back in our apartment, I spent a couple of hours showing him how to use his new phone. For some reason, Drew had never been good with gadgets. That mechanical gene was just not there. For example, if he couldn't get his phone to work for whatever reason, he convinced himself that it was broken and just wouldn't use it again. He didn't seem to have the capacity to figure out why something wasn't working. I made him write down his phone number on a piece of paper and put in his wallet. We added a couple of contacts to his contact list. I had him record a voice mail message and add a ring tone. For a ring tone he wanted something cool. After some brainstorming, he selected The Clash's "London's Calling" as his ringtone. He thought that was very cool.

In the following weeks I spent many hours with him working on how to turn his phone on and off, how to properly answer a call, place a call, and how to check his messages. He practiced like a boy scout trying to earn a merit badge. Finally, after many hours, he learned to master his phone. When a teenagers get a smart phone, they're excited because of their ability to connect with their friends and participate in social media. Drew viewed his phone solely as a way to communicate if there was an emergency, which was fine with me. My gut told me that in a short amount of time he would be inquiring about a smart phone and wanting access to the Internet.

Pickles Part II

PICKLES ENDED UP being a great addition for Drew. He did a fantastic job keeping Pickles fed and always kept his litter box cleaned. Drew loved to go in the pet section at the grocery store and pick out new toys for Pickles. When we got home from grocery shopping, the first thing he did was pull the new toys out of the bag and give them to Pickles. Drew liked to get toys with catnip in them and watch Pickles go crazy. He would say, "Pickles is so stoned." I was certain that during the day while I was at work, Drew played with Pickles for hours and no doubt it was a thin line between playing and tormenting that cat.

After a year and half of Pickles being a member of our household, I returned home from a business trip one Sunday evening. I had been gone for two nights on this trip. As I started browning some ground beef to make spaghetti sauce, I was overtaken by a weird feeling. I knew something wasn't right. Then it hit me. Pickles! Where was

Pickles? Anytime I cooked he came into the kitchen. I hadn't seen Drew yet, so I yelled down to his room for him to come upstairs. I had to yell down again, louder this time. I could hear him moving around downstairs so I knew he was in the apartment. He finally came upstairs and I asked him where the cat was. Quickly and in a matter-of-fact tone, Drew said, "He's dead."

I could not believe what I had just heard. "WHAT?" Drew was silent so I asked, "Drew, what the hell happened?"

"I don't know," he said. "He drank a lot of water for two days and when I came to the kitchen yesterday, he was dead on the floor." I was so shocked I didn't know what to say. Drew's attitude was. "Oh well, he's dead. What's the big deal? Let's move on."

I wasn't thinking too logically at this point, but I had to ask, "Where is he? Where did you put him?"

With a stone-cold face Drew said, "I put him in a trash bag and put him out in the garbage."

For some very bizarre and macabre reason I almost laughed out loud. I thought the situation was nuts. It was like a comedy skit. Drew was the dead-pan straight man and I was there for comic relief. I had to believe that Drew was sad, but he was still not capable of showing any emotion. He'd acted the same way when we found Annie's cat on the railroad tracks back in Jersey, and when Dad and Mom died. I know people react to death differently, but his reaction to death was different from, well, anyone else's. We all go through the normal stages of grief over a period of time; Drew seems to go from death to acceptance in a couple of minutes.

On Monday morning as I was getting ready for work, I noticed that Drew had removed all remnants of Pickles. His litter box, food, and toys were all gone. You'd never know we had a cat in our apartment. I didn't ask him what he had done with all of Pickles things. As I was eating my breakfast, Drew came upstairs and said, "I don't want another cat anytime soon. I think it will be a long time until I'll be ready for another one."

I replied, "Yeah, I think it's best that we lay off having any pets for a while. Pickles was one of a kind." I made a note to myself to call Dr. Cohen first thing this morning. I knew there were still a lot of life lessons to teach Drew and I really needed her help and insight on this one. I was at a loss.

Move On Up

WHEN DR. COHEN AND I worked on Drew's plan for independence, the thought of him being able to live in an apartment by himself seemed almost impossible. Here we were three years later and the time had finally arrived. Drew had made so much progress during that time. His medication had made a noticeable difference. He seemed much more at ease socially, and the majority of his OCD tendencies had disappeared. His current physical appearance did not make him stand out in a crowd anymore. He looked good. He had gained a little needed weight and the clothes he wore were stylish and in fashion. Drew was now able to get around Boulder and Denver on his own, and had a cell phone. He was ready for the next step. He was no longer the older adult with the mind of a fifteen-year-old. I'm not going to say he looked and acted like the man of sixty that he was, but he had certainly matured the last couple of years.

Drew and I made the leap one Saturday and went apartment hunting. After searching around Boulder for most of the day, he asked about the idea of living in downtown Denver. I hadn't thought about him being forty-five minutes away from me but after he explained his reasoning, I understood. He said that he liked Boulder but to him Denver was closer to a life of living in a bigger city, like NYC. He felt there was more to do there. So, we drove down to Denver to see if we could find something.

Drew and I made three more trips to Denver and eventually found the perfect apartment. It was a two bedroom on the ninth floor of a new high-rise smack dab in the middle of downtown. There was a grocery store across the street and a dispensary and an adult store three blocks away. The last two, of course, were high on his list of criteria. With Drew having zero credit and no history of renting, I had to put my name on the lease. For all I know they probably thought he and I were living together. We had two weeks to get ready to move in on first of the month.

On moving day, I rented a U-Haul truck and we loaded up all of Drew's stuff. As we started to take his bed apart he asked, "Do you think I could get a different bedroom set for the new apartment?" I had assumed he would want to keep the same teenage set from back in New Jersey. This was big step forward for him. That bedroom set was like his security blanket.

I answered, "Of course. Let's do it!" With a full truck, on our way down to Denver we stopped by the Furniture Warehouse and bought an entire new queen bedroom set. He was going to have quite the bachelor pad.

Unloading Drew's stuff into his apartment reminded me of dropping off one of my children at college for their freshman year. I was happy he was taking that next step in his life, but had an empty feeling in my gut that he'd grown up and was leaving my protective nest. I had to keep reminding myself that he was sixty years old.

After setting up his apartment, it was apparent he needed some decorations for his walls. He chose what every sixty-year-old college student would want to hang on the walls: posters of the Three Stooges, a sexy super model, Metallica, Bob Marley, KISS, and a Coors Light blinking neon light. When we were finished decorating his place it looked like any guy's college dorm from the seventies, but it was all his own.

I spent Drew's first night in his apartment in the spare bedroom. I just wanted to be sure he was okay and didn't have any second thoughts about the move. I'm not sure what I was expecting to happen, but everything turned out perfectly. The next morning, I made sure that his cable was up and working. I gave him a big "bro" hug on my way out the door and told him how proud I was of him. I told him I would be around regularly to check on him, and reminded him I was just a phone call away. My plan was to check up on him at least twice a week. It would have been much easier to have him living in Boulder, but the forty-five-minute-drive to Denver was his, and my, cost of freedom.

On my drive back to Boulder I kept checking my rearview mirror to stare at the Denver skyline. The Denver skyline got smaller and smaller the closer I got to Boulder. While the skyline got smaller, I could feel my heart getting bigger and bigger.

Work To Do

DREW MOVING INTO HIS OWN APARTMENT was a major step and accomplishment in our plan for his independence. The other major step of that equation was for him to find employment. Drew hadn't worked for thirty-three years. The last job he had was in Greenville working for that cardboard box company. To say he was a little rusty would be an understatement. Now that he was on a day schedule and had his own apartment and the Denver bus system for reliable transportation, it was time for him to get a job.

What kind of job opportunity is there for someone who is sixty, has no experience, and has not worked in thirty-three years? I'm sure Drew would have loved to work at a marijuana dispensary or an adult bookstore, but his previous work history wouldn't have gotten him even one interview. He would never pass a drug test either. We spent a couple of weekends browsing job postings on my computer but either he didn't have any interest or he didn't meet any of the job requirements. I'm not sure how we were going to make this happen. We were both getting pretty discouraged.

Working in Human Resources taught me that it's easier to land a job if you know someone who can get your foot in the door. My next call was to Dr. Cohen. As luck would have it, she knew the director at the downtown Denver location of Goodwill. She didn't make any promises but she was able to get Drew an interview the following week. It's always about who you know, isn't it?

The weekend before Drew's interview I prepped him the best I could for what he might expect. I made sure that he knew to wear his suit, and how important his first impression would be. We also role-played the kinds of questions he could expect to get in his interview. This became rather comical. How does someone answer the typical interview questions when they haven't worked in thirty-three years? "So, tell me about your last job? Where do you want to be in five years? What are your strengths? What attracted you to this company? Why are you leaving your present job?"

His best response came when I was role playing the interviewing manager and asked him, "Tell me about a time when you had to deal with conflict?"

Drew's answer was, "Once I was trying to score a bag of weed from someone in downtown Boulder and was worried that the person may have been a narc." I had to jump in and quickly tell him why this wasn't an appropriate answer, so we tried again.

This time he answered, "Once I was at the Fascinations store looking around, and a guy came up to me and tried to get me to go behind the building and give him a ..." I stopped him in midsentence. We had a lot of work to do to prepare him for his interview.

I had to work the day Drew went for his job interview. He texted me a picture of himself in his suit before he left for his interview. He looked great. Goodwill was only a short seven-minute walk for him. I asked him to call me after the interview was over. I got busy at work and lost track of the time. Later in the afternoon while I was in a meeting, my phone rang. I stepped out of my meeting to answer Drew's call.

In all the years that I've known Drew, I have never heard him so excited. He said his interview went great and that he was hired on the spot. He was to start on Monday, working forty hours a week. Then he said, "You know what the best part is? They're are going to pay me twelve dollars an hour. I was only making three-fifty at Fablok in New Jersey." I had to look it up, but the minimum wage in seventy-eight was only two dollars and sixty-five cents an hour. Again, I felt like the parent whose kid has just landed his first real job. I congratulated him and told him that this weekend we would celebrate. After we hung up, I called Dr. Cohen and thanked her for all of her help in making this happen.

When Drew got his first paycheck, he did something totally unexpected. I was over at his apartment that Sunday morning. We were enjoying a cup of coffee and munching on his favorite—chocolate doughnuts. He had a devilish grin on his face when he pulled out a wrapped gift from under the table and said, "I want to thank you for all the things you have done for me. I wouldn't be here if it weren't for you."

To my amazement Drew gave me a 1967 Mickey Mantle baseball card. I had been an avid collector of baseball cards since the age of five. I still have all my original cards. I was stunned and asked, "Where did you get it?"

What he told me next completely blew me away. "I know that you love baseball cards and have collected them forever. When we lived in New Providence all those years, I knew that the Yankees were your favorite team and Mickey Mantle was your favorite player. You always spent all of your money buying packs of cards. I thought maybe I would like to also start a collection. I bought a couple of packs but never really got into it like you did. One of those packs of cards had a Mickey Mantle card. I think it's from 1967. I thought of giving it to you when you left to go to college, but the time just didn't feel right. When we were moving to Denver, I found that card in my safe and now it feels like the right time." I was left speechless!

After working at Goodwill for over a year, Drew was promoted to supervisor. Imagine that! It just proves that if you show up to work every day on time and work hard every day good things happen. Periodically, I asked Dr. Cohen to call the director at Goodwill to get a progress report on Drew. The feedback was always the same. "Drew continues to be the best employee we have. He is very dependable, gets along with everyone, and works his ass off." What a difference from those report cards he received back when he was in school.

Money

WITH DREW WORKING full time now, he needed his own checking and savings accounts. There was a bank one block away from his apartment, which was convenient for him. At this point, I didn't want to lead him through the process and do all the work for him. He had come this far and it was time for him to get this done on his own. He had an ID now, was fully employed, and had his own address.

One Saturday, I waited back at his apartment while Drew went to the bank. About an hour later he returned with a large packet. Mission accomplished. He was very excited to show me his checking and savings account information. They also gave him a debit card, signed him up for direct deposit, and loaded their app on his cell phone.

I spent the rest of the day showing him how to get all his bills paid electronically through autopay. Now his rent and all his utilities would be paid automatically and I could keep an eye on them if I needed to. It had taken five years, but Team Drew had now accomplished nine of our ten goals for his independence. For all of those five years, I had been focused and aggressive to make sure we were always moving the ball down the field. I had confidence each step along the way. Failure was never an option.

In the back of my mind, I was always nervous about being able to accomplish our last goal. We were asking Drew to go down a road he had never wanted to go down before. Goal ten was the root cause for his life-long anxiety, the reason for his poor performance in school, and why he had habitually made excuses for his entire life. I was going to give it my best shot, but deep down I knew that we might never accomplish this last goal.

You're My Best Friend

WHEN MY KIDS WERE SMALL, they loved to have me read books to them as part of their bedtime ritual. One of their favorites was *Grover Goes To School* by the people at Sesame Street. In the book, Grover learns how to make friends with his classmates.

How do you teach a man of sixty who's never had a friend in his life to understand the value of friendship? We learn those values at such a young age. Drew always avoided putting himself in any situation that would have him in contact with anyone he didn't know. With all the work that Dr. Cohen and I had done with him over the last five years he still had no friends. His anxiety around being in situations with people he didn't know had certainly decreased. Making new friends comes pretty natural to most of us, but not too much ever came naturally to Drew. It was probably easier for him to go through life never experiencing friendship, but I wanted to at least try to give him an opportunity to see what it felt like. If he didn't like it, at least we could say we tried.

Drew had now been working at Goodwill for a year and a half. I suggested the idea of hosting a party at his apartment with some of his coworkers. At first, he tried to come up with excuses for why that wasn't such a great idea. I told him I'd help out to make sure things turned out all right. One of the reasons for his hesitation was that he didn't know how to host a party. He helped me design the invitations. He still had fantastic artistic abilities. He handed them out to over twenty of his coworkers. We went shopping for the necessary food and beer. I put him in charge of the music, but when he brought all of his KISS and Death Metal albums to the living room, we had to talk about what kind of music might be a better fit with the folks he had invited.

The invitations noted that the party was from eight until midnight. At quarter past eight, Drew and I were sitting in his living room staring at each other and waiting for someone to ring the doorbell. I was nervous and thinking to myself that it would really suck if no one showed up. The old Drew would most likely have said, "Screw it," shut things down and gone to his bedroom. Thank God people started arriving at quarter to nine. By nine-thirty, I counted over twenty-five people in his apartment. I had the biggest grin on my face the entire evening as I watched him converse with his coworkers, get drinks for everyone, and show people around his place. I noticed he spent a good amount of time talking with a woman named Jane throughout the evening. I definitely would have to ask him about her later.

Around midnight there were still about fifteen people partying in his apartment. When I smelled pot, I decided it was time for me to bow out. I told Drew I was going to leave and told him he was now officially in charge. He laughed and said, "No worries. I've got this." I left Denver and drove back to Boulder feeling very confident that he did "have this." He also had his phone and could call me at any time.

A couple of weeks after Drew's party I casually asked him about Jane. He got all embarrassed and red in the face like a grade school kid. I could tell he kind of liked her. I think he was experiencing some feelings that he had never felt before and didn't know what to do next. When you're a teenager and have those feelings about someone of the opposite sex, you always have your buddies around to help set you straight. I guess that was my role now.

I suggested that we go on a double date and asked, "Why don't we plan to all go out to dinner and then go to Red Rocks Amphitheatre for a concert?" He loved that idea.

With great excitement, he immediately pulled out *Denver Westword*, a local Denver entertainment magazine, to check the upcoming shows at Red Rocks. He first suggested Slipknot and I told him I thought we should pick something a little more mainstream. We settled on Tom Petty. He wanted to pay for the concert tickets so I told him that I'd take care of dinner. I also told him, "You know, you're taking a risk here. You haven't asked Jane yet and you're all ready to buy tickets."

The next Sunday when I went to his apartment, he said he wanted to show me something. He pulled out his phone, opened his message screen and put it directly in front of my face and said, "She said yes!" He looked just like a little kid on Christmas morning.

We got dressed at his apartment the night of the concert, before we were to meet our dates. Drew asked me if it would be okay to bring a couple of joints with him into Red Rocks.

"Drew, it's Colorado," I replied

He just smiled. Recreational marijuana was now legal in Colorado. I had recently started dating a beautiful woman named Pamela, whom I had met earlier on a plane trip. Pam and Jane met Drew and me at an Italian restaurant downtown. It was unbelievable to sit across the table from Drew and watch him hold hands and trade small talk with Jane. I learned that she had quite a bit of baggage in her past, as did Drew. I thought the two of them were good for each other.

We had a great time at the concert. The beauty of Red Rocks Amphitheatre blew Drew away. I'm not sure of the last concert he and I attended over thirty-nine years ago, but I never could have imagined that the two of us would be together at Red Rocks watching a concert so many years later. I hoped our parents were smiling down on us. I dropped Drew and Jane off at his apartment and headed back up to Boulder with Pam after the concert. On the way to Boulder, I asked Pam, "Do you think Drew will get lucky tonight?" Pam gave me a look; she didn't need to say anything. I said, "Right, TMI." I would have to ask Drew later.

I'm not sure if our last goal of "companionship" was ever to be accomplished. Together, we had accomplished the first nine goals of the plan. The last goal was always going to have to be work in progress. It was a journey and not a destination as Dr. Cohen always said. I believed that I had laid all the groundwork for Drew to be successful in this area if he wanted to be. I had helped him build him a foundation. The ball was now in his court...forever.

Dr. Cohen

Every day I count my lucky stars and say a special little prayer of thanks that I went to the University of Colorado that day looking for help for Drew. What were the odds that I would stumble across Dr. Angie Cohen on her last day before retiring? If I had gone to campus one day later, Drew and I would no doubt have found ourselves in a much different situation. Angie was right that seven years ago we had experienced divine intervention in her tiny office on the University of Colorado campus. I'm convinced that without her help, none of the progress that had been made with Drew over the past seven years would have been possible. Her unselfishness was so exceptional and rare and she had been more generous to Drew and me than anyone I had ever known. She had become a great friend to both of us and I truly loved her.

When Angie told me in late 2015 that she had been diagnosed with stage IV breast cancer I was more than gut wrenched. I was devastated. Cancer always has a way of bringing everyone to their knees. Given the naturalist that she was, she refused any treatment using chemotherapy or radiation. She tried some naturopathic remedies and even went to Mexico for some experimental treatments but her cancer, unfortunately, continued to spread.

Knowing that her time was short, I needed to break the news to Drew. At the time, he was seeing Angie only once a month. His time with her became more about giving her updates on his life and having conversations that any two friends might have. In the past seven years, Drew had lived up to his commitment to her and never missed one appointment. The two of them had become extremely close throughout his journey. When I shared the news with him, he was utterly in shock. Seven years ago, Drew would have been very nonchalant and, at the most, would have said, "Oh, well." I saw a different reaction this time.

He knew the drill with cancer all too well. We had lost both our parents and a few friends to cancer. He had seen the pain and the road to death first hand. He knew what to expect. He asked to see Angie as soon as she was up to it.

I wanted to give Drew some privacy with Angie so when we were able to get some time with her, I dropped him off at her house. He asked if I was coming in and I told him I needed to run some errands and would be back later to pick him up. Two hours later I pulled into Dr. Cohen's driveway and decided that rather than going in to collect him, I would wait for him to come out. About ten minutes later, he briskly walked down her driveway and got in the car. I stared ahead, not sure I wanted to look at him. I waited a moment and then I heard something I had never heard before. Drew was crying. No, he was sobbing...uncontrollably. I turned my head and saw tears streaming down his face. I had never seen him cry before. He didn't cry when Dad passed away or at his funeral. He didn't cry when our mother had passed away. Sitting there in my car crying, he looked so alone. I reached across my console and did the only thing that seemed appropriate at the time. I gave him a hug and told him that everything was going to be okay. I hoped I was right. I wasn't sure but it felt like the right thing to say in the moment.

The ride back to Denver was eerily quiet. About halfway there, I noticed a bracelet on Drew's wrist that I had never seen him wear before. It was made of a black cord and was decorated in beads of all the colors of the rainbow. When I asked him about it, he said that Angie had given it to him and called it their friendship bracelet. In between his tears, he told me that Angie had made it herself and that it was a reminder that she will always be with him. I fought back my tears as I continued our drive back to Denver. It was the last time Drew saw Angie alive.

Two months later on the day of Angie's funeral, I drove down to Denver with the intention of picking up Drew so we could attend her funeral together. When I got to his apartment, I saw that he wasn't dressed. He said he didn't feel up to going. I told him that we both needed to pay our respects and that Angie would have wanted to us to go. "That's what friends do," I said.

In a despondent voice, Drew said, "I'm just really tired of cancer. I'm tired of cancer taking away anyone that I get close to. It's not fair. I fucking hate cancer. Cancer really sucks!"

"Yes, it does, Drew. I don't understand it either. I don't know why some people get it and some people don't. I don't know what causes it. I don't know why we can't find a cure for it. All I know to do is put my faith in a higher power and hope that someday we'll have answers. For now, why don't you get dressed so we won't be late. You know how much Dr. Cohen hated anyone being late."

St John's Church in Boulder was packed. Drew and I got there right as the service started. Angie had quite a following. In life and in death, I have always found that the footprints a person leaves behind speak volumes about the person's character and values. Listening to the minister and hearing Angie's friends and loved ones speak, I knew she was leaving behind two huge footprints in this world. She had impacted the lives of so many.

As Drew and I left the church, Angie's niece, whom we had never met before, approached us. She looked at Drew and asked, "Are you Drew Wilson?"

He hesitated a bit before answering. "Yes."

She continued, "You know, Angie really loved you, Drew. She loved to talk about her relationship with you and how you had come into her life. I honestly believe you kept her going, maybe longer than she would have. Before she passed away, she made something for you and asked me to give it to you." Her niece pulled out a little ornament in the shape of two footprints. She handed it to Drew and said, "Turn it over." He turned the two little footprints over and looked at the inscription. On one of the footprints was inscribed *Souls Forever* and on the other *Drew + Angie*.

On our way back to Denver the car was very quiet. Every now and then I heard Drew sobbing. He clutched that ornament tightly in his hand most of the ride to Denver. I put some KISS on the radio hoping to lift his spirits and distract him. As soon as "Strutter" began Drew piped up, "You know, Angie loved KISS."

For the past seven years I had been comforted knowing that Angie was the real leader of Team Drew. She was the expert and her knowledge and leadership drove our actions and behaviors. She was my coach and mentor through the entire process. Even though we had, for the most part, completed all ten steps of the plan to give Drew independence, I knew she always had my back and would never let me fail. On that drive back to Denver after Angie's funeral, it hit me that we had lost our key member of Team Drew. We were back to just Drew and me again. A feeling of loneliness came over me as we approached Drew's apartment. Rebounding after losing Angie was going to be a tall task for Drew. For the first time in a long time, I was worried.

Love and Happiness

LOVE – *A strong affection for another arising out of kinship or a personal tie. Attraction based on sexual desire. Affection based on admiration or common interest.*
HAPPINESS – *A state of well-being and contentment. A pleasurable and satisfying experience.*

Having gone through a divorce, I had a lot of time for self-reflection. I had been faced with a number of life-changing events that smacked me in my face all at once. Within the same year, I had dealt with the passing of my mother, taking responsibility for and becoming the caregiver of Drew, seeking new employment after my job had been eliminated due to a change in ownership, and getting a divorce from my wife of twenty-six years. Individually, anyone of these events was enough to add a great deal of stress to my life, but having to deal with this 'superfecta' of events might well have sent me over the edge.

Thank God, for the numerous hikes I had done while listening to the words of Peter Gabriel's "Solsbury Hill," and the many rosaries prayed along the way in the Colorado mountains to help me to clear my head and also help me to focus on what was really important. During that year, my friends kept suggesting that I talk with someone but I just couldn't see the value in it. I had many years of regrets along the way and certainly would have done some things differently. I believed if I could just keep moving forward and focus on the future I wouldn't dwell on my past mistakes. I never wanted to look in my rearview mirror. Maybe I was afraid of the pain and just wanted to avoid it. Would some unforeseen event force me to deal with it?

The past seven years of working with Drew had caused me, for the first time, to stop and look in my rearview mirror. There may be a lot of truth in what motivational speaker Tony Robbins preaches in his chapter on Pleasure vs. Pain. I was so busy executing Mom's will, taking on Drew, starting my own consulting organization, and dealing with my divorce that I never mourned Mom's passing the way I should have. In the aftermath of Mom's death, I moved through a checklist as if I was completing a work project. I checked off each task and moved to the next item on the list—Mom's funeral, Mom's will, moving Drew to Boulder. I never shed a tear during her passing or any time in the seven years since. Deep inside I knew this wasn't right and I worried that someday it would all have to come out.

Reflecting on the events that led to my divorce and trying to pick up the pieces and move forward, I kept coming to the same conclusions. At the end of our time on earth, only two things really matter—our relationships and our happiness. Our life is measured by the quality of our relationships. I love my children more than anything in this world. Life is short and after my divorce I made a commitment to always focus on my relationships. Spending time with my children, my grandchildren, and my loved ones and creating experiences for all of them is the most important thing I can and want to do. I live each day working toward my happiness. Nobody can impact my happiness more than me. Life is fleeting, why spend it being miserable? I had spent an inordinate amount of time over the last seven years learning what makes me happy and making sure my daily actions are creating that happiness for me.

Twenty years ago, Dr. Brooks had enlightened me. He'd introduced me to the world of Asperger's and Autism. I had to sit on that information for the next thirteen years until I met Dr. Cohen. For seven years, Angie had guided me in taking Drew from being dependent on me to being independent. He is in a much better place than ever in his life. He has his own apartment, job, and bank account. He pays his own bills, has reliable transportation, and is able to live on his own.

Often, during those years of working with Drew toward his

independence, I wondered if he was truly happy. Many people would say that to have a productive and happy life you have to work, make money, have friends and relationships—to live the American Dream. Most of us, if we're lucky, go to college, get a job, get married, buy a house, have a few kids, bank some money, and retire. If we can get through life without becoming dependent on a substance or not going to jail, we're golden. I often wondered if I was trying to fit or squeeze Drew into some preconceived model of happiness. My happiness, not his happiness. Was I pushing him toward independence more for me than for him? Was I trying to mold him into what my view of normal was? In spite of these questions about my motivations, I believed that we were on the correct path and doing the right thing.

I certainly made a lot of assumptions for Drew along the way. When I visited him in Greenville, I saw a weak man being held prisoner in his bedroom. I remembered that Sunday after we had been living in Boulder for a year, when he seemed to be sliding back to his old life and schedule in Greenville. I simply couldn't fathom how someone could be happy living the life he had been, repeating the same schedule every day for decades.

They say timing is everything. How true in Drew's case. If he had been born twenty or thirty years later, his quality of life would have been so different. He would have been mainstreamed into school and been accepted rather than being bullied. He might have been put on medication and taught how to manage his social anxiety. If he wanted, he might have been able to live the American Dream. There are many examples today of people who are on the spectrum, who have been diagnosed with Asperger's, who have gone on to do some pretty amazing things. I guess I'll never know what he could have done with his life. Timing is everything.

It took many years and a divorce for me to discover what made me happy. I assumed that creating independence for Drew would bring him the happiness he had never experienced before. Drew had so few relationships in his life, beyond his brother, sister and me. It appeared that he was developing a new one with Jane. And Dr. Cohen had been a key relationship in his life. Drew had put all of his trust and energy into that relationship with Angie and had experienced all the usual benefits of a friendship like that. Angie had become his first and only true friend. Drew was now experiencing the pain and grief that goes with losing such a dear friend. This was a new emotion for Drew. Angie was gone. I didn't know what the future held for the two of us.

Part V

Denver, Colorado – November 13, 2016

Part V

Denver, Colorado – November 13, 2016

IT WAS SUNDAY MORNING. I had left Boulder early to head down to see Drew in Denver. I had a lot of things to get done and wanted to get a jump on the day. I stopped and picked up his favorite chocolate doughnuts for him. This had become a ritual every time I came to visit him. He could still down a half dozen of them in one sitting. I entered his apartment and quickly noticed that his bedroom door was closed. I was there earlier than normal so I assumed he was sleeping in. I decided to go into his kitchen and make some coffee for myself. I also wouldn't mind catching up on a little news on TV before he woke up.

I went into the pantry to grab the coffee and noticed that something was different. Something was odd. All the items in his pantry were perfectly faced—lined up with all the labels facing out in a perfect symmetrical order. I hadn't seen this old OCD behavior in four years. Not thinking too much about it, I made my coffee and turned CNN on. I grabbed a mug from the cabinet and found the sugar. Looking for a spoon, I opened up several drawers and did a double-take. All his drawers were perfectly organized, just like in the early days of our apartment in Boulder. I sat down in the living room with my coffee and looked for his other remote. It's hard to describe what I felt next. It was just like that sinking feeling you get when you discover you've made a huge, grave mistake. The sensation you feel that quickly passes through your entire body and then makes you feel like your ears and face are on fire. "Oh, shit!" I yelled. I jumped off the couch, my coffee spilling all over the floor and my pants and ran straight to his room.

His door was locked. I yelled out his name again and again, to no response. In a panic, I found a key pin above his door, resting on the molding. My hands were dripping with sweat and shaking as I struggled to get the pin in his doorknob. I heard the click and opened the door. There was Drew, lying face down on his bed. I pulled the sleeve of his torn and tattered long sleeve shirt up as far as I could and checked his pulse. There was none.

When I was nine or ten growing up in New Jersey in the sixties, there was a cartoon that would be shown on TV once or twice a year. It was usually shown along with a *Popeye, Felix the Cat*, or a *Mighty Mouse* cartoon. The cartoon was called: *The Story of John Henry*. It begins with groups of African American men working and building railroad tracks in the eighteen hundreds. John Henry was a huge, muscular man who could drive rail spikes faster than any other human. He was called "the steel driving man." With his hammer, he could tunnel through rock better than anyone else on earth. The story goes on to tell of the invention of a steam-powered, rock-drilling machine and there was to be a race between John Henry and the new machine to see who could tunnel through rock faster. John Henry hammered and hammered with unbelievable force to win the race, only to die at the end of the race, in victory. He died with a hammer in his hand as his heart gave out from the stress. To this day I can still picture that African American man who stares into the camera after the race and says, "He's dead. John Henry's dead."

Drew's death certificate stated that cardiac arrest—pulmonary embolism was the cause of his death. It was the same cause of death that is found on his grandmother and grandfather's death certificates. His autopsy revealed that no drugs were found in his system at the time of his death. This was surprising, but after I checked his medicine cabinet, I discovered that he hadn't taken his meds in the prior twenty days. I figured out that he had stopped taking them right after Angie had passed away.

In the days after Drew's passing, my Catholic guilt took hold of my every thought. Someone dying of a heart attack at the age of sixty-four might not seem that uncommon but I still searched for an answer to what happened to him. I couldn't let go of the multiple theories and thoughts that continually ran through my mind.

Had I pushed Drew too hard to give him a quality of life and independence? What if this was all actually for me and not for him? What if he really hadn't wanted to change but couldn't bring himself to communicate his feelings to me?

Was Angie's death just too much for him to handle? She was the first and only friend that Drew was able to build a relationship with in his entire life. He had invested so much time and effort in that relationship and in the end she died. Had he just given up? Did he die of a broken heart?

I wondered if Drew's decision to stop taking his meds affected his heart. He'd been on medication for over seven years and just had stopped cold turkey. That couldn't have been good for his system.

Maybe his body wasn't designed by God to handle all the stress that came with the last seven years of change; change that was designed to give him independence. Perhaps the heart God had given him was designed to handle the stress-free life that he had back in Greenville rather than implementing that ten-point plan of independence. I found it interesting that when I found him that Sunday morning in his bed, he was wearing pants and a shirt that were tattered and torn. He must have felt most comfortable and at home in those clothes.

In the end, maybe Mom was right. Mom's always right...right? Maybe I should have listened to her and left Drew alone and "let sleeping dogs lie." She might have known something I didn't. Maybe she had information from his teachers or from that psychologist back in Morristown that she had never shared with me.

The question I kept coming back to was whether I had been trying to make Drew fit into my version of normal. Deep inside we all know what we believe is normal, but it's our own version of normal. My world of normal is not your world of normal. Our life experiences mold what our normal becomes. Who says my normal is right? I had to keep telling myself that I was doing the right thing for Drew.

I beat myself up for a good couple of days with guilt but in the end, I had to come to some resolution. Drew had a heart attack and died.

The verse from Mark 13:32: "*But about that day or hour no one knows, not even the angels in heaven, nor the Son, but only the Father*" helped me to start sleeping again.

Later in the day that Drew died, I called both Annie and Bobby to let them know. They hadn't seen him since he moved to Boulder in 2008. Once or twice a year in calls with both of them they would ask how he was doing. For the first several years before Team Drew was achieving success, I would just reply, "You know, it's just like Groundhog day with Drew. He's fine." Over the past couple of years they had been amazed by Drew's progress and were thankful that he was in Colorado with me. I continued to be baffled that with all the changes in Drew's life they never came to visit him. They both expressed their remorse over Drew's death and said they would try to make his funeral.

Before she passed away, Mom had documented Drew's wishes for his death. He wanted to be cremated. This surprised me because I had thought he would want to be buried in the same plot as our parents. Mom had purchased a place in a new Columbarium that was located on the grounds of the church where she worked in Greenville. She'd also had Drew draw up a will. His will was in a sealed envelope that was in Mom's papers. The will was written on a blank note card and read:

30 July 2012
Annie, Steve, Bobby
Each gets 1/3 of Bank Account
All music, records, CD's, tapes can be shared by those who want
them.
Clothes and furniture can go to Charities.
John Andrew Wilson
Witnessed by: Mary L. Wilson

Drew always used the phrase "even Stephen" whenever anything needed to be divided up. He was always about having everything be even and fair. It's funny in a morbid sort of way, that he always wanted everything to be fair yet the hand he was dealt in life was anything but fair.

After I received Drew's ashes from the funeral home, I finalized and communicated the plans for his funeral in Greenville. I worked with Mom's old church to set up the date and time. There weren't many to communicate with—my kids, Annie, Bobby, and a few people Drew worked with at Goodwill. Many asked me when I was going to fly into Greenville. I told them that I would drive; Drew was afraid of flying.

Road Trip

IN THE BACK of my clothes dresser is a small square cardboard box. In that box is my old wallet that I used as a teenager in New Jersey. In that old frayed wallet are a few keepsakes. There are a couple of old driver's licenses from New Jersey, Florida, and Texas. There's an old receipt from 1974 for the eight-track player and speakers I put in my first car for ninety-nine dollars and seventy-five cents. That was a lot of money back then but tunes in my car were a must! There's also a New Jersey Division Of Motor Vehicles Alcohol Drinking Chart showing how many drinks one could consume before legally being impaired to drive. These were important items for a teenage boy to carry in his wallet. I also found a New Providence library card that looked like it had hardly been used...seems about right. And in the dollar bill section of that wallet are the old concert ticket stubs from all the concerts that Drew and I had ever attended.

My family thought I was crazy to drive the fifteen hundred miles from Boulder to Greenville for Drew's funeral. I thought it would be very therapeutic. I think my kids were worried about my mental state. I was actually looking forward to the three-day journey by myself. I hoped the time alone on the open road across our beautiful country would provide some healing for me. I packed my car for the trip and put the box that contained Drew's ashes on the passenger seat and strapped him in with the seat belt. I never looked into whether it was legal to transport ashes across state lines. I didn't even think about it until I crossed the Colorado-Kansas border.

Before I left, I took all those concert tickets and put them in order by date—our first concert through our last. From The Marshall Tucker

Band to the Allman Brothers to Led Zeppelin, all the way through to Tom Petty at Red Rocks during the past year. I organized my Spotify library to play a live album from each artist in the order of the concerts Drew and I attended. I thought this would be the perfect way to honor him.

The drive did prove to be the therapy I deeply needed. I only made one unplanned stop along the way. As I passed through St. Louis, I saw the red flashing neon lights in the distance, just as Drew had during our drive from Greenville to Boulder. It appears that the Larry Flint Gentlemen's Club was still up and running. I decided to pull off the highway to go in and have one drink in honor of Drew. I wasn't dressed to go clubbing but I didn't care. I paid the entrance fee, dodged a few topless dancers, and made my way to the bar. Drew would have loved this place. The women were beautiful. I sipped my Crown Royal and tried to spend a minimal amount of time with each dancer who wanted me to buy her a drink. I didn't want to be rude, but now was not the right time.

With one sip left in my glass, I asked the bartender if it would be okay to make a toast to my brother who had just passed away. I don't think I had ever asked a question to a bartender whose naked breasts were literally a foot from my face. She said, "Absolutely. In Larry's place anything goes." I stood up and announced that I wanted to make a toast. A few patrons who were sitting at the bar looked up from their drinks and stared in my direction.

I began to speak, "My brother Drew didn't have many friends and he never fell in love. He didn't get to play in this life by the same rules as you and I. While his life on this earth has now ended, our relationship continues to grow. Drew, my brother, they cut you down when you tried to leap high. I will continue to live in you if you'll live in me. Here's to Drew as he begins his new journey."

After a loud round of applause and turning down numerous offers of drinks, I walked out of Larry's Club and headed back to my car. I had put Drew ashes in the trunk of the car before going into the club, so now I put the box back on the passenger seat and strapped him in. I couldn't wait to share my experience with Drew as we continued on our trek to Greenville.

And In The End...

I ARRIVED IN GREENVILLE on a Friday evening. Thank goodness I didn't have any issues along the way. I hadn't been back in town since we loaded up the U-Haul and headed off to Colorado. In all the trips I had previously made to Greenville, I had never had to stay at a hotel. I didn't really know anyone in town. The majority of Mom's friends had passed away. I decided to stay in downtown Greenville, close to the church where Mom had worked and convenient to Drew's service the next morning.

Drew had never communicated what his wishes were when it came to his funeral. In all the years we lived together, he never went or wanted to go church. Mom's church had an entire new lineup of priests who had come since she'd passed away. I worked with the new pastor and we decided to have a short service at the side alter. After the service we could go outside for the interment of Drew's ashes in the Columbaria.

Sitting in the church waiting for Drew's service to begin, brought back a lot of memories for me. Two of my children had been baptized in that church. Both of my parents' funeral services had been held there. Dad had loved serving as a deacon for that church and had spent many hours helping to remodel it. I remembered one December after Dad had passed away, when my entire family had come to Greenville to spend Christmas with Mom, which was also her birthday.

Prior to the trip, I had spoken with Annie about going in on Mom's birthday present together. We decided to get her a new smart phone and Annie would make the purchase and I would pay her back when we were in Greenville. We all went to Christmas Mass together. I sat next to Annie in our pew. During Mass, as the offering basket was making its way to our pew, I pulled out my wallet and noticed the three hundred dollar bills I had set aside to reimburse Annie for Mom's phone. I handed Annie the three hundred dollars. She didn't look at the bills and threw all of them into the offering basket. In a panic, I yelled at the usher, "Stop! Stop! Stop!"

The usher came walking back to me looked horrified as I pulled the three hundred dollars out of the offering basket. I showed Annie the bills and said, "This is to pay you back for Mom's phone." Annie said, "Oh, I thought you gave me, like, three dollars to put in the basket." When I pulled that money out of the basket an elderly gentleman sitting next to me whispered, "You know, *He* doesn't give change."

I knew that my children had flown in for Drew's service but I really wasn't expecting anyone else. Drew didn't know anyone in Greenville. Since Bobby only lived a couple of hours away from Greenville, I certainly thought he would attend. I was sitting in the first pew with Steve Jr., Valerie, and Mark, when Father Kelly started the service. I didn't pay attention to whether anyone else had arrived. Father Kelly didn't know Drew's life story, so while his homily was nice for a funeral, it was a little generic. When the short fifteen-minute service was over, I hesitated to look back to see who else had attended, because in my gut I already knew the answer. Don't we all have the same vision when it comes to our own funeral: a full church, lots of singing, and a slew of people getting up to say how great we were? I saw one other gentleman in a suit sitting a couple of rows back. No one else attended. What was I expecting, The Malaysia Autistic Children's Choir?

Steve Jr., Valerie, Mark, the gentleman in the suit, and I followed Fr. Kelly to the Columbaria. He said a couple of additional prayers and then put Drew's ashes into his final resting place. After Mom passed away, Drew and I had a conversation about the Columbaria. It was built the last year Mom worked at the church. He said, "Mom got me one of the best spots in the Columbaria." To be honest, at the time I didn't even know what a Columbaria was. I had to Google it.

"That's nice. What makes it one of the best spots?"

"My spot is in the shade."

I jokingly said, "Does it really matter when you're dead, Drew?"

"It does to me," he answered emphatically. Drew now had his final resting place in the shade.

After the service at the Columbaria, the man in the suit came up to me and introduced himself as Drew's former manager at Goodwill back in Denver. He told me that he knew about Drew's story from the other team members that Drew worked with. He was moved by Drew's journey and wanted to meet his family. He said that he was going to start an educational fund for people with Autism to find employment at Goodwill in Drew's name. He asked me if I would be willing to help him get the project off the ground. There could only be one answer.

"Yes," I said. I told him we could discuss it when I made it back to Colorado.

After the funeral, my kids asked me to drive by their grandmother's old house on the way to dropping them off at the airport. They had made so many trips here for Christmas and their grandmother's birthday. We parked my car on the street in front of her house, took a couple of pictures, and then shared many grandmother stories on the way to the Greenville Airport. At the airport, amid the kisses and hugs and goodbyes, Steve Jr. asked me if I was going to hit the road back to Boulder now. I told him there was one other thing I needed to do before I left town. I gave them all a final hug, told them that I loved them, and watched them disappear into the terminal.

I headed down Wade Hampton Boulevard. I had a pretty good idea how to get to where I needed to go. I saw the sign in the distance and made the right-hand turn into Woodlawn Memorial Park. I had visited my Dad's grave at least a dozen times while on trips to Greenville. I had not been to my Mom's grave since her burial seven years ago. The Woodlawn Memorial Park is huge, but there is one landmark that helps me know where to park. Right outside the Woodlawn fence on the central west side of the park is a billboard for a religious radio station. I remembered seeing that billboard for the first time at my Dad's funeral on a freezing cold day in mid-January. The last time I'd seen that billboard was at Mom's funeral on a hot rainy day in June.

Close to that billboard was the place to park the car on the road and walk over to my parents' gravesite. I sat in the car for a minute to collect my thoughts before heading to the park to find their graves. I got out of my car and grabbed a small Ziploc bag and a small hand-shovel from the trunk. I walked slowly through the grass to locate my parent's grave.

All the gravesites at Woodlawn look the same. There is a marble stone flush with the ground with a nameplate attached. From the street, the grave markers are not visible, only a field of grass. Since I had been to Woodlawn numerous times, I located my parents' graves pretty quickly.

Mom's nameplate had tarnished a bit since she'd been laid to rest. Dad's nameplate looked the same as I remembered it. I stood in front of both of their graves. I hadn't planned a speech. Maybe I should have said some prayers. While the warm South Carolina sun beat down on my face, I stood in stillness, listening to my heartbeat. A slight wind blew at my back and my legs buckled and I fell to my knees. I began to heave and sob uncontrollably. Words poured from my mouth that I couldn't control.

"I'm sorry, so sorry Mom! I tried. I really did. I tried to do the best I could. I know I've never cried for you…but look at me now. I'm a mess. I love you Mom. I miss you so much! Every Monday I just wish I could call you and hear your voice again…just one more time. You were so brave after Dad died. I know you and Dad are in Heaven doing God's work. If anyone is by His side it's you and Dad. You truly were an angel on earth. You were my saint!

I laid down on her grave and continued to sob. For the first time I felt like I was able to mourn my mom. I released all those thoughts and feelings that had been stored up in me for the last seven years. When some form of composure came over me, I pulled the Ziploc bag from my pants pocket and used the shovel to dig a small round hole in the ground between Mom and Dad's graves. I open the bag and poured some of Drew's ashes into the hole and replaced the soil and patted it down so no one would ever notice.

I stood in front of their graves and spoke out loud. "Mom, Dad, I stand before you, your son. Mom, I know your biggest worry when you left to be with Dad was Drew. You told me that I should 'let sleeping dogs lie' but you also knew that was never who I was. I believe that deep down, Mom, you knew I would try to help Drew. I wanted to give him a better life; a life that held greater happiness for him. I tried my best, as I've done all my life. I did what I believed was the right thing for him. I believe his mission has not been accomplished and that he's still on his journey. I feel like my job has been completed. Now that Drew has been returned to you, we can all rest. I know that there will be a day when we are all back together. I love you, Mom. I love you, Dad." I said a few of the prayers that Dad had us pray in the car on the way to church when we were growing up. I made a final sign of the cross and walked away. I left not knowing if or when I'd be back here again.

It was dark by the time I got back to my car. I had never been at Woodlawn in the dark. The red neon light of religious radio station billboard was flickering, trying to fully illuminate. I took a long deep breath, shifted my car into drive and made a U-turn to head back toward the exit. I stared into my rearview mirror the entire way to the exit, looking back at the rolling fields of green grass and that red neon billboard, now fully illuminated behind me in the distance.